ENDLESS TURQUOISE

Trudy Nixon

A True Communications eBook
Copyright © 2020 Trudy Nixon

eBook First published in Anguilla in 2020 by True Communications Ltd.

The moral right of Trudy Nixon to be identified as the author of this work has been asserted.

All rights reserved. No part of this publication may be reproduced, distributed or transmitted in any form or by any means, including photocopying, recording or other electronic or mechanical methods, without the prior written permission of the publisher, except in the case of brief quotations embodied in critical reviews and certain other non-commercial uses permitted by copyright law. For permission requests, write to the publisher, addressed "Attention: Permissions Coordinator," at the address below.

Any references to historical events, real people or real places are used fictitiously. Names, characters and places are products of the author's imagination.

Front cover image by Esme Mackenzie https://esmackenzie.wixsite.com/illustration
Instagram: @illustrateme
Book cover design by Andrew Fleming
Editing by Alex Mackenzie https://alexmackenzie.uk/
Book design by Polgarus Studio

First printing edition 2020

For Marlene and Malcolm, my Mummy Chicken and Daddy, who loved to read and travel, and who gave those gifts to me.
Thank you for everything. I love you.

PART ONE
ENGLAND

APRIL 2014 READING, ENGLAND

Tracy

"I don't believe the sea is really that colour, do you Mum?"

Rosemary Smith grunted something unintelligible, then took another sip of her drink, without taking her eyes off the telly.

Tracy sighed. Her loving, caring mum, who used to be her best friend, had become a grumpy stranger since Dad died.

She was trying so hard to cheer her up and get things back to some sort of normal, but it was over a year now and nothing seemed to be working. She was losing patience and getting stressed out. The challenges of looking after her mum and grieving the death of her dad while simultaneously running a busy hair salon, managing three rental properties, and trying to maintain some sort of social life, were getting to her.

Tracy called her mum every day to check in and made sure she spent at least one night a week at the bungalow, but Rosemary was still so sad, and negative. It broke her heart. But it was hard for her too! And she was beginning to lose patience.

She missed her dad all the time. He was easily the most important male figure in her life. He was always such an easy person to be around, happy and enthusiastic, unconditionally proud of her achievements and so easy to talk to about everything. She missed his measured advice and positive attitude. His simpler, sunnier disposition had complemented Rosemary's sharp intellect and more reserved nature. Characteristics of hers, which in good times manifested as empathy, a wicked sense of humour and brilliant listening skills. And in bad times, as a tendency to retreat into her shell and worry about things that she had no business taking on.

Reaching down she gave Tigger Tat's bottom a scratch. The beauteous black and white pussycat let out a little 'prrrppp' of pleasure. He was sitting in his favourite spot – curled up on the rug between Tracy's sofa and Rosemary's reclining armchair. The perfect position to receive sensory attention and the occasional devotional offering from his two favourite humans.

Tracy tried again. "It's gorgeous isn't it, Mum? That blue. Well, it's turquoise really. Endless turquoise. I can't actually believe it looks like that. They must have used some special filters I reckon."

Her mum made another noise deep in her throat and then sniffed. Tracy couldn't see her face from her recumbent position, but it sounded like she was crying. Again.

Tracy had chosen the film to watch because they both needed cheering up. Some good old-fashioned escapism.

It was another unseasonably cold and grey night. Instead of enjoying a glorious British summer they were experiencing the coldest May for years. Tracy abandoned the planned barbeque and ended up cooking their M&S burgers on the stove. The film had looked promising. The BBC announcer introduced it as a "high octane thriller set in a breathtaking Caribbean location".

Stunning footage showed clear blue seas and white speedboats racing around. Beautiful people modelled skimpy swimwear while simultaneously avoiding killer sharks, exploring shipwrecks and visiting deserted islands in their quest to find pirate treasure. And they managed to fit in some love action too. It looked lush. Tracy made a mental note to book a beach holiday soon.

"It is that colour," croaked Rosemary.

"Did you say something, Mum?"

"I *said*, it *is* that colour!"

Tracy was confused. "Umm. How would you know Mum? You've never been to the Caribbean."

"I have."

"Err. No. You haven't, Dad always said the furthest away he'd ever been from England was Italy." She softened her tone. "Are you feeling alright?" Then tried to make a joke of it. "Had one too many rum and cokes?"

"I TOLD YOU, it *is* that colour." Rosemary replied witheringly.

Tracy was worried. *Mum isn't seventy yet!* Maybe the strain of nursing Dad for the last few years has really taken it out of her? She's been a bit vague and out of sorts. She'd definitely been drinking a bit more than usual. What if she's going gaga? Getting dementia? Perhaps that's the problem. She would have to find an excuse and take her to the doctor's next week.

"OK, Mum. If you say so."

Every bone in Rosemary's body tightened. She turned and spat,

"Don't patronise me Tracy Maria Smith. I told you it is that colour and it is. It hasn't changed a bit." Then turned back to look at the screen, seemingly done with the conversation.

"Where hasn't changed?" *What on earth is she going on about?*

"Zephyr, it's an island in the Caribbean. Where this stupid story was filmed."

"How on earth do you know that is Zephyr?"

"Because I recognise it. I went there before you were born. Before I met your dad. In another life. And I wish, more than anything in the world, that I never set foot on that bloody island."

JUNE 2014 CLAPHAM COMMON, LONDON, ENGLAND

Charlotte

"Honestly Mummy, I'm fine. Really. Please don't worry. Graham is so ridiculously busy at the moment it makes perfect sense to delay for a few days."

She listened as her mum made some pointed comments about their unconventional decision to leave a gap between the wedding and the honeymoon. Charlotte was bored to tears of hearing it. Time to put her foot down.

"Mummy, enough. It's much better for me actually … Why? Because he'll be able to relax properly if he gets these important things done before we go away. I've hardly had a moment with him since the wedding because everything with the Kennington project is at a critical point."

Oh shit – wrong thing to say. Her mum was working herself up and she needed to calm her down.

"That's enough, Mummy. Listen, I know you are disappointed for me but I'm OK. It's just four days and we will still have a lovely long holiday … anyway, it gives me more time to shop for the perfect bikini which I still have not found!"

As her mum chuntered on, Charlotte lifted the album out of its protective box. It had just been couriered to her from Graham's office.

The wedding was only three days ago, but their celebrity photographer had pulled out all the stops to make sure they had a copy of the best photos before they appeared in the various society pages the wedding planner insisted on sending them to.

She needed to stop listening to her mum telling her that she needed to "start as she meant to go on". And that she must not keep letting him "get away with" putting his work first (Mummy had never understood how important Graham's business was to him). And get on with looking at the album!

At first glance, the pictures looked absolutely fabulous. How lovely to go back to the day and relive it. Including the bits that she had missed. Of which there were many. She couldn't admit to Graham that the whole day was a bit of a blur. Drinking far too much champagne on a small amount of food – not been her best move!

"I really have to go now Mummy. Yes, I promise to call when we get there – just five more days! Yes! It will be exciting. We can't wait!"

She barely heard her mum's last words and signed off with a "Love to Daddy!" before replacing the cordless phone in the cradle with a satisfying clunk. She was a big fan of the cordless phone – you really knew the call had ended.

She was the only one of her friends that preferred using a landline to make calls on when she could. Ali called her the last Social Media Virgin because she still didn't have an Instagram account and hadn't figured out how to post pictures on Facebook. The only thing she really liked using her iPhone for was to find and listen to music.

She made a nice coffee with hot frothy milk and took the linen-bound book to the round table in the bay window so she could really get a good look.

Everyone said the wedding was a huge success. Classy and stylish.

First up, their 'signature shot' as Graham called it. It was a glamourous black and white picture of the two of them walking through a formal box hedge garden, holding hands and laughing. It was taken just after they made their vows. She was gazing up at him mischievously and he was smiling confidently into the camera. It was amazing. She didn't want to be boastful, but they looked like something out of Vouge! Tall, slim, and perfectly matched.

All of the photos were deliberately 'casual', Graham had a fear of doing anything too cheesy. He wanted wedding photos that would light up Instagram. Charlotte just wanted the wedding!

She laughed. *He's such a bloody perfectionist.* But I love that about him. I'm GLAD he choreographed the entire wedding. I would have made some sort of tacky mistake for sure. She'd loved helping with the planning process and the many, many glasses of champagne consumed during it. He'd run everything past her, and she was absolutely thrilled with all his choices.

She adored the photos of the guests enjoying drinks and nibbles in the grounds of the ancient Castle on the outskirts of London – the perfect venue.

Then admired her deceptively simple, but striking wedding dress, an ultra-chic VB gown, specially adapted to feature the same gunmetal grey on the tiny buttons on the cuffs and back fastening as Graham's tie. He looked scrumptious in a perfectly fitted dark grey Tom Ford suit.

"We look good together. That dress suited me perfectly," she thought dreamily. He was right.

Flipping through, she made note of her favourites. A group shot of their mutual 'London' friends – looking all fashionable and sophisticated in their wedding best. A sweet shot of them with her parents – Daddy holding her hand tightly. Then there was a nice one of Graham and his mum, Audrey; he looked like a movie star and Audrey was gazing at her handsome boy with devotion.

There didn't seem to be any of Graham's dad – he probably counted himself lucky to be invited, as Audrey didn't speak to him anymore. There was a brilliant shot of the 'Wiltshire Crew' – Charlotte, Ali, Sammi from the village and a bunch of school friends giggling and mucking around with the bouquet. She was less impressed with the surprisingly large number of photos of Audrey's book club ladies and various bridge partners.

Ali, her best friend forever, had flown in from Spain the day before the wedding – to be bridesmaid. Because everything had been so hectic, they barely had time to catch up and what time they did have was taken up with what they called 'SOS seam-stressing'. A hilarious exercise where they tried to fit her voluptuous redheaded friend into a gunmetal grey raw silk sheath that was a size too small. Ali had provided the wrong measurements, honestly, but misguidedly, believing she would lose some weight in time!

After lots of wiggling and plenty of jokes about how colonics could provide emergency weight loss of up to 10lbs., they finally squeezed her into the gown by utilising the miraculous powers of Spanx and lots of talcum powder.

Charlotte thought she looked amazingly sexy and told her so. Recalling the sight of her curvy friend 'working' the wedding, she smiled. The dress was so tight Ali couldn't sit down, and she spent most of the wedding wandering around in order that no one would notice.

The most glamorous picture in the album was of Graham surrounded by his work team. *I wonder where I was.* Graham was easily the tallest and most handsome person. He had his hand draped casually over his stunning secretary Marian (no need to panic she was gay) and was surrounded by his good-looking team, the modish young designers that worked on his Kennington project.

Taking a final swig of coffee and deciding against making another, she moved onto pictures of the reception.

The gracious 'Great Hall' sparkled with cut crystal glasses and the stunning centrepieces made up of white orchids and antique silver candlesticks. Some arty food shots of the meal, a tasteful homage to the finest organic British produce and, of course, shots of the happy couple sat at the top table toasting each other. The wedding planner had suggested the top table be just her and Graham – not traditional, but romantic. She was glad they did it, as it was the best time they spent together all day. They had gossiped and caught up on everyone's outfits and wondered what they were all talking about at the other tables.

Dinner seemed to be over in a heartbeat – the speeches went by in a blur – her poor dad so nervous in the grand surroundings that he rushed through it, but it was very sweet nonetheless.

Graham's uncle, his best man, made a stirring speech about the young Graham and how much he had achieved by the tender age of thirty-eight! And Graham was fantastic as usual, he loved an audience and was a great raconteur and made everyone laugh. And, when he made his toast, was absolutely lovely about how stunning she looked.

Then there were some photos of them posing moodily in picturesque nooks and crannies around the castle which Graham thought were good, but she didn't think were as much fun as the others.

The best bit of the evening was dancing to the band – Ali, Sammi and her danced their socks off to the eighties tribute band that her mad boss Danny had recommended.

Graham had threatened to book a super trendy jazz/fusion duo or, failing that, a top Ibiza DJ, but she'd put her foot down. She wanted cheesy eighties hits. There would be no negotiation and he'd given in gracefully. The band was the best! Sadly, the photographer had gone by that stage so there were no pictures of her leading a conga line around the room as Graham and his mates looked on in horror!

Honestly, the only thing that wasn't perfect was the wedding night. They decided to forgo their weekend at Le Manoir and had headed home to their Clapham Common home. Graham was at such an important stage in the project that he wanted to put in a few more days' work before they went on honeymoon.

Not to worry, though. She closed the album. We have the rest of our lives and a fantastic honeymoon to enjoy each other. Then went into the guest bathroom to check on the suntan lotion situation.

PART TWO
THE CARIBBEAN

WEDNESDAY 4TH JUNE 2014
ARRIVAL DAY

CHAPTER 1

Tracy

Flying first class to Antigua and then hopping on a smaller plane to Zephyr sounded like a bit of fun when she booked it. Her travel agent hadn't warned her that she would be starring in a reality show called "Extreme airport landings in a nine-seater plane".

The tiny aircraft bounced and lunged towards the island's runway. Hurtling over a lagoon, it only just missed the tops of some innocently moored boats, then went on to fly so close to a road she could almost see the colour of the driver's eyes. And could definitely see if they were wearing a seatbelt or not.

The engines were deafening and as they slowed to land she got thrown forward into the passenger in front. Tracy could feel sweat soaking through both her knickers and the thin fabric of her cotton trousers. Luckily, they were a colourful animal print so there shouldn't be a visible wet patch when she got up.

At forty-two, Tracy was too early for the menopause (she hoped) but had suffered terrible hot flushes throughout the short journey in the hot tin can with wings. The air conditioning simply wasn't up to the job and the seats were *tiny*. It had been a truly hellish forty minutes exacerbated by an unpleasant neighbour, a statuesque woman, in head to toe stretch denim, dripping in costume jewellery.

The woman had been most disgruntled that the stewardess wouldn't let her take an oversized carry-on bag onboard and made her put it in the tiny hold. She also looked less than happy that she would have to sit next to Tracy.

After the woman squeezed her impressive backside into the snug chair, she kicked her platform mules off, and the sweetish-sour aroma of her hot feet had fragranced the journey. A few minutes later one foul smell was replaced by another when she dug a crumpled bag of KFC from her fake Louis Vuitton, and, to Tracy's shock and silent horror, put an entire chicken wing between her pink, glossy lips and chewed and sucked with pleasure.

Taxiing onto the runway, she thought at least I won't have to sit next to her for much longer and tried to think nice thoughts about arriving in a lovely cool hotel room. But the nagging voice that had dogged her for the journey was still screaming that she had made a terrible mistake coming to the Caribbean.

*

Her friend Cheryl picked her up to take her to the airport at silly o'clock this morning. Dragging a pink suitcase filled with summer clothes and wearing her favourite leopard print trouser suit, she almost felt like she was going on a normal holiday. They spent the journey chattering about getting a tan with a Piña Colada in hand and making sure she minimised her white bits. And, of course, they talked about men. Tracy had a 'bit of a record' when it came to holiday romances and Cheryl was encouraging her to maintain that record.

"You've been off your game for a bit, love. Time you had some fun. Go get 'em."

She told her to have lots of hot sex with the island guys. Lots of hot sex. And added, that if she had room in her suitcase, to bring one back for her. They laughed all the way to Gatwick.

It was a fun start to the journey. But the reality was that her friend had no idea why she was really going to Zephyr. And Tracy was increasingly concerned she was doing the wrong thing.

In booking the trip, she'd gone directly against her mum's wishes for the first time ever and now, also for the first time ever, Rosemary wasn't speaking to her. She hadn't spoken to her daughter for nearly a month and it was rubbish. Tracy was still grieving her dad and now she felt like she'd lost her mum too.

But despite Rosemary's telling her not to meddle and to let sleeping dogs lie, she knew – she just knew – she needed to visit the island. Later on, that fateful night, after pushing and pushing her, Rosemary gave her the barest bones of an incredible story. Tracy was still reeling from what she learnt about Rosemary. *I need to know why she did it.* And she needs to face up to what she did. It affects both of us. We need to deal with this so we can get on with our lives.

Ouch! Her charming neighbour was poking her – indicating she would have to get out of the place first. Despite the sun being so low that the sky had turned orange, the heat hit Tracy like a wet flannel as she struggled out and down a step and onto the runway. She looked around. The airstrip was basically a big field, with a strip of concrete down the middle, fringed with coconut trees.

The airport arrival area was tiny and hot and there appeared to be only one immigration officer on duty – and he was looking after the 'Residents' line. Tracy joined the 'Visitors' line and waited patiently as all the other people from the plane went through. Giving her plenty of time to enjoy the delights of the room: posters featuring advertisements for swanky hotels, boat trips and barbeques, a framed photo of a very pleased-with-himself looking man who appeared to be the Prime Minister.

When she finally reached the booth, the taciturn officer didn't return her smile.

"Form?"

"Um I didn't know I had to fill one in?"

He sighed and shoved a copy at her.

She searched through her bag for a pen to fill it out then realised she didn't have one.

Frustrated, she asked the miserable man for a pen and he made a weird noise that sounded like he was sucking his teeth (she learnt later he was doing exactly that) then glared at the ceiling while she completed it.

By the time she'd got her stamp and was free to go, her bag was the only one left. Her shiny pink case sat forlornly on the stationary conveyor belt with only a large cardboard box covered in FedEx stickers for company.

Elbowing her way through some creaky old doors, she entered a brightly lit exit area – where a woman standing behind a podium that said Taxi

Dispatcher, and a short, barrel-shaped man in a black and red checked shirt and a turquoise Miami Dolphins baseball cap on back to front, were arguing loudly.

The man, who had his back to the exit, was poked sharply in the shoulder by the dispatcher when she saw her emerge.

I can't believe everyone is being so unwelcoming. I thought this was a friendly place. I should just turn straight round and go home.

But then a miracle occurred. The taxi driver turned and gave her the widest, most welcoming smile she had ever seen. She grinned back and nearly kissed him in gratitude when he helped her into his white minivan, which, because the engine had been left running, was mercifully chilly.

"Pleased to meet you Miss … my name is Morris," he twinkled as he popped his head through the door to shake her hand before sliding it closed.

"Tracy," she supplied, "pleased to meet you, too."

"Where can I take you today?"

"Mango Bay Hotel, please." She sighed pleasurably. Soon. Soon she could relax, take a shower and get a drink – she was thirsty as hell.

But not quite yet. It appeared that Morris the taxi driver was in no hurry to move; in fact he seemed more in the mood to flirt than drive. He turned round and fixed her in his sights, eyes roaming lazily over her from head to toe, clearly appreciating the view. However sweaty and dishevelled she knew she looked, Tracy could see the cheeky beggar was thoroughly enjoying the sight of her abundant curves and blonde curly hair.

"Wonderful."

Tracy smiled politely, she wasn't sure if he meant her or her choice of accommodation.

"That is one of our most popular hotels. Have you been there before?"

"No, I've never been anywhere here before – it's my first time on the island, first time in the Caribbean actually."

His eyes lit up. "First time on the island? Well, for sure I know you are going to enjoy it. This is the most beautiful place in the world." There was a short pause before he asked carefully, "Are we waiting for your husband?"

"Oh, I don't have a husband, so we can go now," she smiled encouragingly, not minding the attention, but hoping this would finally get him to move.

It worked. Morris pulled away from the airport, but instead of looking at the road, he adjusted his rear-view mirror so he could catch her eye while driving.

"No husband! Don't worry pretty lady, I'm sure you will have found a nice husband by the time you leave."

CHAPTER 2

Charlotte

"One more cheeky top-up before you land?" asked Lorraine the flight attendant, waggling the bottle temptingly to add emphasis.

Charlotte considered her fourth, or was it fifth?, glass of complimentary champagne quite seriously before declining politely. She wanted to enjoy the mesmerising view: a stretch of interlinking islands strung out in a blue, green and white daisy chain below her. It looked utterly, perfectly, absolutely, tropically magical. They were nearly there, and she was excited. In fact, given the tiniest bit of encouragement she would have bounced up and down in her seat like a baby in a pram.

She pressed her nose and forehead against the glass to see better. In the colourful, Pucci-patterned world below, tiny boats made white snail trails across a smooth turquoise sea; islands with areoles of azure, cerulean and jade spawned smaller and smaller slithers of land, and white caps breaking on reefs surrounded by deep, dark navy added contrast to the composition. As the large land mass of their destination slipped under her, she could see that where the sea met the shore, the beaches were the advertised colours – icing sugar white lapped by aqua foam.

Wincing as she gingerly peeled her skin away from the glass, she turned to look around the cabin. The cabin crew were moving swiftly and efficiently through their pre-arrival routine. Over the tannoy, the chirpy Aussie captain was instructing his cabin crew to "kindly take their seats for landing," and her tummy lurched as the huge jet took a sweeping turn to the left, dropped sharply as it slowed to a cruising pace, and then made the horrible crump, rattle and thump sounds that meant the landing gear was being lowered.

It was definitely time to wake up Graham. Her husband was still sprawled in his seat – eyes shut, breathing slowly and deeply, oblivious to the fact they had landed. She'd clearly underestimated how exhausted he was, as he had somehow managed to sleep through not only the landing, but also most of the eight-hour flight.

Of course, he had worked right up until they left – not getting in until minutes to 2am last night and slumping into bed without even saying good night. She assumed he probably didn't want to wake her but wouldn't have minded if he did.

Leaning over to gently shake him awake, she examined her sleeping husband with affection. His long, lean frame was stretched out in the twin yin to her yang recliner seat. He looked so young with his special travel pillow cradling his head and a blanket pulled up to just under his chin. She'd have liked to take a picture of him, but she knew he'd hate it – he vetted all their photos.

He needn't have worried, he was very handsome asleep or awake, and today, with the few worry lines that had begun to appear recently smoothed out by a long sleep, he looked younger than his 38 years. And, exasperatingly, he looked absolutely immaculate as usual – unlike her! *His* mid-brown hair looked as neat as if he'd just styled it. *His* lightly tanned skin looked fresh above the snowy white of his tee-shirt and duck egg blue cashmere sweater. And Charlotte knew instinctively that *he* would still smell as fresh as a daisy and that his dark grey jeans would have just the right amount of Lycra in them to be perfect for travelling – whereas *she*, in her oversized, off-white linen shirt and charcoal cigarette-legged trousers – while stunning in the shop and recommended as being cool and comfortable for travel – looked a crumpled mess now. She put her hand up self-consciously, knowing that her long, dark brown hair, pulled back into a messy low bun, added to her slightly dishevelled appearance, and took a stealthy sniff of her armpit. Not too bad, thank goodness!

This was ridiculous! He *still* hadn't opened his eyes! Charlotte grabbed both shoulders and shook again – this time with force.

"Wakey, wakey, Darling, we've just landed!" A small groan indicated he was still alive.

"Look lively sleepyhead – WE ARE HERE!"

It worked. Graham opened one eye and peered at her. He looked slightly pissed off. He grimaced, yawned, then – finally understanding it was time to come to – stretched out his long limbs, arms above his head first, then legs popping out on either side of the blanket. Charlotte smiled at him.

"Come on sweetie, you have to come back to the land of the living now."

"Uggg ... I feel a bit spaced out. Are we there already? Did I sleep all the way?" She nodded in assent.

He grinned, "Bloody marvellous. Those sleeping tablets were great."

Charlotte pulled the blanket off him and started to fold it up trying to hurry him along.

"You've been dead to the world. No bloody company! You slept the whole way." But she said it with a smile so he wouldn't think she was nagging, then pouted, "AND you missed an awful lot of champagne."

"Hmmm, don't care. Plenty more champagne in the sea."

Charlotte giggled.

He rubbed his eyes tiredly, "I really, really needed that sleep. How was the flight? Did you sleep, my darling? Wow, I can't believe we are here already."

Charlotte nodded her head enthusiastically, "Great, despite my lack of company, it was really very, very enjoyable. Our hostess was fabulous, she was teasing me that I look like Kate Middleton! She said that the captain had given her strict orders to give me as much champagne as I could drink, as they didn't get royal personages on their flights very often!"

Graham nodded approvingly, he absolutely loved it when people compared her to Kate Middleton.

"Anyway, I didn't want to sleep. I was far too excited."

"Excited? About what?" Graham was distracted, not listening properly and patting his pockets frantically, searching around for something. "Where did I put my phone, Charlie?" he added with a note of panic.

"Excited about our honeymoon, silly," Charlotte shook her head in mock despair, "and your phone is in your man bag. Exactly where you put it when you said you were turning it off and didn't want to look at it until we got to the hotel."

"Oh yes, of course." A thought struck him. "The hotel … to be honest …"

The 'bing' that heralded the message that passengers could now disembark interrupted his train of thought. Graham reached up, popped the catch of the overhead and neatly extracted their his 'n' hers cabin-sized designer luggage. He was on the move before Charlie could put on her shoes. Struggling to manoeuvre her long legs after hours of sitting still, a little tipsy from the champagne, and trying not to bash her head when she stood, Charlie followed him – wobbly as a colt.

She stopped briefly to thank Lorraine and the rest of the cabin crew for their generous booze pouring and exited into the stiflingly hot tunnel that linked the plane to the airport. And watched her husband disappear – effortlessly trailing their two smart cases behind him as he raced off, clearly not in the Caribbean mode yet and incorrectly assuming she was right behind him.

"Wait a minute, daddy long legs!" she called cheerfully from the bottom of the tunnel. He stopped, sighed, slumped his shoulders and looked at her with a quizzically raised eyebrow – an expression that signalled Why? without words.

"I've got the passports and forms – you can't get anywhere without me. Bloody hell it's hot!" she gasped, as she caught up.

Because Graham had moved faster than a gold medal winning Caribbean sprinter, they were the first in line, first through immigration and, as luck would have it (their bags were already on the conveyor belt), first through customs as well. They were transferred efficiently from the air conditioned hall to a small boat dock a few hundred metres away. Here they boarded their hotel's speed boat, which would take them to their ultimate destination – a smaller, neighbouring island.

They were helped on to the boat by a muscular, smiley man in a buttery lemon Polo shirt whose gentle hands were the size of dinner plates. He welcomed them, then informed them that he was Captain Danny and that they were waiting for one more couple before they could start the thirty-minute journey. In the meantime, they should sit back, relax and enjoy the view.

Graham frowned at news of the delay but after a nudge and a "cheer up, don't be a grump" from Charlie, got into the mood a bit and stripped off his jumper. He folded it up neatly and gave it to her to put in her oversized shoulder bag. He rifled through his more moderately sized man bag and extracted his new and eye-wateringly expensive sunglasses, which he polished carefully before putting on.

Face impassive, Graham looked around the busy dock area, which was jammed with jostling speed boats. Busy crew members in colour co-ordinated shirts were shouting and wildly gesturing as they scrambled on and off the rocking vessels, hefting towering piles of luggage and their accompanying tourists onto the small boats. After observing the organised mayhem for a while, Graham asked Captain Danny a couple of questions about the transfer process to 'their' island and discovered that they were on the newest, largest and fastest boat the island boasted. Satisfied that they had booked the best possible transfer option, he relaxed back and let the sun caress his face, smiling smugly as he accepted an ice-cold beer from another more junior member of the friendly crew with one hand and draping his other arm over Charlotte's shoulder.

"You did good, hon, our very own speedboat. I hope this desert island you're taking me to is going to be equally good. Quite the adventure you've planned for us."

Charlie snuggled in, glad he was enjoying himself. She was having a little 'moment' of her own, too. This was the perfect and oft-imagined start to their paradise island honeymoon: sunshine, a busy, boat-strewn bay, bright blue sky, friendly crew offering refreshing adult beverages, and a cool trade breeze whipping through her hair ready for the exciting James Bond-style speedboat ride.

"It's going to be amazing, Graham. I know you're going to love it. Cheers!" She knocked drinks with him and gave him a quick peck on the cheek before taking a refreshing gulp of the frosty rum drink she'd been handed – it was delicious!

"Look, I know you're feeling a bit apprehensive, because you would never have let me do the organising normally," she smiled at him knowingly, and he acknowledged her graciously.

"Agreed."

"But there is no need to panic, because …," she held up one finger at a time to underline her points, "*one,* Paradise Point is hideously expensive, has won all sorts of awards and been featured in loads of newspaper articles – *two,* Zephyr island has amazing beaches, fabulous weather and is known to be *very* exclusive – not a grockle in sight – and *three,* Mariah Carey and Robert De Niro can't be wrong." She smiled winningly.

Graham's eyes twinkled. "Mmm, well, I guess if it's good enough for Bob and Mariah, it's good enough for me. But you can't blame me for being a bit nervous. In the brochure you showed me there were pictures with guests wearing thongs! Either they've had a serious eighties revival in the Caribbean, or the publicity shots are a bit dated."

Charlie giggled. "Didn't I tell you thongs are de rigueur at Paradise Point? Don't worry darling – I packed you a couple of pairs!"

CHAPTER 3
Tracy

It took Tracy and the loquacious taxi driver twenty minutes to get to Mango Bay, even though the advertised transfer time from the airport was less than ten. She didn't mind at all.

Since being told that not only would she be happy here but also that she'd never want to leave the island, Tracy had decided to relax and enjoy the little man's flirty company. The journey was comfortable and entertaining – albeit a little noisy. Morris gave a nonstop commentary on things to do, places to go and people to meet, accompanied by long and loud toots of the horn for emphasis every time he passed a bar, shop or person he knew – of which there were many.

He also gave her some helpful, unsolicited advice about the allure of 'island men'.

"Did you know that the men from our island are so powerfully attractive that women often fall in love and leave their husbands for their new boyfriends?"

She looked suitably impressed, so he continued, clearly enjoying himself.

"My good friend plays the steel pan – best on the island. One night he meets a young lady, like you. She loves his playing and they become good friends. This lady happened to be a rich man's wife. Well, when it's time to go home she doesn't want to. She loves my friend and cannot be without him, so she leaves her millionaire, for my friend! – who doesn't have any money. And she gives up her fancy house in America, and moves to the island to live, and they are still together now."

Tracy nodded in amusement. A thought occurs to Morris.

"You should go hear him play, he would like you. He likes ladies like you."

"But I thought you said he was with the millionaire's wife?"

Morris chuckled, clarifying what was obviously an acceptable fact of life.

"Yes, he is. But that doesn't mean he can't talk to other ladies. He loves his lady, but he is a Caribbean man! He has a lot of love to give." And gave her another face-splitting grin.

Oh well, that kind of arrangement wouldn't work for me, but good to know what I'm dealing with here! Tracy got a card from him, then waved goodbye at the hotel. Maybe their paths would cross again – she had loved listening to Morris spin stories in his accented English.

The plane journey and nightmarish airport experience were distant memories – she was ready to move on, to embrace a different, kinder Caribbean, a world full of Morris and his ilk, and hopefully she was going to find that world here – because she'd loved the look of it online.

Mango Bay was as Caribbean in style, and as welcoming in nature, as she hoped it would be. She had searched for a boutique, family-run hotel in the hope that it would give her a better feel for the island and its people than one of the large luxury chain properties.

The receptionist on duty introduced herself as Shelliqua. She was an extremely attractive, confidently overweight, girl in her mid-twenties with immaculate makeup. She flashed Tracy a genuine smile that showed a glimpse of gold in its depths. Her black hair was braided into a fancy pyramid shape which sat towards the back of her head and had a glossy, sculptural look to it. Her multicoloured fingernails were so long they scuttled over the keyboard as she looked up the booking details.

Tracy was very taken with her. "I love your hair; it must take you ages to do that."

The girl giggled. "Oh, I don't do it. I go to the salon."

"How long do they take? It must take ages. It's a work of art!" Tracy gushed.

"Not long, maybe six hours," Shelliqua said, shrugging her shoulders and looking at her quizzically – and Tracy realised the receptionist had probably never had a guest go on about her hair so much before.

"I'm interested because I'm a hairdresser back home, and I don't think I've ever had anyone come and sit in my salon for that amount of time. Was it for a special occasion?"

"No," the girl laughed, "I just like to have my hair nice."

"Well I never. I'd love to see a salon while I'm here. Perhaps you could arrange it for me?"

"Sure," the girl smiled. "But they won't do your hair you know. They only do hair like mine …" she looked at her slyly, then guessing correctly that she could get away with teasing her new guest added, "unless we get you a weave."

Tracy laughed and said she'd think about it.

Once Shelliqua had finished on the computer, she asked Tracy if she would mind taking her own bags because the porter had gone to get something to eat and she didn't like to disturb him while he was eating.

Ah that's how it works. Tracy was amused rather than annoyed by the lackadaisical customer service, as Shelliqua imparted some unfathomable instructions.

"Go down the path so … then go so, and then go east at the swimming pool."

Taking possession of a large wooden key that had both the room number and the Mango Bay logo carved into it, Tracy thought how helpful it would be for anyone wanting to rob her.

Dragging her bag down a couple of small steps, she set off on a path edged on either side with looming trees until she came to an appealing grotto-like pool that featured three mosaic dolphins leaping in a circle in its depths. She took a gamble and turned right (east?) towards a row of small Caribbean style cottages. Night time had arrived swiftly. The sky was black, but the moon and stars were bright, and she could see them clearly because the resort's lighting was discreet and pretty. Twinkly white lights were wrapped around some of the coconut trees and pale lemon lights festooned the balconies of the small cottages.

Tracy paused for a moment, to take in her surroundings. She took a deep breath of the deliciously scented air – a mixture of fresh, salty sea and exotic night flowering jasmine. The silky night air embraced and soothed her, and she felt the last of her travel tensions slip away.

She headed towards one of the cottages. Her room – Number 69. She smirked. *I always liked that number. Must be a good omen.*

CHAPTER 4
Charlotte

Charlie thoroughly enjoyed the speed boat ride, but felt her energy flag during the short transfer to the hotel, despite the comfort of their beautifully cool, chauffeur-driven Escalade. Judging by Graham's pose, slumped against the window on the opposite side of the back seat, he was tired too.

"Not much to see, is there?" observed Graham and started asking the driver questions about where to go and what to do. Charlotte cringed; if she was honest, this was the thing she was a bit worried about. When she booked the honeymoon, she did so knowing that it was a very quiet place. But it hadn't put her off because she was desperate to go to this particular hotel, had been for years.

Charlie's idea of a perfect honeymoon was a simple one – relaxing with her beloved – spending time on a dazzling beach, swimming, laughing, drinking cocktails, eating lots of lobster and, of course, making love. The incipient dread she was experiencing had come on because she wasn't confident that this was what Graham wanted.

Her husband was a workaholic. It was often hard to get him to switch off, and this would be the longest holiday they had ever taken together. They had a great social life. They went out a lot. More than she would like really. Graham worked hard and he played hard too – always wanting to try the coolest new restaurants and to party in all the right places. But they had only done a handful of short holidays in the two years they had been together.

Graham was obsessed with modern design and she'd taken a big risk booking a classic, old school luxury hotel like Paradise Point. She was crossing everything she had that the hotel was as good as the travel agent had promised.

"We reach! Ladies and gentlemen, welcome to Paradise Point."

Charlotte's spirits rose as the driver motored onto a long driveway, lined with colourful flowers and waving palm trees that offered sweeping views of the resort and the ocean laid out below. Graham perked up immediately. Paradise Point was an oasis. A glowing gem nestled in the rough terrain of the rocky island. Ready to welcome them with sweetly and expensively scented arms. The rooms that made up the exclusive resort were laid out like a string of natural pearls along an exceptional, gently curving, white sandy bay. The buildings nestled into spectacularly lush gardens, artfully designed to make you feel that they had grown out of the hot earth alongside the colourful plants.

They pulled up and two smiling young men in immaculate white shirts waited on the steps with no other desire or purpose than to welcome them – pressing delicately and deliciously scented ice-cold towels into their guests' hot sticky hands.

Charlotte thanked the bellmen and walked ahead into a cool, white lobby – a stunning room that boasted a breath-taking view of the sea. The furnishings were exquisite: elegant white wooden chairs with intricately carved legs and arms covered with eau de nil fabric and silky jade and turquoise throws; squishy white armchairs with interesting and inviting cushions; eclectic side tables made of glass and coral, huge table lamps shaped like shells, incorporating petrified driftwood, and beautiful glass 'objets' whose sole purpose was to create colour and interest. The focus of the incredible place was an enormous chandelier made from driftwood, shells, slivers of mirror and sparkling crystal – an exquisite decoration that reflected light and colour from the gleaming ocean. Charlotte gazed around in awe, she'd never seen such an alluring and serene space. Surely Graham would love it too.

A uniformed staff member ushered them into a cool side office where a pleasant receptionist called Jasmin offered them her hand to shake first and a rum punch second.

"Welcome to Paradise Point Mr and Mrs Browning, and congratulations. I understand you're on honeymoon?"

They nodded and smiled "yes" as they settled into seats in front of her desk.

"Well, you've chosen the right place … our hotel is reputedly one of the most romantic in the world," she said proudly. "It truly is our pleasure to have you here. Have you been to our island before?"

"No," said Graham, "it's our first time. Ahhmmmm …" he checked her name badge and asked conspiratorially, "Jasmin. Tell all. What is there to do around here?"

"Well, as many of our guests are honeymooners, they come here for total peace and quiet, and to relax on our beach, which is probably the best on the island; in fact it's been voted one of the best in the world."

Graham, smiled politely. "Well, yes, of course, and the beach certainly looks enticing. But I'm not a big swimmer. Charlotte will love it, though – she's the beach bunny. Tell me about the restaurants and what kind of entertainment you offer in the hotel?"

The girl launched enthusiastically into an obviously well-rehearsed routine, "We have four restaurants and two bars: the beach bar Coconuts, which closes at six, and the lobby bar Sundowners, which closes at eleven. We have a singer in the lobby bar some evenings between six and nine, but not later than that because most of our guests like to go to bed early."

She winked at Graham to underline her risqué reference in case he hadn't got it, then continued, "And we have a very popular Caribbean Folkloric Theatre event on Thursdays – very cultural. Some people get up and dance."

Graham smiled thinly. "Folkloric Theatre. Hmm, not really sure what this is, but I expect we can give it a go." Before continuing in a patient tone, "So, Jasmin, if the folk singers are the highlight of the week and the bar closes at 11, what do we do after that? Is there anywhere else to go? What about the rest of the island – where do people hang out? Is there a nightclub you can recommend?"

Jasmin smiled indulgently, "Oh, no, sir. We don't have any nightclubs, to say of, on the island."

"I see. No nightclubs. Hmmm. What about casinos?"

The girl's full beam smile dimmed then died under the stress of Graham's questioning.

"Oh, no, sir – gambling is illegal – we don't have casinos."

She paused and then in a quiet little voice answered what she anticipated, correctly, would be his next question – before he could ask it.

"We don't really have many shops either. Not any you would have heard of … Sir, our island is really just a very relaxing place …"

She looked hopefully between the two of them, noted Charlotte's worried face and said weakly, "I really hope you enjoy your stay with us."

Charlotte grabbed her bag and followed Graham's stiff back as he walked behind the porter that had been assigned to them. His body language, coupled with the fact he hadn't addressed a word to her in ages, was worrying. Charlie found it impossible to enjoy the journey in the little club car that whizzed them through stunning gardens with tantalising glimpses of turquoise waters beyond, because she needed to know what he was thinking.

When they arrived, Mac, their porter, opened the solid oak door and gestured for them to enter, then said with relish, "Wonderful news, Mr and Mrs Browning … you've been upgraded, from a suite to a villa – this means that not only can you enjoy our wonderful beach, but you also have your own swimming pool too."

He smiled cheekily, "Very romantic and very private. Don't expect we will be seeing much of you on the beach."

Charlotte gasped, "Thank you, that's so sweet … isn't it, Graham?"

She listened for his response, but he'd already stepped in front of her, through the open door and was now inspecting the villa. Without giving Mac the opportunity to do his job he impatiently turned on the TV, fiddled with the air conditioning control and fired questions about wi-fi, safes and keys. Mac did his best to keep up and showed him how everything worked.

While the boys discussed the toys, Charlotte zoned out and looked around the gracious room. It was cool and pretty, with elegant white furnishings, and a fabulously comfortable looking four poster bed strewn with multiple pillows and a sprinkling of flower petals in the shape of two entwined hearts. Floor-to-ceiling windows were framed by decorative shutters and floating muslin drapes and gave a clear view of the sun-drenched beach outside. It was the perfect honeymoon suite. *Surely, he would have nothing to complain about here?*

But it appeared there was something wrong, because after Graham said goodbye to the butler, closing the door with a telling thunk, he walked towards her with a petulant expression on his face, not commenting on the inviting room, or the thoughtful upgrade or their very own private swimming pool – clearly intent on scolding her.

"Darling, are you alright?" she asked, dreading the answer.

"No, I'm bloody not. I'm bloody furious with you. What on earth were you thinking?"

THURSDAY 5TH JUNE 2014

CHAPTER 5
Tracy

This is heaven! Turquoise heaven. The colour is extraordinary and can only mean one thing: I have died and gone to heaven. This warm, golden light gently caressing my skin confirms that I have been transported to the pearly gates as a reward for all those years of being nice to old ladies and dumb animals. Or is it dumb ladies and old animals?

Tracy floated effortlessly on her back with the warm water gently supporting her. Gently lapping waves covered her tummy and legs but left her boobs pointing perkily up out of the sea like two leopard skin covered hillocks. She felt as light as Darcy Bussell and did a couple of twists and turns to demonstrate her weightlessness.

Dropping her feet down she discovered she could float standing up, if she kept her arms wide and flippered her hands up and down. She lifted one leg and pointed her toe, then moved it to the side, delighted with her flexibility. She lifted both knees and used her waist muscles to twist side to side – enjoying the stretch. Then she opened her legs out wide and closed them quickly – aaaaaannnnddd repeat. She was doing a kind of aqua star jump. She liked the way the water whooshed up the inside of her legs and gave her a nice tingling sensation – down there. *Mmmmm*. Suddenly self-conscious, she looked around, a little worried that someone might be watching.

What to do next? She debated with herself. And where should I go for dinner? Should I take a stroll along the beach – check it out? She decided she wasn't ready to do anything much yet, apart from sitting back down on the sun lounger that 'had her name on it'.

She'd discovered her special sun-worshipping spot that morning, at 6.30am when she'd popped out of the room to get the lie of the land and watched the morning light overpowering the night sky. The hotel was very, very cute in the daylight. The cottages ringed three sides of a bright green lawn that ran down to the beach. Said beach was fringed by coconut trees and was the pristine white seen in advertising campaigns for the tropics – the type of white sand beach that is advertised but, in reality, is rarely seen. And beyond that she could see the beautiful, tempting ocean – a strip of pure turquoise sparkling through the trees.

She slipped off her balcony and walked ten steps on springy rough grass and before she knew it was under the palms with her toes in the sand. She looked to the left. The beach was huge – it went on for ages with just a few small buildings in the distance. She looked to the right and saw the same … and best of all, there was no one on it.

In the dappled shade under the trees were two loungers – with deep yellow and white striped cushions – each boasting a lemon beach towel rolled and adorned with a hibiscus flower. Nestled in between was a small wooden table with a bottle of water and drinks menu. "Well, hello, friend," talking to herself out loud, "nice to meet you. You and I are going to spend some quality time together."

Tracy admitted to being the archetypal British traveller. She had a proud history of package holidays in Spain and Greece behind her and couldn't bear the idea of another guest taking her lounger despite there not being another soul in sight. She ran back to her room, collected her book and beach bag and raced back out to mark her territory – keeping an eye out for predatory Northern Europeans.

What a perfect day. She'd swum, sunbathed and snoozed and had hardly thought about her mother. The most energy she'd expended was walking to the restaurant for breakfast. (She WAS going to have a fruit plate to be healthy, but the full American sounded good and she hadn't had *that* much dinner the night before.) Afterwards she discovered the delights of beach service. The only bit of stress was when the nice young woman who brought her a Piña Colada, cautioned her to keep an eye on the coconuts overhead –

as they had been known to fall on a person's head and kill them!

Tracy wished that she could spend the entire time relaxing like this. But at around four o'clock her skin started to prickle almost as much as her conscience, and she knew it was time for a shower and to make some plans.

Later at the hotel bar, smelling gratifyingly of after-sun she fell into conversation with a nice couple from Nu Joisey (New Jersey). Tracy wondered if she would ever find their kind of American accent anything other than a bit grating. She felt terrible thinking that because they kept saying how much they "loved" her accent but was still tempted to respond, "Really? Because I find yours terrrrrrribly annoying." in her best Maggie Smith voice.

It turned out that Brett and Barb were regular visitors to both the island and the hotel. They were delighted to have met a Zephyr 'virgin' and couldn't wait to fill her in on where to lime. At Tracy's look of puzzlement on hearing the term – Barb went on to explain that 'liming', or 'to lime', was a Caribbean expression that meant to hang out.

They were exceedingly enthusiastic and shared so many suggestions, too many to take in, that she just nodded and smiled encouragingly. Spotting her bemused expression, they told her not to stress about trying to remember everything, they would give her a list at breakfast tomorrow. She listened, highly entertained, as they waxed lyrical about their friends on the island – mentioning an array of exotic sounding characters including an Elvis, a Chix and a Binky. Recalling her taxi ride with Morris (who it appeared they knew) Tracy was tempted to ask Barb if she found the men "powerfully attractive" but bit her tongue just in time.

The couple had finished their pre-dinner cocktails and were leaving the bar when a tall, heavyset man in his forties arrived. As he hailed them, he held out his arms and Barb and Brett, overjoyed to see him, indulged in some hugging and back slapping before they exited.

The tall man introduced himself as Freddie, the hotel manager. "Pleased to meet you Ms."

"Tracy Smith."

"Is it OK if I sit here, Tracy?" indicating the neighbouring stool.

Tracy smiled, "But of course."

"Thank you, are you leaving too or can I buy you a welcome drink?"

"No, I'm not going anywhere tonight and yes another Virgin Piña Colada would be lovely, thank you."

He ordered her drink and a fruit punch for himself then turned back to chat.

"I am thoroughly enjoying your hotel, Freddie. You certainly have some very friendly people staying here."

"Yes, Brett and Barb are good people. They love us, love our island and keep coming back. Believe it or not they rebook their room as they leave, to make sure they are OK for the next year – because they always want the same room – the most easterly one closest to the water."

He waved his arm vaguely towards the beach. "They are part of our family now. And they market us for free back home in NJ." He smiled mischievously at her.

"They told me. Very impressive. How long have you been managing the hotel?" Tracy found herself interested to know more about him.

"It feels like most of my life. It's my mother's business – her dream after working in hotels in Florida - where she went to work as a young woman. I saw it being built and I grew up working here. Now my wife works here as the accountant and before long my kids will want a job too, I expect. And I've done every job here I think, from Porter to Chef. You can see – it's not a fancy place but we try hard and people love the location and the family feel."

"Well, I love it already and I know I made a great decision booking it." And she meant it. The hotel was showing its age in spots, the rather haphazard interior design wouldn't win any awards, but her room was spotless, the location amazing and there was definitely something special about the atmosphere.

"How did you find out about Zephyr? – it's not the most well-known island."

"Oh, a friend recommended it to me …," Tracy hedged. Not ready to give too much away yet.

"Well, we must make sure you enjoy your time here. How have you been treated? Have you hired a car? Done any exploring yet?" and spread his arms expansively to underline his point.

She was happy to tell him. "Everyone at the hotel has been very kind –

especially your receptionist and I had a brilliant taxi driver. But arriving at the airport was not nice – I had to wait for hours and they were rude … if you can have a word with the powers that be and arrange for the miserable man at customs to get the sack that would be a great step forward for tourism," she teased. Freddie tutted, and shook his head in despair.

"I wish I could. Believe me you are not the first person to ask me to do that, but he's related to someone high up in government – unfortunately it's a job for life."

Tracy pulled a disappointed face for a moment before she continued, "Ah shame … and to answer your next question, no. No exploring yet. I'm sure I will go out exploring tomorrow, though …" Tracy paused – unsure how to put her next request but realising this was as good a place to start as any.

"Freddie, I wonder if I could ask your advice on something?"

Freddie nodded. "If I can help it would be my pleasure."

"If I wanted to try to find someone here or find out about someone's family history – where would be the best way to start? I'm doing some research for my, em, friend, the one who came to the island before."

He nodded his head. "Well, if you have a name it's easy – it's a small place just ask around and someone will know someone who can lead you to them – and you may be surprised how quickly that can happen. I might know them, who is it?"

Tracy grimaced. "I wish it could be that easy, sadly I don't know the name, I only know some of their circumstances. That sounds a bit vague – but basically, I believe this person was either from here or moved here to work on the construction of the airport back in the sixties and then moved away."

Freddie was beginning to fidget a little – she could see he was too polite to say it but obviously needed to get going,

"Well, that was before my time, and you don't have much to go on really. But perhaps you could start with the museum? It's small but the curator is very knowledgeable about the island and I would guess they have information about nearly every notable event that occurred – and the building of our airport was certainly notable. It changed everything for us because the tourism business started then."

CHAPTER 6
Charlotte

Today is the first day of what should be the best holiday of my life – except it isn't, Charlie thought. Graham was pissed off at her and she was stressed and unhappy.

Last night, as soon as the porter had left, Graham rounded on her. Furious about the lack of wi-fi in their room and dearth of facilities at the hotel. Then he'd started complaining about the simple nature of the island – impressions he'd gathered from the taxi ride and the receptionist.

"What were you *thinking*, Charlotte?" his exasperation showing. "The hotel is charming, I'll give you that, but it's like something from bloody prehistoric times. You know how important it is for me to be able to stay in touch with the office. It's a critical time in the project. Christ, I didn't think I'd have to ask you about wi-fi, it's a fucking *given* these days. And this island. Why on earth did you choose this island? There's nowhere fun to go, no casinos, no shopping, just some cheesy restaurants, some fucking Caribbean Morris dancers and a bar that closes at eleven. What are we going to do with ourselves in the evening?"

Apart from the obvious, given it was their honeymoon. But she didn't say anything, because she didn't really have an answer for him, and that would bring up a whole other can of worms anyway.

She let him rant, then apologised as best she could and then he muttered something under his breath and set off to find the blessed wi-fi signal.

Afterwards she paced around the room until she found the complimentary bottle of aged rum. She mixed herself a stiff drink and slumped into one of the roomy armchairs, staring miserably out of the window as the sun set over the incredible beach and mirror surfaced bay.

When Graham came back, he'd calmed down and was clearly feeling bad about his outburst. He gave her a stiff hug and a sheepish, "Sorry I shouted at you, I can see it's a charming place, not quite what I was expecting but let's just make the best of it."

She said a thankful "I'm sorry, too," then they changed and went out for a quick, subdued dinner.

This morning, pretending to still be asleep, she listened to him dress and grab a coffee from the breakfast tray that room service had delivered, then sneak out – no doubt to use the wi-fi again.

She picked at some fruit and had a coffee as she pottered around the room doing the last of their unpacking and preparing for their first day – praying the first-class service and beauty of the resort would start to work its magic on Graham.

Her new husband was used to things going his way. He was already a successful man: he'd made the beginnings of a fortune in property development and was planning on making many millions more before he hit forty. He had started small with a five-bedroom terrace in Clapham North that he had flipped and resold for three times the money he paid for it. With the profit, he bought two more houses in the same area and did the same thing – but had to move on to Brixton when the returns started getting smaller as the area gentrified. A few years ago, his business took a huge step forward when he partnered with a local construction company to acquire an old factory/warehouse in Kennington. The factory was in an amazing area – just off the coveted Durand Gardens, and he was close to launching a luxury development of flats and town houses that would make his fortune.

Graham was the salesman and visionary. He knew exactly the type of people they wanted to attract, and appointed a top interior design consultancy to work on the project to help sell an ultra-hip lifestyle and reel them in. He had seen the final design concepts a few days before the wedding and he told her he was very, very happy with what had been done. Clearly the designs had made him impatient to get going, and it appeared that the honeymoon had become an unwelcome distraction from getting on with the project.

Charlie was beginning to think that he would much rather be in London going over plans with Andreas, the lead designer, than spending the next week with her, on a tiny tropical island – in a resort, as he had bitchily described as being, "filled with old people and American newlyweds saying 'awesome' every other word."

There was no getting away from it, she'd fucked up royally. She knew Graham's taste, knew what he liked, and she knew in her heart of hearts that she'd booked the honeymoon knowing this wasn't really his sort of place – it was hers. She'd dreamt about coming to the Caribbean and in particular to this classy old resort, for years – after reading an article about it in her parents' Sunday newspaper.

She'd assumed that it would be enough for Graham that it was a place loved by celebs – even if they only came when they wanted to hide from the world!

She loved him, but, truth be told, he was a total control freak. If he hadn't been rushed off his feet with work and planning their extravagant wedding, he would never have let her be in charge of the honeymoon.

Graham had great style, but his one weakness (in her humble opinion) was that he preferred places that screamed conspicuous wealth and success over old school quality and charm.

She finished unpacking their stuff and there was still no sign of Graham. Impatient to work on her tan, she wrote a note on the creamy hotel notepaper telling him where she was then slid the patio doors apart and stepped out onto the beach. *It was utterly fantastic.* He would come round, he had to, it was such a beautiful place and Graham loves beautiful things.

After settling herself on the velvety taupe towels that covered her sun bed, she slipped on her headphones and lost herself in her homemade honeymoon mix. All the songs brought back fond memories.

She had been only twenty-three and hadn't had many boyfriends when she met Graham at a nightclub in London. He was tall and handsome, radiating energy and enthusiasm. He oozed confidence but was friendly and warm, and, best of all, had a warm, twinkly smile. He was also generous with the drinks –

buying their table of giggly girls at least three bottles of champagne.

Charlie wasn't particularly keen on nightclubs. She was much more of a village pub kind of girl. But that night she'd dragged out her best dress (Ali had chosen it), put on some makeup and slicked back her hair and, for once, felt she looked like she fitted in. She was only there because a work friend, Justine, was marrying a DJ called Stevo and it was their joint stag and hen nights. Graham was a friend of Stevo.

It was fate that we met, she thought, probably the only time our paths would have crossed.

They were not a good match on paper, she was naturally quiet and reserved and he was confident and 'out there'. But Charlie had always had a thing for extroverts, and loved anyone who shared her dry sense of humour – her best friend Ali being a good example.

From the moment she saw Graham, she couldn't take her eyes off him. He was taller than her, which made a nice change, good-looking and flirty without being sleazy or lecherous. She was flattered when he sat down next to her and singled her out for special attention, looking at her with frank admiration.

"You look great. I love that necklace – is it Tiffany?"

It was a knock off, but she was so flattered and impressed by him that she would have been embarrassed to admit it was a fake – so, uncharacteristically for her, she lied. "Yes, it was a gift."

"It's beautiful, but so are you. I bet you get told that all the time?"

She didn't actually. Even though she knew she wasn't ugly, she didn't feel attractive. And she always felt like she was the last person anyone would look at. She was tall and flat chested with big feet and boring brown hair. Graham, though, clearly liked what he saw and was so funny and easy to talk to that she relaxed and had a brilliant night. She was overjoyed when he took her number and promised to call the next day. He did, they started dating, and had been inseparable ever since.

Graham's shadow blocked the sun as he bent down to pull her earphones away and whisper in her ear.

"Fancy some lunch, Charlie?"

She smiled up at him. He'd changed into his swimmers and looked much more at ease. It had been good to revisit those memories – things were looking up.

FRIDAY 6TH JUNE

CHAPTER 7
Tracy

As anticipated, Shelliqua, the receptionist at Mango Bay, was more than happy to arrange car hire (apparently she had a friend in the business who would do her a great deal) so after a nice leisurely breakfast and a refreshing coconut water (Tracy's new *favourite* thing) she met Lucy, the car rental lady, in the restaurant.

Tracy agreed to hire a red Suzuki Jeep for the rest of her stay. After they filled in the paperwork, Lucy pointed out some places of interest using the simple map she'd brought with her. The island looked easy to navigate but Tracy couldn't see what she was looking for.

"How do I get to the museum?"

Lucy showed her a tiny M, "M marks the spot," and explained the quickest route to get there.

"But you should call them first. They don't open every day – their information is on the back of the map."

Tracy went back to her room and called the museum – no answer. Rather than change her plans, she decided to go anyway; she had the car, it was still early, and she could do a little sightseeing.

Barb and Brett, her new best friends, joined her for coffee after breakfast and, as promised, provided a very comprehensive list of things to do and people to meet. They also warned her about driving on the 'other' side of the road and the terribly hazardous roundabouts – which they saw as an enormous challenge they had finally been able to surmount after years of practice. Tracy managed to keep a straight face and refrained from telling them the Brits invented driving on the 'other' side of the road.

This is going to be fun, she thought, driving out of the hotel half an hour later, roof down, shades on and with her blonde curls bobbing crazily in the breeze.

She had a good sense of direction and wasn't worried about getting lost, even though the museum was at the other end of the island.

Driving slowly, observing the thirty-mile-an-hour speed limit, it was easy to look around and she was fascinated by how different it was from the UK. No fast food stores or high rises, just small houses. The island seemed very undeveloped. *It must have been even quieter when Mum was here.*

It only took twenty-five minutes to get to the museum, which was, as Lucy had warned, closed. It was also tiny and looked like it may be closed permanently. Getting out of the car to explore more, she could see there was a ratty piece of paper pinned to the yellow and blue painted wooden door which read:

> Closed for the season
> BUT DO NOT DESPAIR!
> Private tours can be arranged ON REQUEST
> Please call Dr Clive "Clinton" Derrick on 878 8785 to arrange an appointment
> A small donation of $5 per person for private tours is suggested

Tracy dutifully wrote down the name and number then got back into the car. *He sounds like a bit of a character.* But that's good news about the private tour. When I get back to the hotel, I'll get Shelliqua to arrange it.

Her spirits lifted. She had tried and, as there was nothing more she could do today, she might as well enjoy herself and explore a bit. She pushed away the thought that the knot of dread had lifted – a bit like when your dentist appointment was cancelled and you got a reprieve.

Consulting Lucy's map she saw that there was what looked like a small town nearby with a beach and restaurants and, most importantly, a petrol station.

Arriving at what was in fact a tiny fishing village, she wished that she had brought a friend along, someone to share the experience with – because this place was brilliant! There was loads to look at. In fact, she was so enamoured of the scenery that she pulled over a couple of times to take pictures – one of a ramshackle wooden house coloured pink and green, then again for the most colourful and prideful cockerel she had ever seen.

She noticed that many houses had a 'no-brand' dog and some chickens scratching around outside. She loved the fact that the small potted plants that brightened up her mum's conservatory grew wild here as huge, vibrantly coloured trees. *Perhaps she keeps them as a reminder?*

Lots of the houses seemed to be unfinished, with unpainted extensions or scraggly sticks of rebar sticking out. Hardly any of them had gates or fences, they sort of ran into the next house or just had stuff stacked up around them – big cages made out of something that looked like chicken wire, wooden boats up on blocks, broken down cars, as well as piles of bricks and building materials.

A lot of people would probably think it's ugly because it's untidy, but I love it. Tracy thought it was charming because of all the colour and the crazily shaped combinations – like a mad sculpture park.

It was definitely a far cry from the tightly manicured squares and toweringly walled spaces that defined a British garden.

There were not many people around, assumedly they were out at work or hiding from the sun, which was also making her increasingly uncomfortable, burning the bridge of her nose and the tops of her arms. She would need to stop and put some more sunscreen on, or put the top up on the jeep, she was running the risk of turning as red as a lobster – not her best look.

On her first pass through the village she drove past the 'gas station'. Hardly surprising as it was disguised as a barbeque stand. Luckily, she glimpsed a half-obscured Shell sign in her rear-view mirror and reversed back to investigate. A tall, elderly man with wet-looking curls, came over and leaned into the car. He smelt strongly of a rich, manly aftershave which she suspected may be Old Spice. He looked very pleased to see her. "Good day, how can I help you?"

"I would like some petrol – I mean gas, please." Proud of herself for learning to speak American.

Even though he was probably in his seventies, the garage man flirted gently with her as he filled up the car. It seemed that friendly chat and a bit of a flirt was as natural as breathing here. Whereas back in the UK no one even looked you in the eye – let alone struck up conversation if they didn't know you.

She asked about the beach in the village, but he recommended that she drive for another couple of miles to a place called Shell Beach where there would be a selection of restaurants to choose from. She could also hire a lounger for the day. "But be sure to come back to visit us soon."

A few hours later, gazing at another exquisite seascape, poised to drop off, soft reggae soothing her ears, belly pleasantly full from a delicious lunch of a grilled local fish and something called 'peas 'n' rice', Tracy reflected that even though she had been forced to come to the island under less than perfect circumstances, she was already feeling the benefit. *I've always thought of myself as a 'glass-half-full' kind of girl but I've been more of a glass-half-empty person recently.* Mind you, it's been rubbish what with Dad dying, then Mum being sad all the time. Haven't even had a boyfriend for a bit. Everyone else is all settled down and having babies. And I work too hard. Yep, I needed a break from work. Maybe it wasn't such a bad idea to come here after all.

Driving home, Tracy decided to take a detour off the main road and visit an area called 'The Strip' before it got dark. She wanted to check out some of the restaurants and nightspots that Brett and Barb put on their list of places to go.

First stop was a beach bar called 'D'wine', where she asked for Chix (as recommended) but was informed that he wouldn't be in till around 9ish, so she drove on to a place called 'Treasure Island'. It was a cheesy name, but it looked inviting enough from the outside with smart purple and white paint. She decided to go in.

The sun was setting and the place offered sweeping views over a bay dotted with yachts and small, colourful fishing boats. It was the perfect spot for a sundowner. She walked to the bar and gingerly raised herself onto a tall bar stool. The barman was youngish, probably in his early thirties, tall and slim with a very cute hairdo (he had put his dreadlocks into two 'bunches'). He wore thick gold hoops in either ear which added to his dashing, pirate-like appearance.

He gave a welcoming smile and handed over a cocktail list, but Tracy was more interested in the big glass container lined with pineapple, at the other end of the bar. The sun slanted in and the vessel glowed, spilling shadows like sunshine across the floor, bar and walls.

"That looks good," she pointed, "what is it?"

"It's homemade pineapple rum. It is delicious on its own over ice, OR I can mix you a cocktail if you prefer?" He raised an inquisitive eyebrow. Tracy shrugged – she didn't know what she wanted – she wanted *him* to tell *her*!

"Here, try a bit to see if you like it."

He poured two shots, one for her and one for him, and raised his glass,

"Cheers! Welcome to Treasure Island," and downed it in one long gulp, licking his lips and grinning as he placed the empty shot glass on the bar.

Tracy took a tentative sip and smiled at him.

"It's very good. Tastes of pineapples and sunshine."

She finished the rest off quickly. "I think I will just have it neat."

"Good idea, but I suggest you have it on the rocks with a glass of water on the side. That way it's cool and the water means you don't go hard too soon." He wiggled his eyebrows suggestively.

Tracy laughed. "Too hard too soon! You make me sound like a serious drinker, sir!"

He smiled, leant across the bar and said conspiratorially,

"Trust me, I speak from experience. I am a bartender that serves the world's most delicious pineapple rum and I promise you it has magical effects. Strong island magic … you best be careful … Miss … what is your name?"

"Tracy. Tracy – without an e," then confessed, "you know, I've always hated it. My name that is. What's yours?"

"Jimmy. Pleased to meet you, Tracy." He held out his hand and they shook. "Tracy is a nice enough name. Why do you hate it?" He seemed genuinely interested.

"Well, it's just one of those names you know. It was a popular choice for girl's names in 1970 – whoops!" she smiled at him, "Gave the game away, but now it's got a bit of stigma attached to it. I much prefer my middle name, Maria. Dad chose that because he liked that film West Side Story."

"Stigma attached to it?"

"Well, there is this thing in the UK that Tracy and Sharon are, well, plebby names."

"Plebby?"

"Plebeian," she clarified.

"Sorry to sound ignorant, but I have a degree in business administration, as well as a PhD from the University of Life and I still don't know what that means."

This bloke's funny she thought, enjoying their banter.

"It means from the proletariat, uneducated, common."

He gave her words some thought, then said, "Well, are you uneducated?"

"NO! Well, I didn't go to university but I could have. I did really well in my A-levels. Just that life kind of took over and I never managed to go … too keen to get out and earn a living …" she trailed off.

"Oh, well then, that must mean you are common," he pressed on with a gleam in his eye.

She burst into laughter. "No! Although it may have been said once or twice in the past." She waggled her finger at him. "*And* that doesn't mean you're allowed to say it. You are rude, young man. No, actually, you are what I call a cheeky bugger."

He looked mock affronted. "What is a cheeky bugger?"

"Well, we won't go into the exact definition, but you are definitely one. You have cheeky bugger written all over you."

She paused and took another sip of her delicious drink.

"Seriously, though, the name thing is exaggerated by the fact that my chosen profession is a hairdresser."

He looked puzzled. "Well, what's wrong with being a hairdresser – clearly you make lots of money because you're here and it's expensive to get here from the UK, right?"

"That's true, and it's also true there is nothing wrong with it. *And* I am good at what I do, but it's perception again. I am a walking cliché." Chirping in a broad 'mockney' accent, "My name is Tracy, I'm a hairdresser, I've got blonde hair and big boobs and I ask people every day where they are going on holiday." She sighed and added wistfully, "When I go to my Drawing class, everyone else seems to be a doctor or a lawyer."

Jimmy smiled. "Tracy, let me offer you some barman's wisdom – you can only be a cliché if you allow yourself to be one. It's clear to me, even though I've only just met you, that you have a lot going on. You're funny and smart and most definitely have a little something we in the Islands call 'spice'.

"Spice?" Tracy didn't quite know how to take that.

"It's OK. That's a compliment," he reassured. "Why did your parents call you Tracy if it's such a bad name?"

"Don't know. Never asked them."

"Well, perhaps you should, then you will know the family tradition, and then maybe you'll learn to love your name …" he looked at her sceptical face and delivered the punch line, "but I doubt it!" They both laughed hard.

"I have news for you Miss Tracy-with-the-big-smile. Here, in Zephyr, we have some funny names too, like Eustace and Randolph and Bummy and Eudoxie."

She nodded, smiling, "And Shelliqua, like my friend?"

"Ha, Ha. Yes, that's one of the modern ones. What we love to do now is to either combine both the man and the woman's name or sometimes combine a part of the parents' name to a 'qua' hence Shelliqua. Her dad is probably a Sheldon. My friend's name is Wayne and his daughter is called Wayneiqua."

Tracy laughed so hard she nearly fell off her stool.

"No way. Stop! My sides hurt."

When she calmed down a little, she took a deep gulp of her delicious rum drink and said, "Jimmy's a nice name, I guess you were christened James, though?"

"No, Jimmy is my nickname. You may not know this, but most Caribbean men usually have a nickname or two. My real name is … Oswald. Which do you prefer?" he deadpanned.

When he said Oswald, Tracy thought she might wet herself she was laughing so hard. His dry delivery just cracked her up. "Oswald," she giggled, "you are a fool."

He grinned. Clearly happy with the response his teasing was having – then his demeanour changed. He leant over the bar, resting on one elbow, stroking his chin and mimicking deep thought. "I have had an excellent idea. I will give *you* an island nickname. From now on I will call you ... duh, duh, duh ... Miss T! What do you think?" He looked at her expectantly.

"Misty?" Tracy was a little confused.

"No. Miss T. Like Mr T from the A-Team? Miss T. Short for Miss Tracy, it's short and sassy – like you. What do you think?"

Tracy nodded vigorously. "I love it. I've never had a nickname before. And you must call me that as long as I can give you a nickname too."

He nodded in agreement, "Cool, what's it to be?

"CB".

He looked puzzled "CB like the radio?"

"No," said Tracy. "CB like Cheeky Bugger!"

She decided to stay for another drink and kept CB company at the bar as the restaurant filled up with people looking for sundowners and dinner. True to his word, he introduced her to everyone that came in as his good friend Miss T.

She talked to a group of friendly expat women, who were around the same age as her, and picked their brains about island life. Then, when they sat down for dinner and she was getting ready to leave, she got collared by a guy.

"Hello Miss, how are you today?"

"Hello Mister," she looked way, way up into soft brown eyes. "Very well, thank you. How are you?"

He smiled. "I am blessed. Even more so now I have met you. Are you thirsty? Hot? You look a little hot. Can I buy you a drink and find you a seat in the breeze to cool off?"

A cool breeze sounded tempting and, hypnotised by the warmth of his smile, and old-fashioned good manners, she found herself willingly taking his hand and being led to a small table on the deck.

He chatted away, talking about the island and how he'd had a great day fishing. The two rums had been enough to make her a little tipsy, but she was sober enough to recognise that he really was gorgeous. And to enjoy the fact that he hadn't let go of her hand.

He was cute, rather than handsome, with closely cropped hair and a mischievous twinkle in his eyes. He smelt delicious. She figured he was a little younger than her, of course – but then every man she was attracted to these days was. His beer and her bottle of water arrived (she'd declined another rum) and he started to ask questions, wanting to know all about her. She flirtatiously deflected them, happy to enjoy the breeze and sneak glances at his perfectly shaped mouth as he told funny stories.

Oh yes. She definitely fancied him, and he seemed to be thoroughly enjoying chatting to her too and it was a tad disappointing when, after a brief phone call, he jumped up saying he had to "go to come back" and left the bar. Treasure Island was still busy, but Tracy decided to go home too. The guy was attractive and he knew it. Extremely easy on the eye and, to be fair, seemed like a really nice person as well, but he probably chatted up tourists all the time.

SATURDAY 7TH JUNE

CHAPTER 8

Charlotte

"I don't believe it. People," said Graham snidely.

He was right, it seemed like everyone staying at Paradise Point, and probably most of the guests from hotels across the island, were waiting to be entertained by the famous folkloric theatre.

The beachfront restaurant was packed with guests enjoying the impressive spread of barbequed lobster and other local delicacies. At the front, ladies in orange dresses with plaid trims and white frills sang up a storm.

"I want mango, give me some of your juicy mango!" trilled the statuesque lead singer who was sporting a large basket of fruit on her head.

"At least she's not singing about a big banana," deadpanned Charlotte, barely holding back the giggles. But Graham didn't respond. He didn't seem to find it as amusing as she did. In the old days, before they got married, they would have had a real laugh about a song filled with double entendres. *Nothing* seemed to be getting Graham out of his funk. As she looked at her handsome husband's petulant face, she felt her giggles die like fragile soap bubbles hitting a brick wall.

The hotel and its amazing beach were everything she had hoped they would be. She had spent another day sunbathing (her tan was going to be spectacular) and enjoying the five-star service – raising a little flag every time she wanted a frozen drink or a bite of something yummy to eat.

At night their room was just as sensual as she had imagined. The problem was that there was nothing sexy about what went on in it. *We've got a private pool for god's sake and we haven't even skinny dipped in it.*

Graham's priority was getting on the internet to read his emails, download financial statements, and pages and pages of plans. Occasionally he would join her on the beach, where he would make a big fuss of applying his sunscreen. Then he'd lie down briefly, before he started to fidget, order a drink and then, before too long, 'go for a walk'.

Lost in thought, she didn't notice that Graham had struck up conversation with the attractive young couple sitting at the next table. And, joy of joys, he looked happy.

"Babe, meet Marvel and Chad – they're from New York and have just been telling me that they come here every year – Marvel's parents own a villa here."

Charlotte leant over Graham to shake their hands. They had firm grips and gave her wide white smiles, from two excellent sets of teeth.

"Pleased to meet you, my name's Charlotte."

"Nice to meet you too, Charlotte. We were just trying to persuade your husband that the island's not all bad. It *is* possible to have a good time here," said Marvel in a conspiratorial tone of voice.

"Oh, thanks. You will be my new best friends if you can do that. What do you suggest we do? I think we've tried everything on offer at the hotel."

"There is a good nightlife scene here, believe it or not – it's just that it's mainly local bars and music spots and the hotel staff aren't encouraged to tell you about it. But we love to go out." An idea seemed to strike the bubbly American. "It would be our pleasure to take you out this evening – Saturday night is normally a good night out. There's a local band that's popular and a couple of other bars to check out nearby?"

"And it's safe to go out of the hotel?" Graham asked Chad, man to man.

"Perfectly safe, dude, and we promise to bring you back before sunrise," (he winked at Charlotte who was beaming encouragingly at him). "What do you think? Up for it? Sounds like you guys need to bust loose of this place!"

Charlotte really wanted to go but she looked at Graham and indicated it was up to him to decide. When he asked if he would be OK to go wearing what he had on she figured he did too.

They popped back to their room to grab some money and arrived in the lobby just in time to meet the American couple. Charlotte climbed into the back of their large silver Wrangler Jeep with Marvel. Graham sat in the front with Chad and the two men swiftly fell into deep conversation about property. Charlotte had her first chance to really study her new acquaintance. The African American girl was petite and very pretty with dark brown skin, long, black braids and wide-set, shiny eyes. She was wearing an off-the-shoulder white top, a long chain decorated with a mix of semi-precious stones and fresh-water pearls, white lace shorts and very high gold cork-soled platform sandals. Charlotte really liked her style and told her so – Marvel gushed that she too loved what Charlotte was wearing (an ankle-length, turquoise, stretch jersey dress that showed off her quickly acquired tan and clung to her long frame, accessorised with silver leather gladiators and chunky matching arm bracelets). They settled into a comfortable gossip.

As the car sped along the empty roads, Marvel told Charlotte that she was "in PR", that it was "awesome" and that she had just got a great promotion with some "amazing" accounts. Charlotte explained that she was the office manager for a chartered surveyor in London – a nice job but not an exciting one:

"To be honest, I'm not a career girl. I know it's unfashionable to admit it, but it's just the way I am. I fell into the job really. I'd always assumed that work would be a temporary thing and that I'd have a couple of babies, a Jack Russell and a nice house in the country by now – like my mother."

She looked wistfully at the back of Graham's head for a moment before turning back to Marvel.

"Do you two have children?"

"No, not yet. Our game plan is to enjoy Manhattan and our jobs for a few more years – Chad's working on a huge project that could set us up. Once that is a success, I can think about getting pregnant but – honestly – I'm not in a rush. I love my job and my life at the moment."

"Graham *loves* his job. He's *so* driven and is becoming very successful. I think he's just beginning. He really does want kids, though – the plan is that he can earn all the dosh and I'll stay home and look after them."

The car slowed; they had arrived in an area Marvel told her was called 'The

Strip'. The jeep cruised past a bunch of busy bars and restaurants – some modern looking and some traditional Caribbean – but all with music pumping. On the side of the road there were groups of people hanging around and chatting by the smoking barbeque stands.

They parked close to a biggish bar that was shaking from the level of the bass that was pounding out of large speakers stacked up by the front entrance. Chad looked over at the building then looked at his wife and made a decision.

"We can go in there later." Then he explained to his guests, "It's really a good place for dancing but it's not the right time to go – a bit early still. Let me take you to our friend's beach bar first. It's a very cool place and probably easier to sit and chat there anyway."

The party of friends turned left and walked along a dimly lit street, the distinctive scent of marijuana permeated the air and Graham lifted up his nose and sniffed appreciatively – like one of the Bisto Kids

"Mmm ... smells good."

Chad smiled, enjoying his role as the perfect host, happy to be of service.

"You want to smoke a little Graham?"

Graham nodded energetically.

"Cool. We can score at D'wine and then we can chillax ... sit under the stars, smoke a reefer, drink a cold beer. Man, before you know it, you'll be an islander!"

Graham laughed and patted Chad on the back.

"Good call old man, bloody good call," hamming it up with his best posh English.

Good call Chad. Bloody good call. Might relax him a bit. Charlotte thought. They approached the entrance to the bar – a sandy alleyway with palms on either side and a glimpse of the sea at the end.

High benches surrounded the colourful bar. There was a low deck to one side, with lots of additional tables and chairs around a small dance floor. There were hammocks slung between the coconut trees and loads of fairy lights and tiki torches provided the lighting. The DJ booth was covered in leaves, built onto the side of a large tree. The DJ himself was a spindly Rastafarian with an enormous 'cat in the hat' striped woolly hat perched precariously on a pile of dreadlocks, which bounced and bobbed on his fragile neck in time to the pounding dub reggae he was playing.

Charlotte fell in love with D'wine on sight. It was the quintessential beach bar she'd hoped to find. Back home she loved nothing more than a drink in her local pub – and the beach bar gave her that same welcoming feeling.

D'wine smelt of barbeque, perfume, marijuana and the sea. The reggae music hooked her, the silky night temperature caressed her skin, sand sneaked into her sandals. The colour and unique vibe of the Caribbean was evident – she couldn't have been anywhere else.

Someone was trying to attract her attention.

"What can I get you to drink?" She met the eyes of a spectacular-looking man across the bar. *When he fills in forms, I guess he ticks the box marked Black*, she thought. But really, he was a dark gold, lighter in skin tone than her – with her new Caribbean tan. He had the most unusual clear green eyes. She put her head to one side and smiled at him.

"What do you recommend?"

"We have everything … what do you like? Sweet? Sour? Wine?"

"I like sweet drinks mainly."

"Rum punch? Ours is famous …" he twinkled at her, "well, I guess everywhere says that – but I guarantee mine is the best."

She raised her eyebrows. "Really?" in her best British accent. "Go on then."

"Yes, really," he laughed mimicking her. "Love the accent by the way."

He turned his back to her and grabbed a large jug with some orangey-red juice mix that he added to the three different types of rum he had already poured into a 12oz cup filled with ice.

"What's in that?"

"A trade secret. Maybe I will whisper it in your ear later. Especially if you keep giving me smiles like that. Try it."

He added a slice of orange, a squeeze of lime and a grating of nutmeg and pushed the jewel-like cup towards her, at the last minute popping in a straw and stirring, before leaving the straw facing her. She held her hair back with one hand and leant over the drink and sipped slowly through the straw. When she looked up, she caught him watching her lips intently.

"Is that good? Are you enjoying it?" he said softly.

"Oh yes, it's delicious," she said flustered.

Conscious that Marvel had disappeared and that she needed to pay, she avoided his eyes and rummaged in her bag.

"That one's on me. It's your first time here, right?"

She nodded.

"Well then, come back and see me and I'll let you buy the next one." And with that he turned around and started making piña coladas for a couple of glamorous girls on the other side of the bar.

Charlotte looked around for the others and just as she was beginning to feel a little concerned about being on her own, Marvel materialised besides her.

"Hey girl, wassup?"

"It's great here, thanks for bringing me. Where did the men go?"

"Oh, they went to score some grass – look over there – with that dude. He's skinning up now. Do you want to go smoke with them or keep me company at the bar? I'm not really in the mood to get stoned so I hope you'll stay with me." She patted the bar stool encouragingly.

"I'd love to stay with you. I don't smoke weed, Graham doesn't often either, but I think he's showing off a bit. He's delighted to have met Chad and have a break from me – he's up for anything I reckon," she finished off sadly.

Marvel looked worried. "Oh. I hope this won't cause an argument with you two love birds? Not on your honeymoon! I'll go grab my man if you want?"

Charlotte shook her head. "No."

"Are you sure? Chad can be a real steamroller – he's very energetic! I can see he really likes Graham. He's just trying to impress him I think." She moved to get her husband, but Charlotte grabbed her arm and pulled her back to the bar.

"No, don't worry. It's super to sit and chat with you and, to be honest, I couldn't be happier that they met. It will cheer him up."

Marvel looked puzzled. "What do you mean cheer him up? What could be wrong? He's on honeymoon with his beautiful new wife. Shouldn't he be on top of the world?"

Sensing an ally Charlotte blurted out, "Oh, Marvel it's all been …" She shook her head, suddenly tongue-tied and ashamed, but wanting to talk to the friendly girl with the doe-like eyes.

"What, honey? Don't be sad … you can tell me."

What a relief it would be to talk to someone. Marvel's face was the picture of concern – and when she reached out and captured Charlie's hand in both of hers, the act of kindness broke through the last shreds of her reserve and the words tumbled out.

"It's been *awful* … a disaster. Oh God, I'm so unhappy and I haven't had anyone to talk to! Graham's been an absolute shit since we got here. He doesn't like the hotel or the island. He says there's nothing to do and is furious that the wi-fi doesn't work properly because he's just obsessed with his work. I wonder if we should go home early. I know he'd love to and he's just waiting for me to bring it up."

"Noooo … you mustn't do that … you poor girl. But why's he being like that? It can't just be work. It's his honeymoon."

"Marvel, I wish I knew. He's been really distant with me. We haven't had sex since we got here and that's not normal. We didn't even go skinny dipping in our private pool!" she ended hysterically.

Marvel squeezed her hand in support. She looked embarrassed for her.

"That sucks."

"I'm terribly sorry to be such a drip and bore you with all this."

"Honestly, not a problem. I'm flattered you're sharing your experiences with me. It's awesome you trust me to hear this and, honey, you needed to talk to someone for sure."

Marvel looked around then nodded her head, "Yep, those guys are going to be gone for ages – I thought I saw Chad sneak up to the bar for some refills. They've disappeared back onto the beach, which means they will be gone some time. Let's get you the next drink."

She started waving at the handsome barman, "Chix, Chix, you hot thing, you, can we get two more of your specials please?"

*

Charlotte took the opportunity to go to the bathroom and tidy herself up. She mopped up her smudged mascara and applied some fresh lip gloss, satisfied that she didn't look like she'd been crying any more. She may be heartbroken but had her pride. She didn't want Graham or that man behind the bar to see her with red eyes and a runny nose.

Marvel was kind and she felt much better for talking to her, or 'sharing'. She was enjoying the differences between the way the Brits spoke English and the way the Americans she met on this holiday (or should she say vacation) spoke English.

Officially they spoke the same language, but she was sure they didn't understand half of what she said – but she understood them, what was that about? And the island language – that was supposed to be English but, in reality, was a whole other ball game. When she heard the staff talking amongst themselves at the hotel, she often couldn't understand a word they said. They put on a different accent when they talked to guests. Still pondering, she walked back to the bar to find another delicious rum punch waiting for her and took a deep, appreciative glug of the spicy, fruity, sugary drink.

"That is soooo good, thanks."

"Agree. What do you think of Chix then?" Marvel nodded her head at the handsome man behind the bar, clearly trying to lighten the atmosphere a bit.

It worked. "Chix? Is that the bartender?"

Marvel nodded and Charlie said enthusiastically, "Oh, stunning. Amazing eyes."

"I know. Good-looking and a successful businessman too – this is his bar."

Charlotte raised an eyebrow.

"He just bar tends because he likes it – doesn't need to do it. Actually, I think he does it because he likes meeting women. And it's good for business. Half the women here came hoping to chat to him. Look around, they are the ones with their tongues hanging out." She smirked.

Charlotte looked round obediently and was amused to see at least three different women gazing enraptured at the barman. Chix was oblivious to them all, chatting to a very old guy whose face had caved in because his teeth were missing.

"He seems very nice as well. Have you known him a long time?"

"Yes ages, since I was a teenager. He's a family friend," she added slightly bashfully and, as it was a night for confessions, said, "he and I used to be close."

"How close?" Charlotte was intrigued at the thought of Marvel and the obviously much older Chix.

"Very close."

"Ohhh. When was that? Please tell me, it will take my mind off my woes."

"Well … if you really want to know (I can't believe I'm telling you this)," Marvel pulled her bar stool closer and looked around to make sure Chad was still a safe distance away and that no one (including Chix) could overhear them.

"Don't worry. I won't tell anyone, I promise. Now spill."

"He popped my cherry." Marvel laughed nervously.

"What? No way."

"Yes way!"

"Oh my god, tell me *everything*. How old were you?" Charlotte was on the edge of her bar stool and Marvel was clearly enjoying her role as raconteur. She leant in even closer.

"I was nineteen – he was in his early thirties. An experienced man."

She wiggled her eyebrows up and down for effect then settled into her story telling.

"I'd known him quite a long time and I liked him a lot. He and my dad get on great – in fact, Pop invested in this bar, which is how he was able to get started and they are still partners, Pop loves his work ethic – Chix is one hundred percent Caribbean man, but is one hundred percent American in his business practices. I think he might even vote Republican – ha! a Republican with locks! Anyway, I'm wandering.

"Chix was always hanging out at our villa. Sometimes he would swing by with fish or lobster for the family and would end up staying for dinner. Mom always made a fuss of him. That afternoon it was wicked hot, and I was in and out of the pool trying to keep cool. He walked past me, and I don't know what got into me, but I decided to push him in. Boy was he mad at me for getting him wet! He jumped out of the pool and chased me. I hid behind Pop, but he grabbed me round my waist and walked me to the pool and threw me in. So, then we got into a big water fight and then we started wrestling and we were touching in the water more and more and then he had his arms round me pulling me about and I just … felt him."

The girls exchanged glances and smirked like teenagers.

"Go on, it's getting good," teased Charlotte.

"Well, I can honestly say it was the first time I thought about him that way – but once the thought entered my mind, I couldn't get it out. And we both had the same thought at the same time. I moved away, but we'd crossed a line. Lunch was unbearable – I was completely over-excited, and I kept smiling at him when I thought no one was looking. Finally, when Mom and Pop were out of the way cleaning up, he more or less says – we have some unfinished business and you better haul your ass to the bar and we can work it out. So later on that night …"

Charlotte was hanging on her every word, completely wrapped up in the story but she needed another rum punch.

"Ok, stop for one minute, I'll get us another drink before we get onto the best bit."

She went to the bar but was served by the female bartender and didn't get to look at Chix, which was probably a good idea because she would have blushed.

"OK, carry on … oh, what about the guys?" worried they would turn up and spoil the moment.

"We're good … Chad just sent me a message."

She held up her iPhone and waved vaguely towards the lights further down the beach.

"They have gone to another bar to listen to the music. I told them we would stay here for a bit but may come and join them. That OK?"

"Yes great, now get on with it – I want all the juicy details."

"I arrive at the bar, dressed to impress, and he gives me this special, crinkly smile. He looked freaking hot as usual. I vaguely remember he was wearing a white linen shirt and some soft looking jeans and his locks were quite a lot longer then and he had them tied back loosely and he smelt amazing."

Marvel's nostrils twitched in sensory memory as she stopped to savour the moment before catching Charlie's impatient nod to carry on.

"A bit later we go to the car and drive down the beach a while – in fact you can see it from here … where those green lights are."

Charlie looked down the beach and nodded when she saw the lights in the far distance.

"We sit in his car and he gives me this talk."

"What talk?"

"The legendary 'Chix talk'. Apparently, he does it with all his girls – but I didn't know it at the time. It goes something like this – only it didn't sound as bad as this … and you have to imagine this delivered in his lovely, sexy voice."

She pauses, deepens her voice and husks, "Marvel, you are a lovely, young woman and I want to be with you, but I need you to understand what it is. This is not love. This is sex and sex is a beautiful game for adults to enjoy."

She paused and looked at Charlotte for her reaction,

"So basically, he told you he would like to have sex but nothing else was going to come of it and it was up to you if you were adult enough to deal with that?"

"Yep. Of course, I said yes and then we sort of worked out the details."

Marvel paused, then added, "I know it sounds a bit practical. But I figured that at least I knew where I stood, and it would be a good way to lose my virginity."

"So how was it?" Charlotte was concerned. It definitely sounded a little 'practical' to her. Not a romantic way to lose your virginity, but apparently, she was wrong.

"OMG it was wonderful. He was patient and gentle with me and made me comfortable. We made out for ages … And then … well, you don't need *all* the details … it just got really hot, you know?"

Charlotte nodded, she could imagine.

"We spent the rest of the vacation together and it was a blast. Then, when it was time to go back to the States, I went to say goodbye and we hugged and kissed like friends. I knew that was it and it was cool. It really was."

Charlotte just nodded her head dumbly – not wanting to be a prude but feeling a bit embarrassed by how frank Marvel had been.

"You know what. I *love* sex and Chad says I'm darn good at it. I think it's all down to Chix starting me off right. Once a woman is given an orgasm, she knows how to get an orgasm right?"

Charlotte goggled at her friend, she was nearly at a loss for words, but managed to squeak, "Does Chad know – about Chix? "

"Nooooooo, I would never tell him that – we laugh about Chix's women all the time. I wouldn't ever want Chad to feel bad around him because we have history. And I can honestly say Chix is like a brother to me now – is that like weird or what?"

"I wonder if I would be more sexually confident if I'd had that sort of experience," Charlie thought as Marvel wandered off to the 'john'.

She'd only slept with a handful of men. Her first time was a night of drunken passion with her friend's older brother – someone she'd had a huge, unrequited crush on for years. It had been amazing and special for her. But he'd rejected her afterwards and made her feel worthless.

The second time was with a very good-looking German guy she met on the last night of a girls' trip to Crete. She couldn't remember his name – or anything about the sex – so it can't have been great. Then she had a couple of short relationships in London – nothing to write home about and then Graham.

Their sex life was good. Not breathtaking, but good – up until a few months ago. *He's always been loving and affectionate until now. And we were always laughing.* But over the last few months, as the project got closer to launch and as the wedding got closer, they had drifted further and further apart. And she, stupid girl, had noticed but had been too scared to say anything.

CHAPTER 9
Tracy

Tracy woke up with a guilt hangover. She'd had too much fun yesterday. First order of business, get Shelliqua to call the museum and set up an appointment for her.

However, when she called reception a different girl answered, and she wasn't nearly as helpful. She told Tracy to do it herself and begrudgingly gave her instructions on how to dial a local number from the room. She dialled. Someone picked up after about five rings but it was a terrible line. It sounded like the person was in a wind tunnel.

"Hello?"

"Hello." She could hardly hear.

"Could I speak to Clinton Derrick, please?"

"Yes."

"Is he there?"

"Yes."

"May I speak with him?"

"Yes, this is Clinton."

"Oh, hello Dr Clinton, my name is …"

"Dr Derrick, but my friends call me Clinton."

"Oh, hello Dr Derrick."

"You can call me Clinton."

Tracy sighed … in theory they spoke the same language but in practice …

"Clinton, I've come from England and I have some research I want your help with. Can I meet you at the museum? I was rather hoping I could come today."

"Yes."

"OK, thank you, what time today?"

"No, you can't come today."

"But … you said 'yes'!" Tracy was getting totally exasperated but trying to remain calm

"I said 'yes' you could come and meet me. I didn't say 'yes' for today. I already have plans."

"Oh, how nice for you," she muttered sarcastically under her breath – then brightly, "What about tomorrow?"

"Maybe tomorrow, maybe the day after that, just call me in the morning."

Or at least that's what she thought he said. The line was getting worse.

"I just want to make an appointment as soon as possible," she shouted, frustration building, "it's really important I see you!"

"Soon," he said, "have a nice day." And put the phone down.

As she had, once again, been foiled in her plans to visit the museum and chat to Dr Derrick – or Dr Clinton, whatever the annoying bastard's name was – Tracy decided to have a quiet morning drawing (she'd recently signed up for an illustration course and was trying to capture some images to take home with her for the course homework). Then she'd do some more exploring.

Yesterday, she'd noticed that The Strip was made up of a long, golden sand bay with all the restaurants at one end and what looked like a deserted beach at the other. She wanted to see more of it.

She parked at D'wine (which hadn't opened yet) and set off to walk to the other end of the bay – relaxed and appropriately attired in a bikini and a short, floaty cover up. She loaded up her wristlet with the car keys and some money just in case she fancied a drink.

It took her about thirty minutes to get to the end – slightly longer than it should because she had to stop and talk to CB who had popped out onto the deck at Treasure Island when he saw her pass.

She tried to keep walking, smiled and shouted she would come in later but he just kept hollering, "Miss T, Miss T, Miss T come see me".

She gave in, walked over, and then he said,

"I just wanted to demonstrate my power over women by getting you here. Proved my point, see you later!" disappearing back into the bar, with a wink over his shoulder, in typical Cheeky Bugger form.

Amused and seriously tempted to stop and have a drink she stuck to plan, determined to get a little exercise. She walked for only a few more moments before she got hailed again. *Amazing. I've only been on this island for three days and I can't walk down a beach without bumping into someone I know already.*

This time it was Shelliqua, she was having a late lunch with a much older man. The spectacular girl was dressed to the nines and had squeezed her voluptuous figure into a hot pink strapless top and matching stretch 'skinny' jeans adorned by a large gold chain belt slung low. Her glamorous (for a night club let alone a beach bar) gold heels had deep platforms and spike heels. Gold and diamond hoops glittered at her ears, they sparkled and flashed almost as much as her smile.

That's a very hot outfit for lunch with Dad!

"Hello Tracy, I would like you to meet my good friend Mr Everette," she winked at her.

Tracy extended her hand politely. "Hello, it's a pleasure to meet you." She noted he had a very clammy handshake and didn't meet her eyes or return her smile. Tracy turned her attention back to the glorious girl.

"Glad to see you having a day off, Shelliqua, you look fabulous in pink. Are you having a nice lunch?" It certainly looked like she was. She had a brimming plate full of what looked like lobster and a frosty, pale yellow drink in a curvy glass in front of her.

Shelliqua smiled like the cat that just got the cream in agreement, and to underline the point stabbed a large, dripping chunk of buttery lobster onto her fork and lifted it up to her glossy lips before making sure her transfixed dining companion watched it disappear with a little mmmm of pleasure. Tracy grabbed the opportunity to wave goodbye and carried on down the beach.

The sand was pale gold and shelved slowly. The blue water hardly broke a wave. Tracy's toes, with their French manicure and silver dolphin toe ring, squished and squelched in the sand. She made good pace along the beach only having to adjust her stride to hop over the occasional rope anchoring a fishing boat and to duck under a dock, where tenders from the large boats moored.

Arriving at her destination, she found it was deserted and magical. Reddish cliffs were home to tough-looking trees that clung on for dear life. Seabirds swooped, then landed on the petrified wooden limbs that stuck out at impossible angles. Parts of the cliff had broken off and tumbled into the water to create rock pools and secret coves.

Tracy hung her cover-up and wrist purse on a convenient rock and waded into the sea, needing to cool off. The beach shelved gently, she had to go quite a long way out until the water came up to her shoulders. It was like a warm bath. She groaned with pleasure as she floated on her back enjoying the late afternoon sun on her face, perfectly content. She decided to exercise a little and ended up swimming backwards and forwards between a scruffy green and yellow fishing boat and an orange buoy that had a magnificent sea gull balanced on it. She did twenty 'lengths' before coasting back to the rocks. She'd been swimming for ages. It was close to sunset and the light was changing – maybe she could stay in the water until then.

This place is really something. I feel great and my libido has returned with a vengeance. The heat and beauty of the tropics was working its magic. The amazing water, the lack of clothes, the rum. And she couldn't stop thinking about that cute guy from last night.

"Need someone to keep you company watching that sunset?" said an amused voice.

She spun round to see who was talking to her and gasped. Standing between her and the beach was a tall man wearing a blue dive mask and holding a spear gun.

"Where did you come from? I didn't see you on the beach," she spluttered.

"Well, you wouldn't. I was spear fishing near the rocks out there." He pointed behind her, close to where she had been floating.

"Could you see me ... swimming?" she asked, mortified that he might have seen her underwater. The water felt wonderful and she'd undone her bikini to let her boobs float free.

"Yes, I saw you swimming," grinning at her. She stared, arrested by his smile; *at least he's a friendly shark.* His teeth were white and straight but stopped short of perfection because of a small gap between the front teeth. There was something familiar about those teeth – but she couldn't be sure because the mask was distorting his features and he was still quite a long way away.

The swine was enjoying himself enormously – teasing her. Despite being cut off from the land by his imposing figure she didn't feel nervous. He turned and walked towards the shore and she watched avidly. An old grey tee-shirt clung to his torso, forming a perfect V down to the baggy red knee length shorts.

When he reached the rocks where her cover-up was lying, he stopped and rested his spear gun on the top, then hung his string bag on a rocky spur. He pulled off his mask and put it beside her bag, then pulled off his tee-shirt and placed it next to her cover-up.

What's he doing? He turned round but before she could get a proper look at his face he ducked under the water and swam gracefully towards her underwater – surfacing just in front of her with a smile on his face.

No wonder he looked familiar. It was the guy from the bar last night.

"Glad to see it's you and not a spear gun wielding stalker," she quipped.

"How was your swim?" he enquired politely.

"Lovely. How was your spear fishing?" she smiled sweetly back.

"Productive. I have seven conch and three pot fish."

Tracy didn't look too impressed. "What's conch like and what's a pot fish when it's at home?"

"Conch otherwise known as lambi is delicious, it's a mollusc," he enunciated the word carefully. "You may have seen the big shells all over the place? It's also, and most importantly, considered by locals to be an aphrodisiac."

As he looked into her eyes, Tracy didn't miss her cue.

"I better try some then!"

"Good idea. Maybe, if you are very nice to me, I will cook some for you one day. I'm a very good … cook. We Caribbean men are all … very … good … cooks."

He moved closer, with a purposeful glint in his eye. Then reached for her shoulders and gently turned her round so he was behind her. The top of her curly head fitted comfortably under his jaw.

"Quiet now. We don't want to miss the show."

He's bold – cuddling up behind me like this – but it feels good, thought Tracy, accepting their closeness and relaxing back onto his chest instinctively. They watched the blazing sun disappear, far too quickly, then waded to shore chatting companionably about the stunning display of nature's beauty. Back at the rocks, collecting their stuff, he asked,

"What are you doing now?"

"I was planning to go and have a drink at Treasure Island."

"You like it there?"

"Yes, it's great. I made a couple of new friends last time I went." She winked at him.

"A couple of friends, eh? I guess that's me and the barman? You like him? You think he's a handsome guy too?" His tone was teasing her but there was an enquiry there too.

Oh no, she thought – *he thinks I'm after CB.*

"Yes, I mean no. I mean I like him. Nothing else you know, we had a laugh, he was very sweet to me."

"Ok. You know he's married?" serious now as he studied her.

"Yes, he told me that. He also told me that Treasure Island was his bar and that his wife is the Maître D. I met her briefly – nice lady. I like him as a friend and I loved the place," she said firmly.

He seemed satisfied with her answer.

"Miss T, I invite you to have a drink with me at Treasure Island."

Tracy grinned. "Thank you. That sounds like a good idea. Hold on – How do you know my nickname?" She may have had a few rums but she knew she hadn't told him her name – just like he hadn't told her his name the night before.

"Ahh, this is a small island. You will learn that soon enough," he said mysteriously. She decided not to rise to his bait.

When they arrived at Treasure Island, she was soon put in the picture. CB greeted them from behind the bar with a knowing expression.

"Hi Bro, how's it going? Well I guess, looking at the company you keep. Hi Miss T, I see you met my disgusting brother. Diver, what have you got in your bag for me today?"

She looked at Diver flabbergasted. CB's brother? And what did he mean Diver was disgusting? Bloody hell this island was small.

It wasn't until CB grabbed the fishing bag and took it into the kitchen that Tracy had the chance to talk to her new friend in private.

"Diver? Your name is Diver? As in scuba diver?"

"Yep, scuba, conch all kinds of diving …" He smiled wickedly.

Oh god, she could sense what was coming. He didn't disappoint.

"Actually, Miss T, there is another kind of diving which I really enjoy … on the whole it's a land-based activity, best practised inside – in privacy, although it can be a lot of fun outside too. I think you might enjoy it. I would be happy to give you a full demonstration when you come round to try my conch?"

They settled in at Treasure Island for a couple of rounds, laughing and chatting as if they had known each other forever. She learnt lots more about the island and plenty about his younger brother, of whom, she realised, he was exceptionally proud. How CB had been educated in the States, had a master's degree and worked as a trainee management consultant but had chosen to come 'home' to give something back to his island by building a business. He and his wife – a stunning and driven Trinidadian girl he had met when he was at college. They had set up the restaurant about two years ago and, on the whole, they loved it and that they hoped to start a family soon.

When she visited the bathroom the excitement of the day suddenly hit Tracy like the proverbial 'tonne of bricks'. Washing her hands, she looked up into the mirror. She was glowing. Her face smoothed of all stress. She had a light golden tan despite being devoid of makeup. Her blue eyes sparkled and although her hair was messy, it suited her in its top knot. Her blonde tendrils curled softly and the height of it elongated her round face.

What am I doing? She had a little talk to herself: I'm having far too much fun. Diver is great, amazing actually, but I'm not here for romance. I've got a job to do and he's just distracting me. And CB's distracting me too. I need to get away from these guys as soon as possible, I can't think straight around them.

She dried her hands. The sensible thing would be to go home. Luckily, circumstances were on her side. Diver was deep in conversation with guests at the next table. She grabbed her purse, squeezed his arm briefly, and echoing his words from the night before said, "I'm going to go to come back!", then hurried out of the bar with a quick "Laters!" to CB.

It was hard to ignore the concerned look on Diver's face or to not hear his request that she "wait" while he finished his business. But she did ignore him and sped down the beach towards her car. Contrarily, although she was the one that had left him so rudely, she looked over her shoulder a couple of times to see if he was following and was a little miffed that he hadn't chased her down the beach.

As she raced off in the jeep, she realised that once again she'd failed to follow her friend's instructions and visit D'wine and meet its legendary owner Chix. *Never mind I've had more than enough excitement for the day already.*

SUNDAY 8TH JUNE

CHAPTER 10
Charlotte

Charlotte woke up to find Graham buzzing around the room, humming along to the music on the TV. What a relief – he's in a good mood – hopefully back to normal!

He poured a cup of coffee and brought it over, placing it on the bedside table, nudging her over so he could sit down on the edge of the bed. He leant in and gave her a peck on the forehead.

"Good morning, sorry I've been such a shit."

She watched his face, he looked contrite.

"I know I've been a bit rubbish, but I'm really pre-occupied by the project, can't stop worrying about it. In retrospect it was bad timing to come away now." He smiled at her, hopeful for understanding and forgiveness.

Charlie smiled back weakly and nodded her head. As she thought. It *was* a pathetic excuse for an apology, but she wouldn't push it – she was just pleased he was in a better mood.

"I understand. Did you enjoy last night?"

He smiled widely. "Well, I probably won't rush back to the Folkloric Theatre but it was excellent to meet Chad – he's a great guy. We really hit it off."

"I noticed. I liked his wife too."

Graham nodded. "Yes, she's a pretty girl. Did you have fun talking to her? I saw you nose to nose over some of those lethal rum punches." Before she had a chance to answer he ran on,

"It was a funny bar, bit scruffy but quite good fun. I enjoy smoking a bit of 'wacky backy' every now and again – took me back a few years. I'd forgotten how much I like it …"

Graham got up from the bed and started pacing round the room, a signal that their moment of intimacy was finished. He started picking up things and putting them down again nervously, he clearly had something to ask her.

"Charlieeeeeee … my new mate Chad said there is this sort of 'island timetable' and that certain places are *the* places to go to on certain days. Apparently, Sunday is the busiest day of the week. He suggested we go to this seafood place at the other end of the island – it has a beach and a band and dancing." He looked at her, "I thought you would love it so I said we would go with them. Is that OK, Babe?"

He's concerned I want to have a romantic time at the hotel instead. He need not have worried. She'd far prefer to spend the day with Marvel.

"Yes, that sounds like fun. What do I need to wear? "

"Chad said to just wear a bikini and a cover-up but I supposed we could take a bag with some dry things just in case we are out later."

"Sounds good, I'll pack us a bag up."

Graham looked relieved. "OK, thanks. I'm going to just do a quick hour online with the office in the UK, I'll meet you in the lobby at eleven."

*

Charlie checked her appearance in the mirror before heading off to the others and for once liked what she saw. She loved her sleek black one piece with the single shoulder strap. She'd paired it with a pair of diaphanous wide-legged beach trousers, a huge black straw hat and some killer red Jackie O's. She felt sexy and sophisticated.

Graham had said the place where they were going had dancing – with a live band – and, fingers crossed, she would get the chance to get her groove on. She loved music, kept up with new releases and was eclectic in her tastes. She really loved the Caribbean music they played at the hotel and had been talking to the beach butler (who worked as a DJ also) about all the different music types. She had learnt a little about the different genres from him, and discovered she loved the soca beat in particular.

The journey to the seafood place was fun – Chad put the top down and Marvel gave them a running commentary on the island. Charlie's hair streamed behind her – she held her straw hat firmly on her lap, and she felt like a movie star.

"Thank you Marvel, thank you. I'm really looking forward to today, it's very kind of you to invite us."

"Honey, it's our pleasure. I reserved a table because it gets very busy there – like Chad said it's THE place to be on a Sunday. My Mom and Pop are going to join us because they would like to meet you both. I'm sure we'll run into some more people too."

Charlie smiled at her friend.

"That sounds lovely."

"I did tell you we have to get on a boat to go there, right?"

"No! But that sounds interesting." Charlie worried, "But is it far? What if I get seasick?"

Marvel reassured her, "No, it's real quick, a water taxi really – but once you're there you feel like you are on a whole other island. It's so special – you'll see. You are going to love it." She smiled smugly.

They'd reached the fishing village and after searching for somewhere to park, squeezed the jeep between two virtually identical white rental cars. The girls climbed out of the car and gazed at the view. A wide bay stretched in front of them and Charlie thought she had never seen so many different colours in one landscape before.

In the water, the natural pattern formed by coral reefs and white sand combined to create an amazing kaleidoscope of green, blue and turquoise shades. The sandy beach was fringed with green and yellow-hued coconut trees that shaded colourful wooden buildings. There must have been more than a hundred boats moored in the water – all different shapes and sizes and in many stages of repair.

In the middle of the bay, a bunch of small children in shorts and tee-shirts were using the jetty as a playground – hanging off ropes and jumping, diving and tumbling into the sparkling water. Beyond the jetty there was a tiny island. A slither of white and green with its silhouette of spiky trees and pointy roofs just about breaking the waves.

After grabbing their beach bags, the group walked down and onto the jetty to hail the water taxi. Charlie took photos of the other three standing at the end – cradled by the bay and wrapped in glorious technicolour. She wanted a record of such a happy day and to be able to remind herself, when she got back to post-honeymoon London, that such a riot of colours existed.

"The owner says just wave your arms and jump round like an idiot and someone will come and get you," said Chad and then started doing just that.

Everyone laughed. His performance worked, because within seconds a long, low boat was skimming over the water towards them. A handsome young man held the boat close to the jetty without tying up and helped the ladies on board, gently reminding them to mind themselves and take it easy as they stepped down.

"Do you guys mind waiting? The band has just arrived, and it would save me a trip."

"No problem the more the merrier," said Chad.

Charlie watched as a white flatbed truck reversed up the narrow jetty. A bunch of guys jumped out and strolled over to the boat.

"Good day," smiled a tall man with his hair tied back in a headscarf, short dreadlocks peeping out.

"Good day," they all echoed back.

The men started to unload the truck and pass the equipment down: speakers, guitars and a keyboard. They then followed by jumping onto the boat themselves, packing neatly into the remaining spaces. One went off to park the truck and waved the boat driver to go on.

As they got closer to the tiny island Charlie could see a low wall running from the beach to the jetty. It had an intriguing texture and gleamed softly pink in the sunlight.

"What's that on the walls, Marvel?" trying to figure it out.

"Conch shells! The whole island is covered in conch shells. It's very unique."

"That's remarkable. What a special place."

"Yes, it is," said Marvel with a proud smile. "Every island has a 'must have' experience and I believe this is ours."

"Our island … you really love it here, don't you?"

"Yes, yes I do. One day, when we are older and we have had our kids and when Chad eventually wants to slow down," she looked affectionately at her animated husband who was gabbling away nineteen to the dozen, high-fiving the band and generally being 'full speed' as usual, "we will come and live here."

"Really?" Charlie was surprised. "Why? I think it's perfect for a holiday, but I don't think I would want to live in a place like this. I don't mean to be rude but I love the seasons. I like to see the colours of the leaves change, I want big green spaces, rolling hills, woods, going for long walks. It's so small, wouldn't you be bored?"

Marvel smiled. She'd heard it all before.

"No. Never, I can honestly say I've never been bored a moment in my time here. But I know it's not right for us at the moment. Anyway, this island has a bit of a reputation when it comes to relationships …"

She stopped herself and looked at Charlie, obviously embarrassed.

"What do you mean?"

"Oh, it's nothing."

"No go on. Please. I'm intrigued. I would like to know."

"Well, they say that if people come here and the relationship is good – it will be a challenge – but it can survive and will grow stronger. But, they also say, if the relationship has any weaknesses the island will expose them. It's all BS I'm sure."

"Why do they say that?" Charlie looked puzzled. "Is it a local curse or something?"

Marvel snorted. "No! No, it's not some Obeah thing – it's actually much more mundane than that. My mum calls it 'the curse of the expats'. Basically, when someone from outside comes here to live – especially if they come from a cold place like the States or England – they have this idea that life is permanently like this," and she gestured at the tanned tourists lying on loungers under palm trees.

"Well, isn't it?"

Marvel laughed again. "Well, it is for someone like you or I because we are here on vacation. But if you come here to work or to retire, unless you want to end your days in the Betty Ford Clinic with a serious case of skin cancer, you can't do what we are going to do today – every day."

Charlie looked sceptical.

"It's hard to believe it but I promise you that you can't go to the beach, drink margaritas and sunbathe all day every day. The biggest issue for some people is – if I don't do that – what do I do? Essentially, the curse of the expats is invoked by boredom."

"But you said you'd never been bored a moment in your time here?"

"Yes, but I do different things to most of them."

Charlie was intrigued. "What do you mean? Ok, how can I say this right, without sounding like an idiot … or sounding racist … is it because you are Black?"

"No, that's OK. I don't *think* so. Chad and I, and our families, we are African American – we don't have any Caribbean heritage and I think your average African American tourist has the same challenges as your average white American tourist.

"Why I think I'm more integrated is because I've been coming here forever, I'm quite young and I have cultivated local friends that live and work here. We are all into social media too, so we keep in touch when I'm away. Then, because I'm into PR and writing, I run a blog and a website about the island and promote some of the places and people here.

"There are a whole bunch of talented people on the island – musicians, writers, artists and producers. I have one friend who is a filmmaker, so I'm trying to help him get work out of some of the local properties who need promotional videos. And then I volunteer for the carnival committee and make sure I come down for that every year. Mom and Pop have been here forever, as you know, and they have always encouraged me to get involved. They go to church – Mom helps with the garden show. We aren't exactly local but we are fairly in tune with what goes on."

Charlie was fascinated. Marvel was so dynamic and obviously good at what she did. She reminded her of Ali. She had amazing friends. What did these career girls see in her when she was so unambitious? She never really had a clue what she wanted to do, apart from marry and have kids.

"What does the average expat do – or not do, then – that brings on the curse? Woooooooooo." She made a silly noise.

"Usually they start to get bored at home after they've finished spending a shit load of dollars building or remodelling their dream house. They start heading out for their sundowners earlier and earlier. They go out to eat more and more, and, as you have probably noticed, our restaurants are *expensive*. They spend too much money and too much time at D'wine or Auntie Mo's. They start complaining about the way things are done here and wouldn't it be better if the islanders did it like this? Then getting upset when they can't change the things they used to love about the place – but which now frustrate them. Then suddenly, before you know it, someone's having an affair or they've realised they don't have enough money to live comfortably anymore, or they realise that the place isn't quite what they hoped it would be. The broken dream kills them. It is sad. We've seen quite a few come and go."

She looked at Charlie's worried face and reassured her.

"But it's only a problem for couples whose relationship is already in trouble, girlfriend. Don't look so concerned. I guess the moral of the story is don't try to use the island to heal a broken relationship … it isn't going to work!

"Ok I need some lubrication – my throat is dry," she pretend-gasped. "Let go get a drink and then we can relax on the beach until Mom and Pop arrive. Hey, did those guys disappear again? That is some love affair that Chad and Graham have going on! People are gonna talk."

They laughed and turned towards the bar, to find a fetching woman in a sunny yellow dress walking towards them, bearing a tray holding two glasses of bright orange rum punch. No wonder everyone has affairs – thought Charlotte, this island's full of amazingly good-looking people!

The girls both took a glass and said "cheers" to each other.

Marvel put on a mock serious voice, "Ms Charlie, because you are my new best friend, I am going to warn you now. This is officially the best and most lethal rum punch in the world. One is good, two OK, three – you're heading for danger ... four, well don't blame me if you find a picture of yourself on Facebook tomorrow, doing a headstand in front of the band with the whole restaurant looking at your panties ... got it?"

"Yes," Charlie laughed, "got it! It's OK, I'm quite a moderate drinker so don't worry about me."

Marvel looked sceptical. "I saw you loving those rum punches at D'wine, girlfriend! But if you say so. I'm telling you – they put something in the first one that makes all the good sense go away ... just saying."

Chad had appeared outside the restaurant area and was waving to attract their attention. "See my crazy husband over there? That means no time for sunbathing – better go have some lunch."

They left the beach and walked up to the restaurant area. There was a bar on one side of the room and a small stage to the left where the band was playing. Around the edges of the room were wooden tables and chairs and in the middle was a clear area – presumably the dance floor. Their two husbands were sitting at a big table opposite the band and there were four other people at the table – an older, but extremely attractive and well-dressed couple in their fifties, who Charlie assumed were Marvel's parents, and two other guys – one of which was Chix.

"That's neat, Chix and Dwight are having lunch with us too. You can get to know him," and she winked at Charlie.

"You're *bad*!" hissed Charlie. "Who's Dwight?" nodding her head at the tall, heavyset man with brown curly hair, hideous sunglasses and a ruddy complexion sitting next to the barman.

"He's a character – as you can see!" The girls giggled at the brightly coloured outfit that was glowing richly from the other side of the room. "He also owns a popular beach restaurant, he's quite the entrepreneur, I can guarantee your man Graham is going to love him. He's a real player too, so don't be surprised if he hits on you, even though you're married."

The whole table got up to welcome them and there was lots of handshaking and introductions. When everything settled down, Charlie sat down with Graham to her right and Chix opposite her. Dwight was next to him and Chad was next to Graham. Marvel and her parents were all the way at the other end.

After treating her to a sweet smile and an "OK love, having fun … it's good here isn't it?" Graham turned to his right and started talking to Dwight and Chad – ignoring her completely.

Chix had gone to talk to someone, so for a few minutes she sat quietly, staring at the band and enjoying a new rum punch – trying and failing to tune out the guys' animated chatter. They were having a loud conversation about someone buying a beachfront property and how there were already plans approved for a hundred rooms, but they wanted to triple that.

Blah, blah, blah, I'm so bored of conversations about buildings, and finances, and sales tactics, and design plans.

Chix came back to the table. As he sat down, he banged into the table leg and Charlie's rum punch rocked and spilt on the table top.

"Damn. Sorry about that, I hope I haven't spilt too much of your drink … here let me mop it up."

He pulled a napkin out of the holder and cleaned up swiftly and efficiently. "Let me get you another one."

"No, that's fine. I have plenty left in here."

"Well, drink up anyway … I'm going to get you another one to make up for it."

She thought, "Sod it – might as well get drunk."

He came back a few minutes later bearing two drinks – one each.

"Cheers! Nice to meet you properly – I remember you from the bar last night. So, how's your visit going? Is this your first time on the island?"

"It's lovely, we are enjoying it. Yes, our first time."

"And, you two are …?"

"Married, just married, we are on our honeymoon."

"Nice. Where are you staying?"

She named their hotel and he nodded in approval.

"That is a special place. And how did you get to meet my friends Marvel and Chad?"

"Oh, we got chatting with them at the hotel and they have been really kind and taken us out and about a bit. We really hit it off."

"Marvel is a lovely girl. I've known her forever."

"Yes, I heard." There must have been something in the way she said it because he looked at her with a curious expression.

Be careful Charlotte … better not dump Marvel in it.

"Yes, well, she said that you were her father's business partner and long-time friend of the family," she added sweetly.

"Yes," he said, "that's right." He relaxed visibly.

"And who is the other gentleman? The one talking with Graham and Chad?"

"That gangster is my friend Dwight. He's a businessman believe it or not, despite his colourful appearance today" (said businessman could not be accused of sartorial elegance. He had squeezed his muscular and rather hairy body into a pair of green, red, yellow and black swim shorts and a matching vest – topped off with a disgusting pair of mirrored wraparound Oakley's and a pair of banana yellow Havaianas.)

Charlie gazed in awe – he had spectacularly bad taste. "He looks very … Caribbean …" she trailed off, not wanting to be rude about his friend but really! She thought Dwight's appearance must be terribly off-putting for Graham, who was very tastefully attired as usual – today's choice being a grey and white ensemble by Diesel – but he appeared to be happy chatting with his new chums.

She looked politely at Chix as he carried on filling her in on his friend.

"He has a very nice beach restaurant called Auntie Mo's. You should go – it's on an amazing beach."

"This island has loads of amazing beaches, I hear. But I can't imagine any are better than the one where we're staying."

"Yes, but this one has a different vibe to your hotel's – buzzier – more like a St Barth's-Nikki Beach vibe. I think you and your husband might like it. You could go for the day – you don't have to go to Auntie Mo's, there are quite a few beach bars that would be more you and your husband's style." He smiled. He'd picked up on her look of disbelief that she could enjoy anything belonging to the colourful character talking to her husband.

"And I have a water sports operation down there. It's the only place on the island where you can rent jet skis and paddleboards. We've got kayaks and snorkel equipment to hire too."

"That sounds good." She smiled anxiously. "To be honest, it's a little quiet at our hotel for Graham – so he would probably like that. I will suggest it."

Charlie looked at her husband and Dwight talking, then questioned Chix, "He seems to be talking to Dwight about a hotel that's being built?"

"Dwight and his family own a fantastic piece of property down on that beach and he has just got planning permission for a hundred-room hotel, which I think would be OK, but he's pushing for three hundred – which I think is far too big."

"Isn't it good to have more tourists? Why wouldn't you want a bigger hotel?"

"Well, this is a small island and if we build too many new hotel rooms I have a belief that it will spoil it."

"In what way?"

"Well, I have quite a few reasons, but the most important one is that, currently, we have mainly local people working in the bars and restaurants and the tourists seem to like that. They like to chat to them about the island and feel like they have made a friend from here. Many people here already have a job in the hotel industry. For us to service three hundred rooms in that area we would have to bring in extra people – either from other islands or from places like Thailand – because we wouldn't have enough people to staff it. A lot of our tourists, who come here every year and spend lots and lots of money, think we have something special going because it's small and personal – old school Caribbean. 'Sustainable', I think is the buzz word now. I think a big hotel like that would change our appeal."

"Oh," said Charlie, "I see." and nodded in agreement. She 'sort of' got it and was terribly impressed with the way Chix spoke. He was a smart man.

"So please tell me some more about the band, I love this music."

"These guys are great. They are just ordinary guys – they work in ordinary jobs during the week, but they love to sing and perform. They have a big following that come here to listen to them every Sunday. They play all sorts – a little reggae, some zouk and then finish with soca. Start off slow and in the background, but they will speed up in a bit and people will start dancing. Do you dance?"

"I love to dance but …" She didn't have a chance to finish because the young man who drove them over on the boat and the lady in the yellow dress had arrived at their table with mountains of food. Charlie had ordered lobster and she couldn't believe the size of the ugly creature on her plate. It was spilling off the sides and its black beady eyes were glaring at her malevolently.

"Looks good, eh? Best lobster on the island, they say."

"Well, it certainly looks amazing. It's a bit overwhelming, though."

"Don't worry it's more spikes and shell than meat, you will manage. Tuck in."

"Are you eating?"

"No, not hungry, I'll probably eat later – over there." He pointed to the mainland.

The plate of food was so colourful and attractive she snapped a picture of it. Then Marvel got up and asked a passing waitress to take a picture of the table.

"One for Facebook," she said.

Charlie really enjoyed the lobster but was overwhelmed by the size and Graham had to finish it off for her. She went to have another swig of rum punch to wash it down and realised she'd finished her third drink without noticing. Chix was looking at her in an amused way.

"Do you want another one of those? Or maybe you'd like water instead?"

Despite Marvel's warnings, she decided she didn't feel tipsy at all – there wasn't anything special about those drinks she thought.

"Yes please, I would like another one of those. I don't know what all the fuss is about, I don't feel the effect at all."

"No? OK, well, I will order you another one."

"Why aren't you drinking another one?"

"I'm a one rum punch kind of guy – I'll usually have one to start and then move onto a light beer. That way I keep my head clear."

The drink was making her bold: she ventured,

"I think maybe you like to stay in control?"

He was amused. "Very good! You must be a student of human nature. I own a bar – I see the effects of too much alcohol every day and I'm not just talking about the tourists. We like our rum here in the Caribbean." He paused, then said,

"My father was an alcoholic – it killed him."

"Oh," she didn't know what to say, "sorry."

"It's OK. He died when I was very young. I didn't know him. He was a sailor, from a neighbouring island, but he went up and down the islands looking for work and spent enough time here to beget me." His words implying a joke were belied by his suddenly sad eyes. "A girl in every port you know. I was raised by his family over there." And he shrugged his shoulders in the general direction of his homeland.

Charlotte sensed that Chix didn't talk about himself that much. She was intrigued and wanted to know more about him.

"What about your mum, what was she like?"

"I never knew her. I was brought up by my grandmother and then, after she died, I was passed on to whoever could be persuaded to have me. I learnt early to look after myself."

Charlie, who had a close and loving relationship with her (both still alive) parents, felt terrible for him.

"That's incredibly sad. You poor thing."

Chix shrugged. "It's OK. I've done OK all things considered." He smiled at her a little sheepishly, "To be honest, I don't normally talk about this stuff. I'm a private person and I don't know why I told you." He paused and looked at her curiously, "You are a good listener. It's a skill – not one that many people have. I suspect you are a special person to make people open up to you that way."

She was flattered but a little embarrassed. "I'm glad you think so, but honestly there is nothing very special about me."

Chix looked at her sternly, he didn't like negativity.

"And pretty and very ladylike. I can see what your husband sees in you. Not so sure the other way around, though." He smiled, but she wasn't so sure he was teasing.

"It's OK," she giggled, "I can see why you would say that. He is being a bit of a pain at the moment but he's a lovely guy really."

"Well, he's quite obsessed with that conversation over there – those guys have been talking business all lunch time."

"I'm so glad you sat close to me, Chix – I would have been bored otherwise. Mind you, who could be bored listening to this music. I love it. "

"As does that lady over there." Smiling widely, he pointed to a short, plump middle-aged blonde, whose big blue eyes were fixed adoringly on her partner and whose slightly mad blonde curls bounced comically. She was dancing up a storm. Her partner, a tall, broad shouldered, happy looking guy, didn't appear to mind that his girlfriend was more enthusiastic than skilled on the dance floor. Every time he twirled her round she giggled in joy, showing a glimpse of her large bottom, barely covered by a leopard print bikini, to the watching diners.

"She looks so happy," Charlie said wistfully.

"She does," he agreed, "she's certainly thrown herself into island life." Watching the couple knowingly, recognising a holiday romance.

He stood up, "Like to dance? I love this song."

"Well, I feel a bit embarrassed. I'm not sure I know how to do it. There seems to be quite a bit involved."

"Don't worry. If you like the music, just go with it and I will show you anyway."

She turned to Graham, "Babe …" he ignored her. "Babe!" she said loudly. He looked up, guiltily.

"Sorry darling, yes?"

"I'm going to dance with Chix."

"Well, enjoy," barely acknowledging her before returning to his conversation.

"Not exactly the jealous type, is he?" Chix murmured as he took her hand and led her onto the dance floor.

It felt strange at first, dancing in the sand in the middle of the day. And dancing this close to a man that wasn't Graham, but Chix was both a gentleman and an excellent dancer, and she soon relaxed and found the beat. He held her lightly, one arm round her waist the other holding her hand quite high up. It was almost like a waltz: old-fashioned and definitely more courteous than the dance the other people on the floor were performing.

She couldn't help but notice that the enthusiastic blonde and her partner had their hips welded together for the entire song. They even indulged in a long lingering kiss at one point, much to the delight of the band, who whooped and hollered at them.

When they finally returned to the table Chad, Graham and Dwight were still nose to nose, talking business. Marvel and her parents had moved to another table and were chatting to some friends.

Her friend caught her eye and mouthed, "You OK?" and Charlie raised her thumb and smiled.

Chix went to the bar and came back with yet another rum punch and a small bottle of water. As he handed her the drinks he said,

"You can have the next one if you drink the water first."

She giggled and gulped the water down fast, then slammed the bottle down on the table defiantly.

"See? I'm a good girl. I drank up all my water. Honestly, I feel sober as a judge."

"Hmm, well, let's see. Luckily you had some food. I'm a bit hot. Do you want to go for a walk on the beach and cool down?" suggested Chix.

"Yes, that would be lovely. Can I swim? I haven't been in all day."

"Sure. Let's go."

They walked onto the small beach. He held her drink as she quickly stripped off her black trousers and placed them onto one of the conch-covered walls.

"Take it in with you," he said, handing her glass back to her as she walked towards the water.

"I've never had a drink in the sea. What fun! Ohhh … it's lovely and warm. Aren't you coming in?"

"No, not today, actually I won't probably go in the water 'til August – our summer. It's a bit cold for me. I only go in when I have to."

"Really?"

He shrugged his shoulders at her bemused expression. "I have spent years helping on boats and slogging away doing water sports, I've sort of lost my love of the water. You have fun, though, I'm going to catch up with some friends. Catch you later."

Charlie wallowed around in the water, watching a group of inebriated tourists who were making a meal out of climbing back onto their boat charter, obviously a little worse for wear after the rum punches.

Swish, swish, swish what a lovely, lovely day. Chix is so kind and thoughtful and very VERY, attractive. She remembered the story Marvel had told her last night and wondered what it would be like to be with him. If he made love with as much skill as he danced then – well, that would be something. She thought about dancing with Graham and making love with Graham and concluded that Graham made love just like he danced, technically very well, but there was no … she didn't know what the word was … but when Chix danced he definitely had it.

A cool breeze whipped over the water. the drunken passengers sped off in a roar of engines, a cloud rolled over the sun and suddenly the euphoria of her day wore off. She felt sad. Thinking about some of the things she had learnt that day. About Chix not having a mum or dad and about that horrid thing Marvel said about couples coming to the island and splitting up.

Could a thirty-year-old marriage really be torn apart by boredom? What if that happened to Mum and Dad – that would be awful! She wondered if she and Graham had any hope at all. To be honest, the chances didn't seem good at the moment.

She cheered up when Marvel and Chix arrived and insisted they took a picture of her –teasing and calling her a supermodel. As a teenager she had been tall, skinny and awkward. And, until her braces worked their magic, very goofy too. In her mind she was the proverbial 'ugly duckling' that had turned into a swan – but still didn't truly believe it until she met Graham. He loved the way she looked and had really helped her choose clothes to flatter her, rather than make her blend into the background.

Charlie knew women envied her slim figure and long legs, but she still had memories of being the tallest, gangliest, most flat-chested girl in the class. She'd also always felt slightly overshadowed by Ali, her bubbly friend who, despite being a self-proclaimed 'ginger' with the classic, big bottomed, English 'pear shape', got tonnes of attention from guys because of her pretty face and outgoing personality. *Graham is the first man to make me feel beautiful.*

Chad and Marvel dropped them home to the hotel just after sunset. They decided they were too drunk and tired to go back out, so they ordered room service. The butler delivered a huge silver tray laden with delicious club sandwiches, chocolate brownies and a refreshing jug of frosty homemade lemonade. Lounging around in the fiercely air conditioned room, enjoying its cool comfort on their overheated skins, chatting companionably about their day, was the best time they had together for ages. When they got into bed Graham reached over to kiss her.

"Good night my darling, sleep well."

Charlie tensed. *I don't want to make love …* The thought popped disloyally into her brain. Her wish was granted. After kissing her briefly on the lips, he moved over to his side of the bed and fell asleep immediately.

CHAPTER 11
Tracy

Tracy and Diver – with a combined age of close to eighty – were snogging like teenagers. In public! As she came up for air she started laughing.

"What?" said Diver and raised his eyebrow in a Sean Connery-like way. She laughed some more.

"What?"

"I can't believe I'm behaving like this, snogging and carrying on like a teenager in the middle of the day."

"That's good – me too."

"Really?" She looked sceptical. "You're exceedingly good at it which makes me think you might do this all the time?"

"What – coming for lunch?"

"No, you idiot. I'm wondering … do you bring a different woman here every week? Are you a gigolo?"

She smiled to lighten the question but, in reality, was deadly serious – the thought having occurred to her that picking up tourists was probably a regular activity for him.

"Because if you are you will be sorely disappointed – I haven't got any money, despite my wealthy and sophisticated appearance," she raised an eyebrow at him.

Diver looked pained. "Now you're insulting me. What have I done to deserve this? I try to be helpful and take you out to a nice place for lunch and you reward me by insulting me. It's not fair."

She noticed he hadn't actually answered her.

"Diver, when was the last time you brought a woman here to this island?"

He thought about it, then pretended to just remember, "About two or three weeks ago."

"Two weeks ago! You dog!" and began moving away, shocked at his nerve, he was a terrible flirt and she could see he was 'a bit of a one', as her mum would say … but to come out and admit it.

He grabbed her back, laughing. "Yes, Jimmy and I brought Granny here for lunch on her birthday." He looked smug, "That is the nice kind of thing I do for the women in my life." And he inched closer with the clear intention of kissing her.

"So, you don't bring all your women here?"

Tracy kept scooting back. Determined to maintain a healthy distance. She couldn't think straight when he was too close.

"What makes you think I have lots of women?"

"Just the way you are. Because of the professional way you have pursued me. I think you must have had lots of practice?"

"You think I am a gigolo because I have been good at pursuing you? Hmmm, very interesting. I guess I should take that as a compliment."

Not to be deterred, he still hadn't actually answered her question, she asked again,

"Well, have you?"

"Have I what?"

"Had lots of practice, God you are annoying."

"No, I'm not and I don't think you think that I am annoying at all. I think you think I am interesting and exciting and … sexy," emphasising the last word huskily. "I can tell you like me."

"Why do you think I like you?"

He smiled, reminding Tracy of the cat that got the cream.

"Because you say things like 'oh, I can't believe I'm doing this!' And 'oh, I don't normally behave like this'," in a terrible approximation of Tracy's British accent. "Therefore, I conclude that you think I am a powerfully attractive man – like James Bond – with my sexy moves and powers of persuasion."

She burst into a new set of giggles and shook her head in wonderment.

What am I going to do with him? He's bloody gorgeous and I can't resist. She leant forward to give him a kiss on the cheek. "You're not bad I suppose."

"I will take that as a compliment from an understated English woman. Can I get you anything Miss T? Anything your heart desires? I hope you know by now that your wish is my command."

"Actually, I would like a drink."

"Rum punch?"

"No … no, thank you, I've had enough of those recently to last a lifetime. Can you get me a coke or that grapefruit thing … or something soft, please?"

"Sure, one Ting coming up. I won't be long, *don't move*. I don't want to come back and find you gone again." He couldn't quite resist a little dig about her behaviour yesterday as he headed off.

Tracy watched him leave, admiring every inch of his tall frame – especially his long, strong legs. *What a sweet, sexy, affectionate man.* She was incredibly attracted to his looks but the thing she liked most about him was his sense of humour – he made her laugh a lot. She was so glad that they'd got together today.

Diver had commandeered a small tiki hut with views of the ocean. It was close to the bar but not overlooked. They spent the afternoon glued to each other – hand feeding morsels from the brimming plates of lobster, laughing, chatting and canoodling.

She couldn't blame him for his dig about yesterday. She would never have had this wonderful day if he hadn't persevered and come looking for her.

*

She had woken up that morning feeling low. Also, a bit guilty about running away from Diver the night before. But still determined to concentrate on and fast track her plans to find out more about Mum's time on the island.

She tried calling the museum man's phone but there was no answer. She tried again – still no luck. She promised herself she would give it another go after breakfast and after that, if she didn't get through she would take a drive to the airport and see if she could find someone who'd worked there back in the day. She knew that would be a very long shot, but at least she would be doing something.

But then she walked into the restaurant and found Diver sitting at 'her' table. Bold as brass. He'd asked the waitress (who of course he knew) where she normally sat and waited patiently for her to turn up.

"Good morning," he said brightly

"Good morning." Tracy felt a bit flustered, if she had known she was going to see him she would definitely have paid a bit more attention to her appearance.

"How are you?" In an extremely polite voice.

"I'm fine, how are you?" She could be polite too. She sat down gingerly and looked at him from the safety of the other side of the table.

"I feel much better for seeing you in one piece. I was worried that you'd had an accident – or something bad had happened to you."

"No. I'm fine. Why would you think that?" she asked, playing dumb.

With a serious face and searching eyes he said, "Well, normally when two people who like each other are in a bar, having a drink and getting to know each other better, and one says to the other 'they are going to come back', the other person waits for them to come back."

Tracy looked guilty but didn't say anything. He carried on.

"Picture my distress when I waited at Treasure Island for hours before having to admit I'd been stood up. My brother found it amusing. He told me you are a nice woman, not normally rude. Therefore, I am giving you the benefit of the doubt and am assuming you must have had an emergency to deal with back at your hotel?" He looked at her for an answer.

Tracy felt guilty. But attack was the best form of defence.

"I was only treating you the way you treated me!"

"What do you mean?"

"Well, the night we met you did the same thing to me. We were having a nice chat, you got a call, jumped up and left."

"Yes, I did. And I also told you I had to go to come back. And I did. Come back about five minutes later. And you weren't there."

"You came back that night?"

"Yes, because that's what 'go to come back' means. I just had to go see a man about some fish, then I came back."

"Oh ... I didn't realise. I just thought you'd gone."

"Like *gone* gone? No. I'd gone to come back."

Ah. She got it now.

"Sorry. We don't use that term in the UK. I misunderstood."

"So ... are you OK?" Diver looked a little less serious now.

"Yes, I'm fine. Look, I'm sorry, I really am. I don't know how to explain it. I was having a lovely time, but I suddenly just needed to go. Really needed to go. I am sorry if I was rude, though, truly sorry."

He looked concerned, "Are you better now?"

He thinks I had a tummy upset or something. Should I set him straight? She debated quickly while he took a sip of her orange juice then poured them both a cup of coffee from the pot that had magically appeared. Her mind was working overtime: He's very easy to talk to. I could tell him about Mum, I'm sure. But I'm just not in the mood for loads of questions now. And it's so good to see him. It's really, really nice that he came to find me. And he is incredibly cute. And Cheryl said I should have fun. And I work hard all the time. And I could still call the Museum later, though it probably doesn't open again until Monday. *Oh god ... what's happened to my willpower!*

She gave in to temptation. "Much, much better. Maybe I could buy you breakfast to make up for my behaviour last night?" She smiled enticingly.

It looked like that was all that was needed. Diver's eyes were alive with mischief again, and the charming gap between his teeth was back in evidence.

"Only if you let me buy you lunch later. I know this great little place."

She laughed, the man really had her number, and put her hand out to shake on it.

"It's a deal."

MONDAY 9TH - WEDNESDAY 11TH JUNE

CHAPTER 12
Charlotte

Charlie was happy. Graham was back to normal since their fortuitous meeting with Marvel and Chad. Granted, they hadn't 'been intimate' and he was still spending lots of time hunting down wi-fi and calling the office, but he was a lot more relaxed and that made her happy too.

They'd seen Chad and Marvel every day since they met them and were now firm friends with the two Americans, who were keen to show them every aspect of 'their' island.

Graham was starting to see potential everywhere, as the island was under-developed and unspoilt with amazing beaches that were currently empty of (what he deemed) appropriately-sized property. As a result of his chats with Chad and Dwight, he was now seriously considering the possibility of investing in the island, once he was a bit further on with his own project. The plan for today was to view some land options.

They chatted over a leisurely breakfast, enjoying views of the beach and the colourful Hobie cats lined up by the water's edge.

"There is definitely room for a large luxury hotel here. This hotel is charming but it's small and dated, a bit like Joan Collins," he joked.

Charlie felt a bit put out on Joan and the hotel's behalf.

"I think it's perfect as it is."

"I agree that it's lovely, Babe, and the beach is amazing, but it needs an upgrade. They need wi-fi throughout, good TVs and more contemporary design – a beachy version of what I'm doing in Kennington. Andreas says that people are so particular about their own homes these days, that they invest huge amounts in domestic interior design – that they expect similar quality, or better, from their hotel rooms. I'd love him to get his hands on this place. He would work wonders."

"Well, let's just agree to disagree."

Charlie didn't want to rock the boat, but she didn't really give a fuck what Andreas would think about their hotel.

Paradise Point is unique, she thought. It's developed its own style. It's quirky, timeless and incredibly comfortable. I don't always want to be somewhere that looks like my flat in London – much as I love it – I'm in the Caribbean and I know it – but if Graham and Andreas had their way this place would feel like South Beach.

Just after 9am, the force of nature that was Chad turned up. After greeting every staff member and saying a friendly good morning to all the guests, he gave her a kiss on the cheek before whisking Graham off.

She was looking forward to another quiet day on the beach, working on her already nut-brown tan. Since they met Chad and Marvel, the holiday had flown by and they only had today and tomorrow as full days before they went home. She enjoyed two full hours of soaking up the glorious sunshine and listening to cool island beats courtesy of DJ Sweets – aka Karim the beach butler – and was just beginning to feel peckish for something to nibble on when a shadow blocked out her sun. Looking up she saw a grinning Chix standing in front of her.

"Hey lady, I've been sent to collect you, by Marvel and the gang," he said.

"Oh, nice surprise. Where are they?"

"Over there …" He pointed behind him at a large white, grey and silver motor yacht moored in the bay.

"What? … on that boat? … Wow, … fancy."

"Yep, look …" he turned to them and started moving his arms out and together over this head, "can you can see them waving at us?"

"Yes, how wonderful. How do we get out to them?"

"On that." He pointed to a small inflatable boat pulled up on the beach a few yards to her right. "I suggest you run back to your room, grab Graham's swimsuit and whatever you need to see you through 'til sunset because we are going to a place called Prickly Pear Island for lunch."

"That sounds painful," she joked. "Where is it?"

"Na," he said, playing along with her, "it's quite comfortable actually, and very beautiful. It's about four miles off shore, uninhabited. No electricity, no running water, just an amazing beach, some palm trees, lots of birds and lizards and a little restaurant-bar run by some of my friends."

Archly raising an eyebrow, she said sarcastically, "You have friends there? Wow! What a surprise … NOT – honestly Chix, do you know everyone?"

He smiled and shrugged, "It's a small place."

"Well, it sounds amazing, I'd love to go. Whose boat is it?"

"Dwight's."

She raised her eyebrows again, this time quizzically.

"You're surprised he has a boat like that?"

She nodded.

"Look, I know he's a bit of a rough diamond but he's extremely successful. And that boat is a status symbol – it's his pride and joy. You have to look beyond the terrible taste in clothes and sunglasses."

Charlie felt guilty; she didn't want Chix to think she was a complete snob.

"He's a good guy really. He came from a regular Zephyr family but what he did right was understand that tourism was the way forward for the island and that our beaches were going to be our biggest asset. A family member left him a tiny parcel of beach land. At that time, most people didn't understand its value and preferred to be inland because it was better farming, but when he was very young he somehow scraped the money together to put up Aunty Mo's – and the rest is history. He worked hard and he's kept adding to that land every opportunity he could. Now he's worth millions and that boat tells everyone he has done really well for himself."

"Well, that is very interesting and it's incredibly kind of him to take us. Graham will love it I'm sure. Give me five then – I'll try and be as quick as possible." And she ran off to their room to get their stuff.

Back in her room Charlie decided to change swimsuits (to minimise strap marks) and put on the divine, metallic gold bikini. Graham had bought it for her from the hotel shop and she hadn't had a chance to wear it yet. It was a simple design: plain Brazilian cut bottoms with a little ruching at the back and a plain bandeau top – the beauty being in the perfect cut and stunning colour. She put large gold hoops in her ears, popped on her favourite smoky grey Tom Ford Sunglasses and a pair of delicate gold thong-style sandals. She grabbed her woven beach bag and added two large hotel towels, Graham's grey Diesel swimming trunks, a plain white tee, some money and their camera. Finally, she walked to the wardrobe and selected a gossamer thin, charcoal grey cover-up with a discreet, gold thread pattern at the neck and at the bottom of the sleeves. The flimsy silk chiffon confection was another costly present from the hotel shop, and it floated lazily down over her body until it almost reached the floor, its long side slits leaving her deeply tanned legs free to move. The gold bikini gleamed enticingly underneath.

I really do look good, she thought, flicking her glossy, dark brown hair over one shoulder then giving herself a final check in the mirror before locking the room and heading back to the beach.

She ran over to Chix, who was sitting under her umbrella trying unsuccessfully to keep out of the fierce midday sun.

"Well, you were certainly worth the wait." He wolf-whistled appreciatively. "You look a million dollars. Prickly Pear won't know what's hit it."

"Oh, this old thing?" she smiled. Teasing but delighted by the compliment. "Anyway, you look rather spiffy yourself. I wouldn't want to let you down."

"Oh, this old thing?" He was dressed casually in a pair of turquoise long shorts and a long, tight white vest top which went over his shorts to the top of his legs. His gold chain had a turquoise and diamond encrusted seahorse on the end and it sparkled in the sun. He had tied his locks back and they were completely covered with a turquoise and white headscarf, which she found amusing. She tried to imagine the average English man in a headscarf and couldn't.

"I like your headscarf," she teased as she sat down on the side of the boat and gracefully swung her legs up, over and in. Chix pushed the boat further out into the water then jumped aboard and started the engine with one quick, efficient move. The trip across the sparkling turquoise bay was almost over before it began.

Charlie was helped onboard the yacht by the crew, while Chix secured the tender. When Charlie joined the others on the top deck, Marvel let out a gasp of appreciation when she saw her outfit.

"Girlfriend, you look fierce, that is one – sorry for the crude language – freaking, amazing look."

Graham beamed at her. "Babe, I must agree, you look delicious. That gold bikini gleaming under the grey silk reminds me of a caramel waiting to be unwrapped. I knew it would look wonderful on you."

Marvel's jaw dropped and her eyes bugged.

"Graham, you picked that out for her? That is awesome. Wow, you have great taste, a really good eye for fashion."

"Thanks, I love to buy clothes for her. When I met Charlie, she was a blank canvas waiting to be turned into a masterpiece."

There was an awkward silence.

I don't really know how to take that … Charlie thought and could see the others thinking it too. Was it a compliment or an insult? Was he saying she was beautiful or just looked good because of the clothes? What kind of weird way was that to talk about your wife? Luckily the irrepressible Chad broke the silence and said cheerfully,

"Well, I'm just your average guy and I don't really understand all that art crap, but I am a red-blooded man and, Charlie, I think you look hot."

Playing to the crowd he attempted to mimic a sexy stripper routine – licking the tip of his finger and pointing and winking at his wife flirtatiously.

"Baby, we are gonna have to go find you one of those gold bikinis and when it gets cold up in NYC we gonna turn up the heating and you gonna slip that on so you can do a little private dance and warm me right up."

"I hope you'll tip me," Marvel pouted.

"I gotta big tip for you, honey," Chad leered.

Everyone cracked up and the tension in the air evaporated – but Graham's comment hurt. *Why can't he just say I look sexy?* Fighting back the tears but not wanting anyone to see, she moved to the back of the boat and leant against the railings, pretending to look at the rapidly disappearing hotel. Sensing someone behind her she turned, hoping for Graham, but it was only a crew member asking if she wanted a drink.

Prickly Pear was only a few miles away from the mainland and before long the boat was racing along the side of the tiny island. Downstairs, Dwight was steering the huge yacht. Upstairs the two crew members, a captain and first mate, served drinks and hung out with the guests. Looking at the happy scene, Charlie thought what a good-looking and interesting bunch they were, a mixture of ages, cultures and colour – all attractive in their own way.

The stretch of white sand eased into a cove. The boat swooped in and slowed down to a snail's pace as it got close to the shore. Limpid pale turquoise water lapped the beach lazily, tempting the passengers to immerse themselves as quickly as possible. Chad threw himself off the boat as it was still moving, even though Marvel told him not to.

Halfway up the beach Charlie could see a small tiki hut style bar, further up, nestled under gently swaying coconut palms, was a small restaurant painted red, gold and green.

"Where's Robinson Crusoe?" asked Graham, pretending to look around. Charlie giggled.

The purr of the engines quietened and was replaced with a mechanical whirr as the huge machines were raised out of the water. It was suddenly all action as Dwight skilfully manoeuvred the yacht to its mooring spot fifty metres from the beach. There was a creaking noise as the huge chain uncoiled and the heavy anchor slipped down to the white sandy bottom of the sea.

Satisfied that everything was in order, Chix pulled the tender round and started organising them all. Charlie and Graham tendered in with him and arrived without getting wet. The others jumped off the boat to join Chad and were swimming in.

Would you ever get immune to all this beauty? The white, white sands, that ridiculously blue water, the picturesque coconut trees, the whole 'Treasure Island' thing? Charlie didn't think you would. She studied a flock of small white birds with big feet rushing comically along the water's edge and didn't notice Graham coming up behind her until he put his hand on her shoulder.

She turned and smiled at him. He was grinning and shaking his head with disbelief.

"What a waste. What potential. There's nothing here! Imagine putting a boutique hotel here – and a spa – that would be incredible."

Before she could answer that she didn't think it would be a good idea to spoil such a perfect place at all, a dripping Dwight emerged from the sea, and walked towards them shaking the water out of his ears. Charlie tried not to look at what was highlighted by the clinging, wet fabric of his banana yellow surf shorts.

Dwight joined in, nodding his head enthusiastically,

"I hear you Graham, and I would love to do that here man. It would be a licence to print money. But them people that own the island well …"

And once again the two of them jumped into another animated discussion about the perfect hotel.

And once again I feel left out and inconsequential. Charlie watched as the men walked off towards the tiki bar without a backward glance at her.

CHAPTER 13
Tracy

Naked, splayed like a starfish that had washed up on crisp, white sheets, Tracy stretched each limb in turn.

The days have flown by since I met Diver, I'm very, very glad he came into my life. Every single part of me loves being here and being with him.

Her skin felt smooth and tight because Diver kept insisting that he rub suntan lotion into her. Her hair was the perfect shade of saltwater blonde and the humidity helped it curl just right. The sun brought out her freckles, which she'd been reliably informed enhanced the ocean shades in her sparkling baby-blue eyes. *He looks at me like I'm the most precious thing in the world and I melt inside when he smiles … And those kisses.*

Sublimely comfortable, in no hurry to get up, she luxuriated in her memories. After an amazing day at Shell Cay, Diver had driven her home to the resort where they hung out on the moonlit beach for hours. Somehow he managed to fit both of them onto her favourite sunbed by lying down first and pulling her back to relax – settling her head comfortably in the dip of his chest. His long legs framed her. He made the best sofa ever, and they lay for hours watching the bright sky – pointing out shooting stars and fast-moving satellites. He whispered nonsense in her ear and dropped light kisses on her heated neck until they feel asleep. Tracy woke as the dawn broke but didn't want to disturb the soft rumble of Diver's steady breathing. Nature called so she tried to extract herself from his arms without waking him. It didn't work. As she unlaced his fingers from around her waist, he protested by snuggling her back into him.

"Let me go, Diver, I've got to go!"

"No."

"Please. You will regret it if you don't."

"I don't want you to leave me," he pouted, "I'm so comfortable."

"Me too, but when a girl's got to go, she's got to go." And she ran into the sea.

He followed her in – diving under the water to grab her legs and tip her up. Then they mucked around for ages. Ducking and jumping on each other like kids in the early morning light. When he was finally ready to stop teasing and tickling her, they agreed to a leisurely breakfast. They feasted like kings on delicious savoury, saltfish-filled johnny cakes, cinnamon spiced cornmeal porridge and sweet bush tea. Local dishes she'd noticed on the menu but hadn't been brave enough to try.

After breakfast she thought he would ask to come back to her room. Despite the attraction between them, they were taking their time. She wasn't a prude, she loved sex and wanted to be with Diver – but it was such a treat to be wooed this way. All the kissing and touching had her body alive with anticipation. She was a little disappointed when he told her he had some Monday chores to do but would come back as soon as possible. But everyone knows that good things come to those who wait.

She had a lovely morning, wandering the garden with her sketchbook and pastels, hoping to capture the colour and beauty of the resort. She did quite well with the vegetation – drawing a coconut palm and hibiscus flower with some aplomb.

She was just finishing up a club sandwich and putting the final touches to a sketch of the neighbouring islands from 'their' sunbed, when a low riding turquoise boat with orange and white trim, motored into the bay and stopped in front of her. The captain was waving at her. It was Diver.

She recognised him because, even though she couldn't see his face (he was wearing something that looked like a long black snood on his head), she would have recognised his muscular upper body in the clinging white rash guard anywhere.

He jumped lightly off the boat, gave her a kiss and cuddle, then sent her to change into something suitable for a boat trip round the island. She returned in her favourite push-up tiger print bikini and a skimpy black cover up. He gave her a lingering look, then laughed and told her to go back and put something a bit more robust on otherwise he wouldn't be able to concentrate on steering. Adding that she should also bring something warm as it could get nippy on the water and to 'borrow' the cushions from her balcony furniture to sit on, as his fishing boat wasn't built to be a tourist boat.

They were out on the boat for hours – all the way around his island. He pointed out places of interest. Some, like Shell Bay, she had already visited, but most were new to her. He showed her his special fishing and diving sites, including an area where there were at least three sunken Spanish Galleons; the channel where you could most often see dolphins; a mangrove forest in a secluded bay; a tiny rock island that was home to a huge colony of seabirds and a pristine beach where the original inhabitants of the island had settled first.

She loved how knowledgeable he was and how safe she felt in the small boat. The sea was very choppy when they reached the far end of the island, but he handled the boat masterfully and looked so perfectly at home riding the waves she couldn't imagine him being elsewhere than on Zephyr. When she tried to picture the two of them walking through the centre of Reading – his tee-shirt covered by a winter coat. She couldn't. Or introducing him to the girls at her salon, or taking him to meet Mum. Equally impossible. That made her sad. She was really going to miss him.

By the time they'd got back to the small marina where he kept his boat, and he'd done what he needed to do to secure it, they were both exhausted. Back at the hotel he suggested she grab an overnight bag and come home with him, but she refused. She didn't want their first time to be spoilt by the fact that her bum hurt from hours of bouncing up and down on the waves and she was feeling slightly nauseous. She wanted to look and smell nice for him. She needed a nice long shower and to shave her legs.

She felt comfortable enough with him to tell him that, and, although she could tell he was disappointed, he cheered up when she gave him a lingering kiss goodbye and told him good things come to those who wait.

He called her on the room phone an hour later to wish her good night then added mischievously,

"I'm cuddled up in bed now with my Sweetie Pie. Bet you wish you were here."

"Who's bloody Sweetie Pie??"

"Sweetie Pie is the love of my life. It's a good job I have her to come home to as otherwise I, like you at the moment, would be very, very, lonely."

"You have some girl called Sweetie Pie who loves you unconditionally and lets you go out and spend the day with other women? I'm guessing she's not your secret girlfriend then?"

"She's my dog."

"You didn't tell me you had a dog."

"You didn't ask."

"Oh well, I hope she doesn't sleep in your bed."

"Why not, are you jealous?"

"No."

"Yes, you are. You are jealous of my Sweetie Pie. Well, she sleeps under my bed. And as she's waiting anxiously for me to give her some attention, I better go. Good night, Tracy."

"Good night, Diver".

*

The next day, knowing that Diver had plans and they wouldn't meet again until the evening, she was determined to get back on track with her quest and dialled Museum Man for the gazillionth time.

It rang five times and then went to the Museum's answer phone. Bloody great! She thought about putting the phone down – then decided to hold on and hear what the world's most annoying person had to say.

There was a lot of disturbance in the background, some muffled shouting and slapping noises – maybe the Museum doubled as a martial arts centre? The sound was so bad that she could only hear about one in four words over the kerfuffle.

"Slap … muffle … slap … is Professor … Derrick. I am … muffle … muffle … slap take your call … muffle, muffle … muffle … muffle … slap …

arrange a visit to the museum … muffle … slap … call back on Monday 16th June. I have a … slap, slap muffle … personal … muffle, muffle slap … unfortunately … not open this wee … muffle, slap, slap … patience and I look forward to muffle, muffle, slap, the museum soon."

The 16th was the day after she left the island.

"Bloody man! Bloody, bloody ANNOYING Museum Man."

Despite longing to kick something in frustration, she took a deep breath and decided instead to take a long relaxing outdoor shower. Because being naked outdoors felt really good. Massaging loads of delicious smelling coconut conditioner into her rather crispy blonde curls also felt really good. And looking at birds play in the air currents far, far above as you washed your body made you feel really good. Yep, she felt really good.

She hummed "feeling hot, hot, hot." as she gyrated out of the shower, wrapping her hair in a towel and slipping into a cotton wrap. *Good to go!* She had shaved and plucked everything she needed to and was now ready, desperately ready, for Diver. She started making coffee and then it hit her.

I'm happy – as happy as I've ever been. And tonight I'm going to be even happier. I've only got a few more days to spend here with Diver. I should concentrate on that and enjoy our time together. Do I really need the stress of meeting up with that annoying man who probably won't tell me anything anyway? Do I really need to try to find a long-lost half brother who will probably hate me? And what am I going to say to him anyway? What if he asks to meet Mum? What do I say then? That she doesn't want to see you?

She went to the safe and took out her passport. Tucked into the red leather cover was a handwritten letter: neat, navy blue letters on pale blue Basildon Bond notepaper. Her mum's favourite.

Once she was settled on her chair with her coffee in easy reach, she opened up the letter and read the familiar words:

Tracy,

I deeply regret telling you about Zephyr. I drank too much that night and I was feeling very low, missing

> your Dad, and that film took me by surprise. I shouldn't have said anything to you.
>
> What happened to me there was a long time ago. In another life.
> I am not proud of what I did, but I did the right thing for me at the time. As your mother I expect you to abide by my decision. DO NOT try to find him. This is not your problem to solve.
> You loved your Dad, PLEASE DO NOT disrespect his memory. He never knew about this and I DO NOT want any of our friends or his family knowing about it.
>
> I love you, I don't want to row with you, but if you persist in your plan to visit the island and stir things up, you will hurt me deeply.
>
> Mum.

Tracy gazed around the room without seeing it. The letter arrived a few days before she left for the island. When she opened it, she felt, in turn, angry, sad then even more determined to go to Zephyr.

On the fateful night it all came to light, Rosemary had told her the barest of facts about her trip to the island in the sixties, about staying with a friend who helped to construct the airport, about parties and good times and the upshot – a baby. A baby she abandoned because she wasn't married. A baby she never attempted to find and who no one else knew anything about.

Shocked to the core, Tracy had pushed her mum for more information but Rosemary simply refused to say anything else. Tracy, frustrated and angry that her mum wouldn't talk, threatened to go to the island to find out more if Rosemary didn't fill in the blanks. She carried on calling her for days, begging her for more information until one day Rosemary slammed the phone down on her and refused to answer any more calls. Tracy, furious at

Rosemary, booked her ticket. The letter came two days later.

Now, a couple of weeks later, happy and relaxed, she looked at the letter with fresh eyes. Rather than seeing her mum as being high-handed, cruel and uncaring, she saw desperation, pain and fear. Rather than dictating terms, she was defending Dad. Tracy could see now that Rosemary was petrified – scared to death that her carefully constructed life was crumpling and was lashing out in defence. Nagging and putting pressure on her had been the worst thing Tracy could have done. Two strong women. A rock and a hard place.

She knew what she needed to do. She called her mum's number, got the answerphone and left a message.

> *"Hi Mum, hope you are OK. I love you. I miss talking to you … I'm sorry. You're right. It is your story, not mine. I should never have meddled. I want you to know that I do understand how easily it must have been for you to get swept along in something. This place is intoxicating. I hope you'll talk to me about it when I get back but I won't pressure you if you don't want to. I can't believe how brave you were to come here all alone. How hard it must have been for you to keep a secret like this from Dad and me for all those years. I'm glad you told me – I really am – but I'm going to stop looking for him now. I'll be back on Saturday, early. Can't wait to see you. Love you lots."*

She really did love her mum and she couldn't go on arguing with her. She might not agree with what she had done but it was Rosemary's decision. And it was up to Tracy to be a better person and support her. She couldn't lose her too. She would do what her mum asked. She would leave it alone and get on with just enjoying the rest of her time on island. With Diver.

CHAPTER 14
Charlotte

No one had thought to pre-order lunch for eight, so their meal was going to take some time to appear. As the wait for lunch lengthened – the crowd around the tiny bar got more raucous.

Charlie and Marvel alternated having a drink with having a dip in the ocean. The men sat around the small bamboo covered bar, joking and chatting with the barman – a laconic Black Englishman with long, luxuriant braids. They were drinking beers, following each one with some kind of shot. Everyone was hanging on the barman's every word – laughing at his jokes and exchanging gossip. Everyone, apart from Graham, who, for once, was out of his depth. The men's voices got louder and louder and their island dialect became stronger and stronger. There was lots of slapping of the bar top and sucking of teeth and, although she couldn't understand everything, she enjoyed listening to them. "You lie", "for real" and "bwoy" punctuated the conversation.

Graham wasn't used to being side-lined. He turned his attention to Charlie.

"Do you fancy going for a walk?"

"Sure darling, it's getting a bit heated round here."

"Bloody is. Honestly, I can't understand a word they're saying."

"I think it's about a friend of theirs and some woman."

Graham looked sceptical.

"Really, you could pick that up? I'm impressed darling, you have a better ear than I do. I didn't understand a thing."

They reached the water's edge and paddled along the beach towards the horizon.

"It really is something, this place. Just when you think you've seen the best beach, they take you to another, even more magnificent one."

"Do you really like it here, Graham? I'm glad. I didn't think you did to start with?"

"Yes, Babe, I do." He looked guiltily at her. "I'm sorry I was hard work those first days … it's no excuse but it was just when we got here it was so … simple … and unsophisticated. Honestly, it was a nightmare realising I had no wi-fi … I don't know, maybe I'm just not the relaxing type?" He looked around and shrugged sheepishly. "This all seems very far away from London … from everything I know and what I like to do."

She nodded encouragingly, it was the most he'd opened up to her in days. "Yes. I know."

"Even Chad and Marvel – don't get me wrong – they are lovely, but they are just so bloody … enthusiastic. Everything is 'awesome' and 'amazing'," he mimicked badly.

"Don't be mean, Graham."

"No, no, I'm not. Well, I don't mean to be, actually I don't know what I would have done without them, stuck here …" Graham petered off, noticing her stricken face.

Charlie's heart was breaking.

"Stuck here, Graham? Stuck here? Is that what you really think? That you're stuck! It's your honeymoon! Is it really so terrible being stuck here with me, Graham? Is it such an awful thing to be stuck here with me on your honeymoon?"

She looked at him, feeling a mixture of despair and disgust.

"I can't believe you said that, Graham. What the fuck is wrong with you?"

She stared at him, angry and needing a reaction, but he just stood there, not answering, looking at everything but her.

He looks pathetic. "Tell me!" she demanded, "Tell me what the fuck is wrong with you! You've been horrible since we got here. In fact, when I think about it – it's been bad between us for weeks."

And then it hit her.

"You are doing that thing that men do, aren't you? You're being vile to me so that I force the issue. Being so awful that I'm the one that speaks up when it's really your fault."

She paced the beach, pointing and shouting at him. "You are putting me in a position where I have to force whatever the problem is out of you – because you're TOO COWARDLY TO ADMIT IT!"

He didn't answer her, but she could tell that she was right by his guilty expression and resigned stance.

"What is it, Graham? Clearly you don't love me anymore. But what else? Don't tell me you've fallen for someone else? Is that it? That you are having an affair? It's such a cliché. ARE YOU HAVING AN AFFAIR?"

She shouted at him, willing him to answer but frightened to hear what he had to say. She'd crossed a line and there was no coming back.

He moved a few steps away from her to the water's edge and stared at the ocean. When he finally started talking it was in a quiet, sad voice, the voice you only use when you tell someone really bad news.

"I'm sorry. Very, very, sorry, Charlie. You're right. I did have sex with someone else."

He heard her intake of breath, and turned round, frightened to see her reaction.

"I never meant for you to find out. For it to hurt you. It was just a distraction. Something to take my mind off the pressure of the wedding and finalising the building plans – all that planning rubbish I went through. It was only a fuck, just sex. I thought we could just carry on as normal, but I guess I got that wrong. It reminded me what I was missing, what I might miss."

"Charming. Who is it?"

"It doesn't matter."

"It does to me. Who is it? I need to know. It's someone at the office, right? You've been on the phone to them the whole time. Who is it?

"Look, you don't need to know the details. The 'who' is irrelevant. What you do need is to know why. Why is because I realised too late that I am not ready to settle down and be a family man. I have too much I want to do. The project is creating so many opportunities for me. It's the wrong time for us. I shouldn't have married you. It's not fair. I can't give you what you want."

Charlie was stunned. "But … why on earth did you go through with it then? You must have had doubts earlier than that?"

"To be honest, I did, but I just kept pushing them aside."

Charlotte was glaring at him, furious.

"I'm not blaming you, but you could have picked up the signs if you think back." He went on, "Do you remember when we went out to the OXO Tower that night a month or so ago? We talked about the wedding? I asked you if you had any doubts? I hoped you would say 'yes'. But you didn't and … I just couldn't say it myself."

"You are a coward. I remember that conversation. You asked me if I was excited about getting married. And I said 'yes' and then you asked why and I said …"

He finished her sentence, "… 'so we can get on with having a baby or two without Mum disowning me.' That is when I lost the nerve to tell you. Plus – I'd put so much time into the wedding already." He smiled weakly. "You know as soon as I saw you I thought you'd make the perfect mother of my children. I'd be mad not too. You are beautiful and sweet. I honestly believe I wanted kids as much as you did at that moment. That's what made me chicken out of telling you and decide to go through with it."

"But I still don't understand what you're saying? What could have changed? Don't you want kids anymore? Is that it?"

"I still love the idea of having kids, it's just that's not the lifestyle I want right now."

"You want to be young, free and single? Or is it to do with your affair? You want to marry her? I'm confused."

"It's complicated. I didn't want to tell you who I've been sleeping with because the affair was just a catalyst. I'm not in love, I just know I need more than we have."

"Who is it? I won't stop asking 'til you tell me."

He sighed. "Andreas …"

"Andrea? Who's she? Do we know an Andrea?"

Graham shook his head, "No, not Andrea, Andreas."

Did she hear right? This is a nightmare. "Andreas? The Designer? Your Designer? Male Andreas?"

He nodded.

"You're gay?"

He looked awkward. "No. I'm not gay ... I just like to have sex with men sometimes."

"Since when?"

He shrugged, "For a while."

"You what? You want it both ways? To be straight when it suits you and gay when it suits you?"

This is in-fucking-credible! Charlie shook her head, unable to speak for a while, then spat out,

"You've been talking to Andreas every day since we got here! I let it go – because I thought you needed to keep up with work." Charlie walked around in tiny circles, breathing high up in her chest, "But all the time you were ... talking to your BLOODY LOVER – on our honeymoon!"

I'm so naïve. Now I know how Princess Diana must have felt, when she worked out there were 'three in her marriage'.

Another thought occurred to her, "I hope you bloody well used a —"

"Charlie don't be like that. Anyway, I haven't slept with you since I had sex with him the last time." The faintest note of impatience was creeping into his voice. Graham wasn't the type to be cowed for long.

Her head was pounding. She was going to be sick. The sun beat down, the bright sparkle of the water was blinding her. She needed to get off the beach and lie down somewhere dark and cool. Actually, what she really wanted was to turn back time – to breakfast at the hotel this morning. She'd felt optimistic then – now her life, her situation, was inconceivable.

"What do you want? What do you want me to do?"

Graham interrupted her thoughts.

"What do you mean?"

"Well, do you want a divorce? Do you want me to move out of the flat?"

Charlie couldn't believe what she was hearing.

"Graham, I don't know what I want! How can you expect me to know what I want yet? You've only just told me that you don't want to be married and that you have a gay lover! You have to give me some time to digest this. At the moment I just feel sick and tired. Disgusted with you for lying to me, for being unfaithful and for making a mockery of our life together."

CHAPTER 15

Tracy

"I don't like to see that sad face …"

Tracy, who had been thinking about the fact she was leaving soon, looked up to see Diver looming over her with a concerned look on his face. He was here! She beamed.

"Oh, there's my favourite smile."

She was so pleased to see him she jumped to her feet, wrapped her arms around his neck and laid a big noisy kiss on him.

"Guess you missed me, eh? I think I'm going to learn something from this. I might start playing it cool, if this is the kind of welcome I get when you don't see me for a few hours. My time away from you has been well spent. I've made us a lovely dinner, I caught a couple of nice fish and picked up some crayfish. It's all ready and waiting at my house. "

"Are we going now?"

"Of course, come on let's go, I'm hungry." He winked at her.

"Me too. Ok, let me get my handbag."

"I'd prefer it if you grabbed your overnight bag."

"Of course! It's already packed." She smiled at him cheekily over her shoulder before sashaying off in the direction of her room, fully aware of his eyes on her departing behind. She stopped and turned, suddenly needing to get another look at him.

God, you're gorgeous! Diver looked smart in a bright red polo shirt and some baggy cream shorts. His skin gleamed with health. His intelligent brown eyes were bright and brimming with admiration for her. His large feet planted solidly wide in their Fila slippers. *What a happy, handsome, strong man. A real man … my man.* She felt an anticipatory thrill run through her and hurried off to grab her bag, impatient to leave.

They held hands for most of the journey to his house – only breaking contact so that he could fiddle around with the CD player and put some music on. Tracy relaxed back in her seat and listened to the words. The song was lovely and it struck a chord, a man was singing about how people were going to talk and say bad things about them being together, but that wouldn't matter because they were in love, and to not 'worry what the people say'.

She'd heard the deep, sweet voice before but couldn't place it. "Who's that?"

"Beres Hammond, Beres is *the* man. One of the Caribbean's best. This style of reggae is called 'Lovers Rock'."

"I love it," she sighed. "I guess some people would say a lot of things about us being together?"

He smiled. "No need to worry about that. I just played it because I thought he'd be just the thing to get us in the mood." He squeezed her hand.

"Not that we need much encouragement," she giggled back.

They drove the ten minutes or so to his house in companionable silence, content with the music, and the simple, affectionate contact. Tracy looked at Diver's profile and lifted her hand to stroke a small curl on the back of his neck that had broken loose from his neat hair.

She pulled and released the curl gently, he sighed in pleasure.

"Pull it as much as you want. It's yours to do whatever you want with."

"I don't know what else I can do with it. But I know I love this little curl that somehow escaped the shears … Don't cut it … you might lose your strength."

"Like Samson in that Bible story? No – I won't risk that. I won't cut it. I will leave it there just for you."

She moved her hand away from the curl, back towards her lap and Diver grabbed it and pulled it onto his thigh.

My hand the erogenous zone – I don't know when one small hand has had so much excitement. Her lucky digits were achingly aware of Diver's muscular thigh. The atmosphere in the car thickened. Both thinking about what was going to happen next, the best and most natural thing in the world.

The car slowed, Diver indicated, and they passed between some tall, skinny oleander bushes into a large grass and tree covered yard with a low pink house in the middle of it. The car came to a gentle halt.

Diver cleared his throat, looked uncharacteristically nervous and said in a soft voice, "Well, we're here. I hope you like it."

She looked out the window towards the house and saw a small, sandy-coloured dog jumping around crazily outside the car.

Diver pointed at it and said, "Mind you … if Sweetie Pie doesn't like you, and if you don't appreciate my cooking, I may have to send you home."

She laughed and leant over to kiss him on the side of the mouth. "Now I really am scared. Any tips on wooing her?"

"Just let her sniff you first. Don't go to her. Don't try to touch or make a fuss of her and whatever you do don't try to kiss or hug me … she will definitely bite you then."

"That's just great. I might have known you would have a jealous dog. And, of course, she had to be a blonde too!"

"You know I like my blonde ladies," he winked. "Let me go first and I can formally introduce you."

Diver got out of the car and the little dog went into overdrive, yelping and leaping and running around in ever decreasing circles. He calmed her down using soft words and she was soon lying on her back offering a fluffy ginger and white tummy for his attention.

Tracy got out of the car to get a better view of the big man bending over the small dog and talking nonsense to her. It was clear they adored each other. Heeding Diver's advice to wait, she looked around, noticing that the house, although simple in design, was quite large, nicely painted and well kept.

The 'yard' that surrounded it had a mixture of scrubby grass, trees and flowering shrubs. There was a red and blue boat resting on some kind of support, a motorcycle with one wheel missing, a pile of tyres, orange and white buoys and a whole bunch of what she now knew were lobster pots.

Although there was lots of 'stuff' around, everything was neatly stacked up and the plants and trees looked healthy.

She became aware of a slight tickle on the back of her calves and then something cold and wet touched the back of her left knee. She squeaked in surprise.

Mutually shocked, both 'ladies' jumped back and looked at each other suspiciously for a while, before Sweetie Pie decided that Tracy was no threat and scampered back to her dad.

"I've got your bag, and the dog hasn't mauled you to death, so you better come in."

She walked round the car and joined him, he grabbed her hand again and they walked up the three shallow steps and onto a wide tiled porch. Diver had to let go of her hand to unlock the door and swing it open into the living area but quickly grabbed it back and pulled her into the house.

"Welcome, my love, welcome to my home. I hope you will be very comfortable here." He dropped her bag on a wicker armchair by the door and pulled her into his arms, kissing her thoroughly.

They broke apart at the sound of a persistent and annoying noise. Sweetie Pie was sitting on the floor by Diver's feet, alternatively licking his leg and whimpering – in a flagrant attempt to pull his attention back to her.

"Ignore the jealous bitch – she better get used to this," he laughed before pulling Tracy back to him for more.

"Well, that wasn't bad for starters," teased Tracy, "What's the main course?"

"Well, funny you should say that, because although I would like to … well, you know, I'm starving." Diver's tummy rumbled just then to underline his point.

"I think we should go and investigate what's in the kitchen, so I have the strength to get through the night. I think I'm going to need all my strength to keep up with you."

Tracey stepped back in mock annoyance then reached round and whopped him on his bootylicious bottom.

"You keep up with me? You're the sex-mad one."

"Well, that's not my fault, that's yours for teasing me. Don't start tickling me in all my most sensitive places if you're not going to finish what you started," he warned then tried to steer her into the bedroom.

But Tracy had decided she was hungry too, so she scooted out of his way, then walked into the kitchen and gasped. *What a sight!* There was enough food to feed a small army. The shining work surfaces were covered in different sized and coloured casserole dishes and covered pots – each filled with delicious-smelling food.

"As you can see, I have prepared a sumptuous feast for you, my love."

Diver walked around the kitchen, lifting each lid and smelling it proudly, using his hand to waft the fragrance towards Tracy's nostrils. Sweetie Pie, not to be left out, had jumped down from the sofa and followed behind, sitting down each time a different lid was lifted and licking her lips every time a tempting, new smell escaped.

"I see that, it looks incredible, I'm overwhelmed by your skills. Diver, exactly how much food do you think I can eat? I know I've got a healthy appetite but this is, well …"

He chuckled, "Don't worry. We don't have to eat it all now. I've made enough so that we don't have to leave the house for forty-eight hours – we can just eat the food, eat each other, repeat!" He leant in for another kiss.

She was close to tears. *What a lucky girl I am. I've had lots of love in my life, wonderful parents, great friends, and some lovely boyfriends in the past, but this feast of love is the most thoughtful thing anyone has ever done for me – hands down.*

Standing in Diver's kitchen, surrounded by his incredible, edible gifts, Tracy understood just how much he meant to her. Diver was no holiday romance, he was the real deal. *I hope he feels the same, I'm pretty sure he does.* To distract herself from blurting out "I love you", and potentially scaring the poor man to death, she asked him a safe question.

"Well then, what have we got here then?" and pointed at a clear Pyrex dish filled with a red coloured sauce.

"This is Creole conch, conch stewed in a rich, spicy, tomato sauce – I actually made that yesterday, in anticipation of your visit, because it tastes better the next day." He moved his hand to the next dish. "This is my famous baked kingfish – a big steak cooked in a green seasoning mix which has peppers, onions, garlic, parsley and other special ingredients, you just have to watch out for the bones on that one. This is our national dish – 'peas n rice', long grain rice cooked with pigeon peas and seasoning to give it flavour. This is macaroni pie, which is basically baked pasta and cheese. This is a salad with tomatoes from my garden and lettuce from the Rasta dude down the road. And over there in that pot are the lobsters." He pointed at the large silver Dutch oven that was sitting on the side. Its lid was twitching. She could see the creatures' antennae moving. That was what was making the lid rattle. She shuddered.

"What are you going to do with those poor things?"

"You won't say that when you eat them. You will just be enjoying how delicious they are."

"I know, but I feel a bit guilty seeing them alive like that."

"Don't worry, I'll kill them humanely. I'll just fire up the grill a minute, mix you a drink and then, when the coals are good and ready, we can grill them."

She still looked dubious.

"Drink? I made you some local juice." He went into the big American style fridge and pulled out a jug of cloudy, golden yellow juice. "This is golden apple – have you tried it?" She shook her head.

"No? Well, it's delicious." He put two glasses under the ice dispenser, topped them up with the juice and handed one to Tracy. She took a long appreciative swig. It was indeed sweet and delicious.

"It doesn't really taste like apple – more like a tropical fruit with a touch of apple," she observed, intrigued by the new flavour.

"You like it?"

"Love it, thanks."

"Do you need some rum in it?" She shook her head no.

"Good, we are all set. Now, come with me." He grabbed the drinks and they went outside. Sweetie Pie followed reluctantly, not keen to leave the kitchen with all its promise of fishy delights.

He settled her down on one of the low seats on the porch, fussing over her until she was comfortable, and her drink was within easy reach.

Tracy leant back, relaxed and happy just to watch him lighting the coals. It was another wonderful Caribbean night. The air was the perfect temperature to sit outside, the stars were bright and she was hungry – for the mouth-watering feasts to come, of food and fleshly delights.

"Is that an old cooking gas tank?" she asked about the barbeque.

"Yep. Cut in half with some legs welded on. No fancy shop bought grills for us. This one has years of smoke and layers of flavour residing in it," he said proudly.

Residing … nice word. Diver's got a really good vocabulary for a fisherman.

"Did you go to school here Diver?"

"Yes – until I was eighteen. Then, when I got my scholarship I went to Barbados and lived with my cousin's family."

"You got a scholarship?" intrigued at his answer.

"Yes! Of course I did. It was the only way I would have been able to complete my degree." He looked at her curiously.

"You have a degree?"

"Of course I do. Well, two – because I have a master's … how else could I do what I do?" he finished.

"I don't mean to be rude, Diver, what do you need a master's for? You're a fisherman – what do you need any kind of degree for? – well, unless it's in fish husbandry or something." Tracy was intrigued. The signs of a good education were there, in the conversations they'd had.

Diver looked puzzled. "Tracy, you really think that I'm a fisherman? You think that's my job? What I do every day? That fishing is how I earn a living?"

"Well, … yes … of course … you never told me any different. You … I-I-I just assumed …"

"*You* never asked. For true? Wow. I just *assumed* you knew what I did." He scratched his head in wonder. "Hold on, you spoke to my brother, he told you about me."

"When?" She looked at him. *I must be going mad, when did CB tell me about Diver's job?*

"That first night you were chatting with him at Treasure Island. He told you about his big brother who he followed up to school in Boston. He told me that he'd told you."

"Sorry, I must be losing it. I had two rums that night and you know I don't drink a lot. I do vaguely remember the conversation – but I just assumed he was talking about another brother."

"Another brother?" incredulous. "Why? Because you didn't equate Diver, the fisherman, with some educated guy that went to University?"

She was shocked at his tone. He was clearly pissed off with her. When he spoke next his voice literally dripped with sarcasm.

"You didn't notice that I may be just a LITTLE more sophisticated than your average fisherman?"

Oh lord, she had hit a sore spot. "Honestly, I don't know. I guess I didn't think about it. I haven't met a fisherman before. I just knew you were very funny and clever." She smiled, continuing with, "And I guess you just turned me stupid with your wicked good looks and manly charm," in what she hoped was a winning way, then spoilt it by saying, "I knew you had, a sort of 'native' intelligence."

He stood up straight, face screwed up in disbelief, and started shaking the box of matches at her to add emphasis to his words.

"A 'native' intelligence ... what is that supposed to mean? God Tracy, that's so patronising. No, patronising is not strong enough. I have to call it racist," he spat out.

Then, in a horrible singsong English accent, he attempted to mimic her, "I had a little thing with this cute guy – oh, just a fling – he was a fisherman. Crazy about me, terribly sexy and ever so funny. He was quite interesting, in his own way, with his NATIVE wisdom and funny local accent."

His voice went icy cold. "Well, I haven't just got native intelligence, Tracy – I've got a FUCKING PhD!" He turned his back on her and stood staring at the glowing, red coals. Shaking his head in disbelief. "Three more degrees than you," he finished.

Tracy felt awful. She wished she could go back five minutes and take back her words.

"Diver, Diver, look at me." He wouldn't, so she walked up to him, grabbed at his tightly folded arms and tried to get him to turn and look at her. "I'm so sorry."

He resisted, shrugging her off. Undeterred she stood behind him and wrapped her arms around his belly and leant into him. This time he didn't throw her off – even though his tense stance hadn't softened at all.

"Diver, I am really sorry. I assumed that … Well, you know what I assumed. Stupid of me. I didn't ask the right questions and I've been wrapped up in myself and not thinking about you. My head is full of stuff at the moment and probably that is why I've been so bloody stupid."

He was still letting her hold him, so she thought she would risk telling him what was on her mind. She talked softly into his back.

"You don't know yet why I came here. There's something I need to tell you too. I should have told you from the beginning. But I was just enjoying you and me too much. I should have told you, but I was just avoiding reality, going with the flow. I've been so happy here, Diver, mainly because of you, but also because I love the island – relaxing on the beach, going into Treasure Island and meeting CB … everything was so special it made me want to forget what I came here for."

Her voice broke, *it couldn't end like this*. She held him even tighter and talked through her tears. "It's no excuse I know, but I wasn't expecting you. I was just looking for a nice distraction. A holiday romance. Someone who I could have fun with before going back to my life in England without a backwards glance. I never thought I might meet someone special like you. You know I think you're lovely. I'm never going to forget you."

She had inched her way around and he had finally uncrossed his arms and they hung by his side. Not holding her – but not pushing her away either.

In a consolatory voice she said, "What about if we both calm down and start the conversation again? You can tell me all about yourself and I can tell you all about myself. Let's start at the beginning, fill in the gaps. No more assumptions between us. I think it's wonderful that you have a great education. I wish I did. Tell me," she said coaxing him on, "what was your degree in? What do you do here when you're not fishing?"

She could sense he didn't want to stay mad at her, but because she'd more than dented his pride he needed to set her straight. She took his hand and he let her lead him back to the sofa on the balcony. Sweetie Pie watched them closely, a worried expression in her deep, chocolate eyes. She hated it when Daddy raised his voice.

Diver took a long drink of juice and took his time before telling her his story.

"I studied archaeology at the University of the West Indies, and then I went on to do a research fellowship at Boston. I have a PhD and my specialism is the Indigenous people of the Caribbean."

He sounded like his normal self as he got into his subject. "Did you know that we have a number of significant Arawak sites here? I'm applying for a grant to help us protect them and ultimately get World Heritage classification for some of the most important ones. I plan to raise funds to do a proper excavation and full documentation. I'm a bit late in the game sadly, some of the major sites have already been looted. Luckily there are still great things to be learnt and pieces to be uncovered."

"Diver, that's fantastic. How interesting," she was hanging on his every word, genuinely impressed by him.

"And I have a day job too. I run the local Museum."

What the fuck! Tracy looked at him in horror. Had she heard him correctly?

"Did you say you run the local Museum? The one by the Salt Pond?"

"Yes, that's it. Did you try to go?" a puzzled look on his face.

"Try to go?" she said in a tight voice. "I've been trying to go ever since I got here, but that bloody man Dr Derrick or Clinton or whatever …" she ran out of steam and looked up, two plus two suddenly making four.

Diver was looking at her with what could only be described as a shifty expression.

"You are Dr Clinton Derrick?" she said wonderingly.

"Ahem, yes, guilty as charged."

"But then that means we must have spoken? I kept calling trying to get an appointment. I needed some information and they said at the hotel that you would help me. But I kept ringing and there was no answer or I got that bloody antiquated answer phone. And the receptionist said she called too.

How could I not have known it was you? How can you not have known it was me …?" she trailed off.

"I only spoke to one person looking for information last week and she didn't give me her name. Anyway, I don't think we had spoken much or even met by then, and I recall, you sounded very different then."

"And I couldn't hear a word you said – your phone reception was terrible. What do you mean 'different'?"

"Well, you were all posh sounding, like the Queen. Not friendly at all –"he mimicked an upper crust English accent, "'I demand an appointment!'—"

"I *was* friendly, I'm always friendly, and I did … not … sound … like that."

"Yes, you did, and when I tried joking with you – you got irritated. You were lucky to have found me at the museum at all. That day was a public holiday and I had already made plans – to go fishing," he said with no trace of an apology.

"You decided not to open up the museum to a paying visitor because you didn't like the sound of someone on the phone and wanted to go fishing? That's not very professional," she said incredulously.

"I decided not to open up because it was a public holiday. That's my call. Anyway, I don't like disrespectful white ladies," he said with an angry shrug.

"Disrespectful white ladies! Bloody great. Now who's being a racist?" She shook her head in disgust.

Her eyes stung as she looked away from him and into the distance. The house was on a hill and she could see the lights of a neighbouring island twinkling far away. *I've never felt less twinkly in my life.* She was so disappointed in herself.

Don't be surprised Tracy, he's basically a stranger, however close you may have felt to him. You know hardly anything about him and yet you let him – and the island – weave a spell on you.

"I came here to do one thing and one thing only and because of you," she spat, "I've failed."

"I'm so sorry," voice dripping with sarcasm and obviously not sorry at all, "but I fail to see how anything I have – or haven't done – at the museum could affect you."

"I just needed some information. That's all I wanted … some bloody information. And you could have helped me, but you didn't."

She started crying, anger and frustration spilling out in sobs.

Diver looked guilty, stricken and cross at the same time. "Stop crying, woman. What? What information?"

"I … I don't want to tell you now. You're so angry with me … you won't help me AND I DON'T WANT YOU TO ANYWAY!" sounding like a little girl watching her teddy bear get strangled.

"Don't be so stubborn, woman. What did you come here for? – stop beating about the subject."

Tracy couldn't hold it in any longer. She had to tell someone. "I came to find my brother. Well, my half brother," she whispered.

"Your brother? You have a brother on the island?"

"I don't know. I don't know where he is, but this island is the only place I know where to start looking for him."

Intrigued despite himself, he asked, "What's his name? How old? Which family?"

"He will be 46 or 47, but I don't know anything else. It's probably a wild goose chase," her voice sounding increasingly hysterical as she continued with the story.

"A few months ago, Mum and I were watching TV and this programme comes on. Turns out it was filmed on this island and 'it reminds her' – though how on earth she could ever have forgotten … – that once upon a time, in a far distant land, many, many years ago, she had a baby that neither me or Dad knew about," she looked at his incredulous face. "D-d-don't laugh, it's true."

She sniffed back a tear and then it all came flooding out. "I've got hardly anything to go on. All she said was she came to stay with friends in 1962, who were here to build the airport. She met some guy, got pregnant and then left the baby here – because they weren't married presumably. She won't tell me any more. And she's really angry with me for coming and trying to 'dig up dirt' as she calls it."

"Some story," he said, reluctantly impressed.

"I know," she agreed enthusiastically, forgetting she was mad with him for a moment. She looked up at Diver's face. He was intrigued and there was a slight softening around his generous mouth, which up until that point had been set in a hard line. It gave her the courage to carry on.

"I wanted to find out who had worked at the airport then. Maybe see if there were any guys around that worked on the project who might know a bunch of white people, you call them 'expats' I think. Mum's friend was working there at the time. I'm assuming the baby's father was—"

He cut into her, suddenly furious again. "A white man? Why are you looking for a white man?"

"Because Mum would—"

He cut her off before she could finish, "—'because Mummy wouldn't have been with a 'Zephyr man' I assume?"

"No!"

She shook her head helplessly. That wasn't what she was trying to say. She was trying to tell him her mum would have been visiting with some expats, but he'd leapt to the wrong conclusion.

How could he think I would think like that? I give up, he's so angry and I'm tired of arguing. We keep saying the wrong thing to each other and … *I don't do arguing!*

But Diver had more to say, lashing out at her so there could be no turning back. "You don't have an answer for me? I guess that means you thought your mum was too good to have sex with a local, let alone have a baby with one. Like mother , like daughter. You know, you just admitted I was great when I was just a fisherman who, as you so charmingly put 'you could have some fun with and forget'. You don't like it now you find out I'm more educated than you will ever be! You're nothing special you know, Tracy. You're only a hairdresser and you should really think before you speak if you don't want all your new friends to think you're a racist."

Tracy was horrified. She couldn't really blame Diver for attacking her before about his job, she hadn't asked him the right questions, she'd made assumptions, and everyone knew assumption was the mother of all fuckups. But this tirade was out of order.

"Diver, that's not fair … you're the one that's assuming now …" she trailed off into silence as he'd already stomped into the house and was ignoring her.

What was the point in trying to explain? She was leaving the Island anyway and he'd made it perfectly clear they had no future. I've been disrespectful and much, much worse, he thinks I'm a racist, even though I never thought I was. How could everything have gone so wrong?

Diver reappeared with her overnight bag in his hand.

"Please get in the car Tracy, I want to take you back to the hotel now."

THURSDAY 12TH JUNE

CHAPTER 16
Charlotte

"Charlie! Charlie, wake up …" She woke, completely disoriented.

Where am I? I don't know this room! Oh, of course, the stateroom on Dwight's yacht. She'd crashed onboard last night – unable to face going back to the hotel or Graham.

"Charlie, can I come in now?" demanded Marvel.

Dragging her head off the downy pillows and into consciousness she croaked, "Sorry, come on in, just trying to make myself decent," she swung her legs over the side of the bed and onto the floor, pulling on a monogrammed white robe. Then she staggered over to unlock the door.

Marvel burst into the room waving a brown paper bag. She was wearing a turquoise sundress and delicate silver thong sandals that showed off her toned legs to perfection.

"I got fresh croissants. How are you? I'm worried about you! Did you sleep at all?"

"Amazingly *yes*. How about you? How was Chad when you got home? So sorry I kept you out so late."

"Don't worry. Gave him the time to make a big pot of chicken chilli and we binged on that when I got in."

She looked around the room with a twinkle, "Was it comfortable in Dwight's sex palace?"

"Oh my god! So comfortable. This bed's amazing. This room is extremely luxurious, and the bathroom – it's heaven. Check out my robe … Did you say sex palace?"

"Yep. This is his L.O.V.E. nest, this is where he brings all the 'special ladies' he wants to impress and from what I hear he has quite the success rate."

"Too funny. Well, some of that 'sex palace mojo' may have rubbed off."

"What do you mean?" Marvel asked shrilly. "Don't tell me you seduced Junior? Poor child!"

"No, you silly. I wouldn't seduce anyone, let alone the boat crew! But I did have a sexy dream. Weird, or what? After what went on yesterday. Maybe it was the dehydration."

"You are joking. With who?"

Charlie looked deeply embarrassed. "I don't think I can tell you I'm so ashamed!"

"Not my man I hope?" she said mock angrily, hands on hips and head to one side.

"No! Chad's safe."

"Chix?"

"No, although I sort of wish it was. I might feel a bit less squirmy. Well, saying that, I probably wouldn't be able to look him in the eye again if it was him. No, it was … Dwight."

Marvel started cracking up, "Dwight! Ha, I really didn't think he was your type. In fact, I distinctly remember you saying he made you shudder – and not in a nice way," Marvel teased, glad Charlotte could smile about something today – she'd been heartbroken yesterday.

"So, what did he do to you then?" Marvel asked once they had finally mastered the Nespresso machine and were outside enjoying a delicious cappuccino and a buttery croissant.

"It's more what I did to him! Honestly Marvel, it was like I was a different person in that dream. I was this confident siren who knew her power, knew what she wanted and abused his manhood to get it." She shook her head in wonder. "Honestly, very out of character for me. I feel a bit ashamed now … please don't tell anyone, she finished quietly, shy again.

"Who am I going to tell? Don't worry about that. But you know what, sweetie. I'm glad you had that dream. You need someone to make you feel sexy and powerful after what happened to you. Maybe you should make it happen in real life?" She winked, lightening the mood again.

"With Dwight?" she squeaked, "Noooo waaaay!"

"If you say so, sweetie, if you say so. Personally, I think you dig those wraparound Oakleys and that big hairy chest! Now if you'll excuse me, I'm just going to check out that luxury bathroom experience that got you so fresh last night."

It felt so good to laugh. Yesterday had been a real nightmare. After her confrontation with Graham, she had to get away from him. She ran down the bay, in the opposite direction of the restaurant. Five minutes later she reached a part of the beach where a ridge of spiky coral stone made it impossible for her to walk any further in her bare feet.

Disconsolate, she slumped onto the hot sand, wrapped her arms around herself and started to cry. Tears pouring down her face. Snot streaming out of her nose. Her tummy churned and she felt like she would throw up if she didn't stop crying. His rejection. The undeniable tension and stress of the last few weeks and the dawning realisation that her comfortable life would never be the same again overwhelmed her senses.

The afternoon sun beat brutally on her hatless crown. She had a splitting headache and was gasping with thirst. *I've been abandoned*, she thought piteously. Nobody cares about me. I could die here of sun stroke and dehydration and no one would know. *I wonder if Graham cares at all or if he would be happier if I died.*

Then she heard a noise, the thrum of an engine and someone shouting. She looked up. A small green and yellow motorboat was chugging along, laden down with coolers, boxes and some men including the bartender, Chad and Graham.

The boat slowed. Graham looked at her briefly then turned away tight lipped. It was Chad who spoke – pointing back to the restaurant and shouting,

"The girls are waiting for you down there." Only after she nodded her head to show that she had heard him did the boat speed off – Graham didn't look back.

Well, I guess he's not coming to tell me it's all been a huge mistake and beg my

forgiveness then. Time to face the music.

It was a hard slog back. As she neared, Marvel ducked out from the bar and came to meet her, concern written all over her face, then opened up her arms to give her a huge hug.

"It's OK sweetie, it's OK," She nodded to a lovely looking dark-haired lady behind the bar, "Sue and I are going to look after you." With that, Sue handed her a cold water to drink which she gulped down thankfully – she'd never tasted anything as delicious.

"Chix and Dwight are having a little sleep under the tree, but they will take us home when we are ready," Marvel said soothingly.

"I don't care if I ever go back. In fact, I don't ever want to go back and see him Marvel. I'm so fucking angry." She managed a weak smile. "Can't I stay here, Sue?"

Sue grinned, "Oh, yes love, if Dwight's OK with us sleeping on his boat we can stay here all night and go back on the boat in the morning. I'd love a sleepover! We've got food and plenty of beers."

"Well, it looks like our ride is out cold for a while. But it's probably good for you to sit here a while and cool down. Do you want to tell me what happened?" she asked gently.

"You know what, Marvel, I will tell you but … I don't think I can just now."

"No problem honey, take your time."

"Thanks, you've been so kind, a real friend. Really, I don't know what I would have done without you, I'm sorry you and Chad have been dragged into our drama."

"Honey, Chad and I love you both already and we just want what's best for you. It was obvious there is something wrong. Graham was shaken up, and you weren't with him. The other guys were preoccupied with lunch, so they didn't notice. Chad and I figured out something had happened, so he made up a story that Graham was feeling a bit sick and that he'd take him home early. I think he might suggest he stay at our place tonight."

Chix and Dwight woke eventually, they all boarded the yacht and made their way back to the mainland. By the time they got to the mooring,

Charlotte was exhausted and really didn't want to go back to the hotel on her own. Then Marvel told her that Dwight had offered her the use of the luxurious boat for the night.

"Stay here? That would be amazing. But won't that be inconveniencing him?"

"No, he says that's fine. Junior, a member of the crew, sleeps here anyway – so there will be someone here to keep an eye on you. There's plenty of drink. Not much food, though."

"That's perfectly OK! I'm not in the slightest bit hungry … you know Marvel, if that's OK with Dwight I think that would be the best solution. I don't want to inconvenience anyone anymore. I want you to go home and see Chad. I will just stay here quietly for the night."

Marvel had tried and failed to hide her relief. Clearly wanting to go home but also still determined to make sure her friend was comfortable.

"Well, if you are sure you will be OK?"

"Absolutely sure. I think some alone time is exactly what I need. And Marvel … thank you – I don't know what I would have done without you. You're amazing."

Speak of the Angel. Her lovely friend was back from the bathroom and waxing lyrical about the marble and brass fixtures and fittings and L'Occitane amenities.

"What do you want to do now, Charlie? Shall I take you to the hotel – maybe we could hang out for the day?"

"I guess I should go back and pack. We leave tomorrow morning. And I'd love some company if you can deal with my miserable face." She paused then asked, "Did you talk to Graham? Will he be there? I don't want to see him."

"He said he would make himself scarce. I didn't talk to him, but Chad did," then added, "we had to let him know that you were safe when you decided not to go back to the hotel. He was worried about you."

"So he should be."

"He's suffering, Charlie, I can see that. I still don't know what it is between you two but Chad says he feels terrible."

CHAPTER 17
Tracy

If the drive to his house had been as close to getting to heaven as Tracy had ever experienced – the drive back to Mango Bay was as close to hell as she ever wanted to go.

Her lovely Diver had never been so big, so distant, so serious, so hard to read or as implacably silent. As soon as the car stopped she jumped out, slammed the door and didn't look back. She avoided reception by taking a side route and ran through the grounds as quickly as she could, praying that she wouldn't meet anyone that she knew.

Emotionally exhausted, she collapsed on her bed and eventually fell asleep for a couple of hours. When she woke, her trusted self-defence mechanism kicked in. Like a Tracy-Terminator she found herself filled with steely determination to do what she had to do in the one full day she had left on the island.

Shelliqua was on duty that morning and, when Tracy went into reception to say good morning, the girl could see she was upset and motioned for her to stick around until she finished checking out some guests. She finished her shift at three and was going to the hairdresser's and invited her to keep her company while she had her hair done. Tracy agreed – thankful that she could kill two birds with one stone: see a local salon and keep thoughts of what should have been her and Diver's last wonderful day together at bay.

Back at her room she looked for Morris the taxi driver's business card and booked him to take her to the airport the following morning. Then, on a whim, asked him, "Morris if you were trying to track down someone who lived on this island about forty-five years ago – where would you start?"

It became immediately apparent that if Tracy had asked him that particular question on the day she arrived – she would have saved herself an awful lot of trouble. When he learnt she didn't know the person's name or anything much about them apart from a connection to the airport he suggested that she could try the Government Immigration Office – because if the people she was looking for had lived or worked on the island for any amount of time he was confident they would have a record of their work permit. Tracy secretly thought it was a long shot but decided anything was better than sitting around contemplating what could have been with Diver.

Morris said it would be his pleasure to take her and within the hour had picked her up from the hotel, suitably attired and equipped for a business meeting, and sped her into the island's capital – The Bottom – which was, of course, the butt of many jokes.

She spent an interesting hour at the Immigration Department talking to Morris's 'good friend' Isilma, who happened to be the deputy director. Isilma was a steely, attractive lady in her sixties, who was obviously extremely fond of Morris judging by the way her face softened as she set eyes on him. Tracy was impressed by the lady's smart, grey suit and fiercely air conditioned office and also pleasantly surprised that Isilma was interested in what she had to say. She expressed a passion for the island's history. Morris joined in the meeting, (Tracy didn't have the heart to ask him to leave) egging Isilma on to "help out the nice lady who might have family here".

Isilma promised to look back through the records to see if she could find information about the project team that built the airport. She told Tracy she may be in luck, because it was a notable government project.

It wasn't much, but it was something, and Tracy felt a tingle of excitement at the thought of making even a little progress. A tingle that was quashed when Isilma went on to say that although she would like to help she wouldn't be able to do anything for a while, as she was due her annual vacation – she was going to Florida to visit with family for a month or more. They exchanged cards and Tracy thanked her profusely but privately doubted she would hear anything from her. She kicked herself for not acting quicker, because if she had met with Isilma earlier in her stay, there was a chance she may have found something out before she left.

Morris refused to take any money from her for driving her around, but indicated he would accept "a little refreshment", so they stopped at a couple of his favourite local haunts to grab a cold beer or two and a takeaway lunch box. Tracy got the distinct impression the taxi driver was showing her off to his friends as he squired her from bar to bar, chatting and introducing her to everyone. She smiled and joined in, but her heart wasn't in it. Every time a red vehicle passed them, she tensed wondering if it was Diver.

By the time she got back to the hotel and finished packing her bag it was already time to go out with Shelliqua. The hair salon was packed with women, and the smell of product and hot hair was soothingly familiar. She watched, fascinated, for hours while Shelliqua had her hair done in an updo of spectacular complexity. For such a small island she was impressed by the size and quality of the establishment and the sheer number of women spending money on hairdos, cosmetics and nails.

When she got back to the hotel, Desiree, the grumpy receptionist, handed over the checkout information, grabbed her car hire keys and warned Tracy that she needed to be out by midday or face a fine.

"No problem. Any calls for me?" she asked hopefully.

"No," said Desiree, leaving little room for doubt.

And when she got back to her room there was no flashing red light indicating Diver had left a message on her answer phone either.

FRIDAY 13TH JUNE
DEPARTURE DAY

CHAPTER 18
Charlotte

After successfully avoiding Graham since 'Prickly Pear-gate', Charlotte's first glimpse of her husband in nearly two days, hit her as hard as a punch.

They met up, as co-ordinated by Marvel and Chad (who had been absolute bricks), in the lobby of Paradise Point, and got into the waiting taxi without looking at or speaking to each other. A strained silence accompanied them throughout their journey as they cleared customs at the island's seaport, and boarded the speedboat over to the airport on the neighbouring island – all the steps needed to catch a plane to take them back to their home in London. To a home life that no longer made sense to either of them.

Charlie found it easier to stare at the disappearing shoreline of an island that had shattered her dreams than to meet the gaze of her husband. She watched her dream hotel, on its white curve of beach, get smaller and smaller. She could even see the faintest outline of Prickly Pear – a light grey smudge on the top of the sea – in the far, far, distance.

At the airport, Graham commandeered a porter and for the first time in two days spoke directly to his wife. Getting her attention by tapping her on the shoulder, "Follow me," and strode past the all the other people queuing for their flight before stopping in front of the first-class desk – behind a model-thin, deeply tanned, French couple with matching Burberry luggage and artfully distressed, white linen clothing.

When it was their turn, she snatched his passport from his outstretched hand and handed it along with hers to the young woman behind the counter.

"We'd both like window seats please," she said firmly.

ENDLESS TURQUOISE

The girl peered at her computer screen. Her spectacular turquoise nails clattered over the keys as she sprang into action.

After a few seconds she said apologetically, "I can do that Mr and Mrs Browning but I'm afraid you will be sat at different ends of the cabin."

Charlotte nodded and gave the girl a tight smile.

"That will be fine." At exactly the same time Graham opened his mouth and said the same thing.

They stood awkwardly side by side while the girl weighed their bags and gave them their passports, boarding cards and gate instructions.

Once past passport control, Graham said in a quiet voice, "Seems that they have a first-class lounge here – shall we give it a try?"

"Sure," said Charlotte, too weary to come up with an excuse not to go with him.

It was a new airport and the first-class lounge was attractive, spacious and flooded with light. They found a quiet corner by a huge window that overlooked the ocean and sat down at opposite ends of the long couch with plenty of space between them.

At the other end of the room, a dark wood, marble-topped bar ran from one wall to another. The lounge's sophisticated look was offset by the fact that the room smelt faintly of floor cleaner and stewed meat. There was also piped music – loud enough for Charlotte to recognise the song as one by a famous calypso singer called Mighty Sparrow.

He was singing saucily about his girlfriend wanting '*a little, little piece of his big bamboo*'. The song almost made her smile, then almost made her cry, thinking about the night of the Folkloric Theatre. *Discovering Caribbean music and making friends with Marvel are the only good things to have come out of this terrible excuse for a honeymoon.*

Feeling the need to get away from Graham, Charlotte grabbed her handbag and wandered over to the bar without asking him if he wanted anything. She ordered a spicy Bloody Mary and distracted herself by looking at the complimentary appetisers, which the bartender had pointed out listlessly.

There was absolutely nothing appetising about what she saw: the small display consisted of grey meatballs sitting in a pool of glossy brown sauce –

now she understood where the smell of meat came from, pieces of deep-fried something in bright orange breadcrumbs, and some tired looking chicken wings drying up under the strong heat lamps. All the 'delicious' items had helpful signs to identify them 'Meatballs in barbeque sauce', 'Fish bit's with tartar sauce' and 'Jerk chicken wings'. At the end there was a pot of cocktail sticks, some napkins and a pile of small plates to encourage you to sample them.

"I don't want to think about what bit of the fish that is," stage whispered Graham behind her. She giggled forgetting for a moment that she hated him – temporarily united by their shared sense of the ridiculous.

"Or what meat those balls are made of," she deadpanned. He laugh-snorted.

"Tempting, but I think I will give the 'Jerk Wings' a miss – what about you?" Graham asked, raising his eyebrows.

"Agreed. I'll take my chances with the in-flight dining – at least that's hermetically sealed."

She picked up her drink from the bar and they walked back to their seats together.

Charlotte made herself as comfortable as possible on the hard, faux-leather sofa. Nursing her drink while watching a motorboat trail streams of white and aqua on the lagoon. Sensing that Graham was looking at her, she turned her shoulders to avoid catching his eye – as far as she was concerned 'pax' was over.

Graham wasn't to be put off. He scooted closer along the sofa.

"Look, Charlie. I know you are terribly upset and angry with me. And that you don't want to talk to me, but I need to know what's going through your head."

She turned and looked at him blankly.

"Do you know what you want to do next?" he asked anxiously.

Charlotte sighed. *I wish you would leave me alone – I'm so tired – too tired to know what to say.* But he just kept staring at her, waiting patiently for her to answer.

"Graham, I don't know. I wish I did." She folded in on herself and looked down at her hands, sans wedding ring, clasped in her lap.

His voice was uncharacteristically gentle. "I want to say to you that whatever you want is fine with me. If you want to stay in the flat and for me to move out that's OK; I can go to a hotel or stay at a friend's."

"What friend? Andreas?" she snarled.

"No not with Andreas. That's not appropriate."

"What do you mean not appropriate? More like he doesn't want you," she goaded.

Graham tightened his lips and looked pissed off. Charlie wondered if she had managed to touch a sore spot. *Good! I hope he called Andreas and got the brush-off – serves him right.*

"No, Charlotte, it's complicated. Listen, I'm trying to be fair. I want you to know you can stay in the flat as long as you want and take as much time as you need to make a decision about what's next."

"Big of you."

"Look, I'm not trying to force your hand, but I think I'm safe saying you don't want to live with me at the moment … or be married to me anymore?"

She nodded. "Darn right. I want a divorce as quickly as possible. It shouldn't be too difficult to get one on the grounds of non-consummation, or just plain infidelity," she spat.

"Of course, I will do whatever I can do to make things better between us. Charlie, I would love it if we could still be friends."

She shook her head in disbelief. "Friends, Graham? Really? I doubt we can ever be that. I just keep thinking thank god we didn't have those children yet."

"I don't. I wish we had. We would have had good-looking children. You would make the perfect mother, and I know I would have been a great dad."

"And that's why you married me? So that you could have some perfect children, keep me around to raise them right and have a man or two on the side whenever you want some adult fun?" she finished bitchily.

"Oh, you don't understand. I'm not gay." Voice raised in barely reined in frustration.

"Well, let me try to understand. Because I am very confused. You say you are NOT gay however you prefer sex with men? That's gay in my book Graham."

"I'm not alone in this you know. There are lots of guys like me out there. We even have a name – MSM – men who sleep with men."

"Unbelievable!"

"It's true. I read an interesting thing last year. It was a sex survey of working men in New York, a big survey. The results said nearly ten percent of the married men they spoke to had had sex with another man in the preceding year, and nearly ten percent of men who identified as heterosexual were having sex exclusively with men."

"I still don't understand. Why don't you just come out as gay or even bi-curious? There's nothing wrong with being gay. It's just a fact of life. There's no shame. And it's fine to adopt children if you are gay – you didn't need me to have a family. I just don't get it."

"Because I don't want to. I don't want to be defined by sexuality. It's no one else's business. Would we have dated if I told you from the beginning I also slept with men?"

He had a point. She wouldn't.

"Sleeping with a man, for me, it's just a sexual preference. I decided a while ago that I don't want to be a part of that gay world – the scene. I don't fit in. To be honest, I don't feel like I fit anywhere," he continued. "I like men, which means I'm not straight enough in the straight world, and I don't feel gay enough in the gay world. I guess that's why I got us into such a mess."

"Graham," she said quietly, "what about girlfriends? I think you had some before me."

"You know I did. I've had plenty of sex – and relationships – with women, who I have liked *and* fancied."

She plucked up the courage to ask the burning question. The thing that made her cringe every time she thought about it.

"But what about the sex you had with me? That's what's killing me, Graham. Were you just going through the motions then?"

"No, of course not. I loved being with you. Try not to blame yourself or overthink it Charlie."

She hadn't said it to him but of course she had thought it was to do with her not being sexy or good enough for him. Who wouldn't?

"For me, sex is about exploring all the options. I have a healthy sexual imagination and sometimes I like to get naughty and explore a bit. I'm not gay, I'm curious. The world is changing and apps like Grindr make it easier to experiment without commitment." He shrugged his shoulders. "There is a whole smorgasbord of sexual experiences out there and I want to try them. You'd be amazed how many straight men are using Grindr to—"

He cut himself short, realising by the look on her face it was too much information too soon, "But, I shouldn't have …"

"You shouldn't have married me," Charlie concluded for him sadly.

"No, I shouldn't have. I was selfish. I wanted it all."

They were both quiet for some time before Graham broke the silence.

"I was very happy when we met, and I was attracted to you. You were, you ARE so beautiful, but you have never really understood that. I loved helping you change your style and grow in confidence. Of course, you are great company too. I loved spending time with you."

So, I didn't just dream it all?

"Remember, when we first met, we had sex regularly but then it just petered off until … well, I don't know if it was all me, either … I felt like you wanted to less and less also, but I didn't question that. Perhaps because it suited us both?"

He looked at her enquiringly, she didn't agree or disagree, just carried on looking at him. *Was he finished or did he have more to say?*

"They say time will out, and I think that's what has happened to me. When I met Andreas, I knew immediately I was attracted to him. I didn't act on it to start with. I knew it would be bad for the project and unfair to you. Maybe I should have walked away. Changed designers – but I think he came into my life for a reason, Charlie."

She stared at him blankly, *Surprise, surprise*! *He worried about the project first and me second.* With Graham there always is – and always will be – a project. She wanted to shout out loud "I hate that bloody project and I hate Andreas too!" but instead, jealousy and grief stabbing her like a pair of knitting needles, she began to cry.

Graham looked stricken. Moving closer, emboldened by their frank talk, he dared to reach out and pull Charlotte close into his side and wrap his arm around her protectively. She didn't resist. He nestled her head under his chin and spoke quietly into her hair.

"Ohh Charlie, what a mess. What a horrible fucking mess. I won't blame you if you hate me. I hate myself at the moment."

They sat together until the PA system announced the last call for London Gatwick. They boarded the Jumbo and sat at different ends of the first-class cabin. Charlotte reclined in her seat, replaying the revealing conversation in her head. *Maybe if we had both been a bit more honest from the beginning – none of this would have happened.* Perhaps if I'd asked him more about the project and what he was doing. She dismissed the thought immediately as being his fault – not hers – but what a mess. What would she do next? How would she tell everyone? How could she go into work? How would they live together? Could she carry on sharing a house with him?

"Glass of champagne, Miss?"

She didn't know what to do next in life but she did know what to do in that moment, take the attentive young man up on his kind offer, and not think about Graham or what next, for the rest of the flight. London was eight hours away after all.

CHAPTER 19
Tracy

Tracy slept badly on her final night at Mango Bay. Dropping off then waking up, tossing and turning for hours. The worst thing was that every time she fell asleep, she dreamt of Diver, then felt the pain fresh when she woke and remembered what had happened. I would have been brokenhearted this morning anyway, having to leave him, but at least we could have kissed goodbye.

When the sun rose at 6.30am, she headed to the beach for a final float in the perfect ocean – but her heart wasn't in it. She looked at 'their' sunbed. It looked insignificant and sad. Not the scene-setter for a great romance.

The morning passed quickly. She had her final breakfast and bid a brave goodbye to Freddie the manager, who came in specially to wish her bon voyage. She left tips for the restaurant staff, who she had become very fond of. They were so sweet, hugging her up and saying they were sure that she would come back "because you're a local now". She got through it all without shedding a tear, amazed at how strong she could appear on the outside. Inside her heart was breaking. She knew it was goodbye. She would never come back to this special place. It wasn't just Diver she'd fallen in love with.

At reception she paid the bill, handed over her room key then gave Desiree an envelope to post. She also handed the perennially sour-faced receptionist a $20 note to sweeten the task. Desiree looked at the envelope as if it was infected with the bubonic plague, and barely grunted a response when Tracy asked, for the second time, if she "could do that for her?"

It was addressed:

For the attention of Dr Clinton Derrick, the National Heritage Museum.

She'd made the last-minute decision to write an explanatory note to Diver after breakfast. She needed him to hear what she had been trying to say that night. To set the record straight, that she had made assumptions that were wrong – but he had too.

The note was brief and to the point. Even though what she really wanted to do was to spill her heart out and tell him how much he meant to her. That she would miss him terribly because he'd stolen her heart. But she didn't.

Maybe when he reads it, he will understand and get in touch. I've written down my contact details – he knows how to find me now if he wants to. I can't do any more, she concluded as she turned for one last look at the receptionist before she headed outside to meet Morris.

It would have been better, much better, if her friend had been on duty that morning and she could have handed her the note to post. Hanging out together the two women had created a nice bond, but even though Tracy liked her very much, when they parted company and Shelliqua made a comment about Diver coming to the Hotel to climb in her suitcase and go home to England with her, Tracy trivialised their affair.

"Oh no, we won't be seeing each other again, It was just a bit of fun. He's much younger than me and, well, he lives here and I'm in the UK, so it would be impossible to keep it up. Yep, it's for the best."

"Don't forget, 'age is just a number', Tracy."

"Indeed. And it was fun while it lasted, but it's back to reality now. Back to normal, not this 'Fantasy Island' existence I've been living. Life can't be a beach every day."

*

Morris talked nonstop all the way to the airport – undeterred by Tracy's uncharacteristically monosyllabic responses. She stared out the window, soaking every little detail in, imprinting the island in her mind. Hoping, yet dreading that she might see Diver or CB drive past – it was such a small place it was entirely possible.

She held it together until they reached the airport. After Morris got her bags out of the car and she tipped him, he held out his hand to shake hers then leant in for a kiss on the cheek.

"Safe travels and see you soon then, my friend."

"See you soon," she choked, eyes welling behind her mirrored sunglasses.

Her flight departed on time and the connection to the big plane was as smooth as silk. Clearing customs in the UK she looked for and found the familiar face of her regular taxi driver (and Rosemary's next-door neighbour), Reggie. He was holding a sign saying, "Welcome Home, Tracy".

Beside him, scanning the arriving passengers with an anxious expression, was her mum. As soon as she saw her, Rosemary's face relaxed into a broad, pretty smile. Tracy ducked under the barrier and wrapped her arms around her tiny, fragile form – hugging her tight and breathing in her familiar smell.

"I'm very happy to see you, Mum, I missed you a lot."

PART THREE
ENGLAND

CHAPTER 20
Charlotte

During a long, uncomfortable journey home in a cold and rattling black cab, Charlie and Graham discussed their situation, and came to a joint decision – to do nothing for a while. The thought of telling their friends and family that they had split, and why, was just too much to deal with now.

Charlotte paid the driver and Graham dragged their bags out of the cab and up the stairs of the imposing Victorian mansion block on the 'right' side of Clapham Common. She paused at the door of the 3rd floor apartment she used to call home.

Once inside Graham busied around, disarming the alarm system, and unlocking the windows of the graciously proportioned, light-filled living room that smelt faintly of old roses. A dappled greenish light filtered through the mature oak trees that guarded the outside of the building and spilt into the room via huge bay windows boasting the original sashes.

The room was a perfectly eclectic mix of modern and traditional – paying homage to the wonderful Victorian 'bones' of the room yet feeling fresh and modern. Their 'great room' was the envy of all their friends and the perfect expression of Graham's exquisite taste. Looking at it with fresh eyes, Charlie realised, with a jolt, that it said absolutely nothing about her – her personality – her taste. It was all Graham. And she didn't know where to put her cases either. She certainly was not going to sleep in the master suite with Graham.

She made them both a cup of tea while Graham quickly unpacked and had a shower. He emerged from his dressing room immaculately suited and booted ten minutes later. Charlotte looked him up and down critically – as usual he presented the perfect façade – his face was tanned, handsome and completely unreadable. No one would ever know the emotional strain he was experiencing. He gulped his tea back in a couple of thirsty swallows and smiled weakly at her.

"Business as usual then."

"You're going to work?" Charlie questioned.

"Yes. Thought it would be best. Give you some space." He looked at her quizzically, obviously wanting approval for his decision.

For a split second, Charlie considered being bitchy and creating a scene to stop him going – but it suited her if he left. "Yes, probably."

He smiled – obviously thankful to have a 'get out' card. "See you later then."

"Yes."

"Bye, then." He gave her an awkward kiss on the forehead, grabbed his (she'd always thought) ridiculous man bag and keys from the hall table and disappeared. Charlie barely had the chance to say 'bye' before the door closed firmly behind him and she heard the whir and clunk of the lift descending.

She finished her tea and washed up their cups. *What now?* She felt lonely and restless. She gazed out the window, trying to think of something to do. Clapham Common was buzzing with its normal weekday crowd: red buses were loading and unloading trendy and not-so-trendy 'Claphamites'; uniformed school children from the private school close by were playing football in the weak sunshine; two fetching 'yummy mummies' in skinny jeans and colourful pashminas were chatting and drinking take out lattés, while pushing strollers along the paths; a personal trainer was putting a panting 'city type' through his paces and a couple of homeless men were drinking Special Brew on her favourite bench under a chestnut tree.

Charlotte sighed – the sight of the common usually filled her with pleasurable anticipation but suddenly none of her normal pursuits had any appeal. She didn't want to go have a coffee at the nice French place because she might run into someone she knew; she didn't feel like going to the gym - she was too tired. She didn't fancy the cinema – sitting in the dark would depress her. She was at a complete loss.

I'd quite like to go into work too. That would be a distraction, but she wasn't due back at work until the middle of next week. Anyway, she couldn't deal with Danny's raised eyebrows – as soon as he saw her moping around he would get the truth out of her in seconds.

The house phone rang and broke her reverie. In two minds about answering she was glad she did because, joy of joys, it was Ali at the end of the line.

"Hello, my lover," her friend said in the broad Wiltshire accent they used between themselves sometimes. "You're back, hurrah! How was it? Are you really brown? Bet you are. Can you still walk after all that honeymoon sex?"

Charlotte felt her eyes pool, "Hi Ali," she said quietly, willing herself not to cry.

"What's up? You don't sound too chipper – bad journey home?"

"And some."

"What's going on? My spidey senses are twitching. Is something wrong?"

"It's complicated." Charlotte should know by now she couldn't hide anything from Ali.

"Tell me." Concern in her friend's voice.

Oh shit, Charlie was dying to spill the beans, but knowing that she'd made a pact with Graham not to say anything just yet she said weakly, "I can't really."

Ali grabbed hold of the hesitation in her friend's voice like a terrier would a rabbit, "Hold on Charlie – what do you mean can't? You know you can tell Auntie Ali anything."

"I can't tell you this," she said sadly, balling up her fist and stopping her mouth to prevent herself blurting out the truth.

Charlie could sense Ali thinking at the other end of the call, before breaking the silence with: "God, now you're really worrying me. I wish I could come round and drag it out of you, but I'm in Wiltshire at the oldies."

Charlotte's body perked up – anticipatory as a meerkat, "You're in Wiltshire? How long for?" and held her breath hopefully. She was in luck.

"Until tomorrow. I was due a visit, so I decided to hang around after your wedding. I'm so sorry I won't see you."

Charlotte suddenly knew what to do. Ali was the only person she wanted to see and who she could trust to talk to about this. Bugger her agreement with Graham; she couldn't miss the opportunity to see her friend.

"You will," she said.

"What do you mean?"

"You will see me. I'm coming to Wiltshire. Just decided. I'll see you tonight at The Lamb. 9.00pm. After dinner."

Ali let out a whistle of surprise, "Ooooookkkkk. You and Graham?"

"No – just me."

Ali asked, confused, "Am I to understand you are finishing your honeymoon a few days early and coming on your own to Wiltshire to see me? That doesn't sound right." Her next questions tumbled out in a breathless and indignant rush, "Why isn't he coming? Is he back at work already? He's a bloody workaholic! – can't he take a break? Is that why you're upset?"

Charlotte just made a noncommittal noise – she didn't want to go into it now, "Like I said, it's complicated so I will tell you later. Nine o'clock at The Lamb. Don't be late." She hung up before Ali had a chance to ask any more questions.

Fired up and needing to get out of the flat as soon as possible, she made a quick and deliberately vague call to her dad, who said he was delighted they were coming to stay, then swiftly packed a small bag with clothes, toiletries and her parents' holiday gifts.

She had a nice long shower and washed the last lingering deposits of the Caribbean from her hair. She dried it roughly, tied it back in a high ponytail, slipped into a pair of all-purpose jeans, a pale blue long sleeved tee-shirt and some butter-soft, brown leather loafers. She then sat down to write a note to Graham, which she left on the kitchen counter, weighted down by a bottle of Californian red.

> *Graham, we both need some space. I couldn't see the sense in staying. I'm going to Wiltshire to see Ali. See you on Sunday. Charlotte.*

Five minutes later she was striding across the common towards the underground and she felt a whole lot happier. A short tube journey, an hour on the train and she'd be home.

CHAPTER 21
Tracy

The arrivals area at Gatwick was crowded and even though people were busy with their own life dramas – long-lost lovers reunited, excited travellers embarking on international adventures – Tracy's gulping sobs were too loud to be ignored. To paraphrase her Auntie Dorry, she was 'causing a bit of a scene'.

Tracy's mum and Reggie exchanged worried looks but didn't say anything. Reggie grabbed her wheelie bag and her mum held her hand as they ushered her up some ramps, out of the airport, through to the short stay car park and into the car. Sniffing and snorting into the lavender scented hankie her mum had provided, she curled up on the back seat like a child, until they reached the bungalow. She uncurled stiffly then gave Reggie a rather sniffly hug and an embarrassed thank you for collecting her.

She didn't even put up a fight when Rosemary suggested she stay at the bungalow that night. Although her own flat was much nicer, she didn't want to be on her own. She needed her mum right now.

They sat for a while in the cosy kitchen with its oatmeal-coloured tiles, lemon walls and flouncy net curtains. Tracy's mum busied around putting on the kettle and darting concerned looks at her daughter as she flipped through the previous day's Daily Mail.

To make her mum happy she managed a cup of tea, some dark chocolate Hobnobs and a little superficial conversation before making her excuses and crawling up to bed. It was a bad idea to go to bed at midday (it was going to take ages to get over her jet lag) but she hadn't slept on the overnight flight and couldn't stay up any longer. She fell into a deep sleep almost as soon as her head hit the pillow.

She woke up four hours later after sleeping as well as every child does (whatever their age) when they know their mum is close by watching out for them. Desperately thirsty with a mouth like a sandbox, she gulped down two glasses of tap water then ran herself a nice deep bath with lots of bubble bath Her mum popped her head round the door, having heard the tank firing up for the hot water, bringing in a soft peach towel from the airing cupboard and one of her dressing gowns to put on after the bath.

Half an hour later she joined Rosemary in the living room where she was watching TV. Deciding she felt a bit peckish, she explored the fridge and made them both a prawn cocktail sandwich with juicy prawns, pink sauce and a fancy lettuce mix from Marks and Sparks. They split a packet of plain crisps between their two plates. She located her mum's wine box, poured them both a glass of cold Muscadet, added that to their TV trays and took them into the lounge.

Her mum looked up and smiled gratefully as she grabbed the tray and settled it on her lap. "Oh lovely, prawn sandwiches. You're spoiling me."

Tracy laughed, "You're spoiling me, more like. I know you brought those prawns for me, Mum."

They watched Gardener's World and munched their sandwiches contentedly – discussing the show but not talking about anything much. When they finished the sandwiches and wine, Tracy took the trays into the kitchen and picked up a box of Maltesers from the 'chocolate drawer' and they shared those while watching a show where a famous actress traced her ancestry back to discover that she was distantly related to the royal family.

It's a little close to the bone, she thought, watching a TV programme about tracing your long-lost family.

Her mum didn't seem to notice the irony, though, and as she never really wanted to talk too much when she was watching the TV, they spent most of the evening in companionable silence – until her mum heaved herself out of her armchair and went to bed at 11.00pm, yawning and stretching.

"See you in the morning, love. We can catch up then. Hope you can sleep." She bent over and gave Tracy a light kiss before heading along the corridor to her bedroom.

Not tired enough to go to bed after her siesta, Tracy reached down from the couch and picked up Tigger. She needed a cuddle.

"What am I going to do Tigger Tat?" Tracy asked her furry friend sadly. "What am I going to do?"

She felt as deflated and useless as a punctured beach ball. The rollercoaster of emotions and situations she'd experienced over the last few weeks was overwhelming. The thought of going to the salon on Monday – going back to her normal life – didn't give her the sense of pride and purpose it normally did.

The following morning, she gave her mum an edited version of the trip. Rosemary expressed a polite interest while she waxed lyrical about the beaches and how friendly the hotel was and about all the great people, she'd met – but that was it. True to the message on her mum's answer machine, where she promised to give up her quest to find the child, she didn't mention the abortive attempts to visit the museum or her meeting with Isilma.

Rosemary didn't ask any questions at all after Tracy finished her roundup. She seemed happy to move on to other safer subjects and Tracy was keen to get their relationship back on track. They passed a pleasant hour eating toast and marmite, drinking instant coffee, catching up on the neighbourhood gossip and what passed for news in the Daily Mail.

Looking vacantly out of the car window as Reggie drove her back to her own home, Tracy thought back over their conversations and realised there was something about Rosemary's behaviour that didn't sit right.

Is she playing me? Showing me her poker face? It was entirely possible. I've learnt a lot about her these last few months. She's incredibly hard to read and very easy to underestimate.

The time on Zephyr had made her see Rosemary from a whole new perspective. Her mum was braver, bolder and more adventurous than she'd ever imagined. And secretive. And if she can keep a secret, so can I. I'm not telling her a thing about Diver until she spills the beans about what really went on with her too.

CHAPTER 22
Charlotte

Charlotte's parents, Peter and Helen, lived in a picture-perfect Wiltshire village called Puddlington. The village was arranged around a large, tree-fringed village green and boasted a population of approximately five hundred. Puddlington was so attractive, architecturally harmonious and authentically 'chocolate box' that the BBC had used its ancient stone houses and verdant village green as the backdrop for a number of the quality "period dramas" that enthral the British viewer most Sunday evenings.

The village cricket team, in their grass stained whites, were regularly photographed, hitting the ball for six, for articles about living in an authentic rural idyll. The local pub had been turned into a gastro pub of such outstanding quality that minor royalty were often to be found there. All in all, it was a very desirable place to live, less than two hours from London, but deep in ravishing English countryside.

Charlotte's parents hadn't always lived in Puddlington; the family had moved from a large, modern estate house in a suburb of Swindon when she was thirteen, but the charming village had felt like home to the little family from the moment they moved there. She'd met Ali on the day they moved in. Ali – being a gregarious child and the daughter of extremely sociable parents – had been sent over with a 'welcome-to-the-village' Victoria sponge cake and an invitation to drinks the following day. The next evening the three of them wandered over shyly to say hello, not knowing what to expect from their new neighbours. After sharing four bottles of wine (the grownups) and a litre of Taunton cider mixed with lemonade (the girls) and assembling a makeshift supper of cold cuts and cheese from the fridge – Ali and Charlotte, and their respective parents, had bonded, staying firm friends ever since.

As the GWR train shuddered to a long slow halt at Mawksbury, Charlotte felt her throat tighten at the sight of her parents waiting on the platform. She loved them so much and thought they looked very smart in their matching dark green Barbour jackets and sensible trousers. They were scanning the passing windows for a glimpse of her.

She stepped off the train a few metres away from where they were standing but as they were looking in the opposite direction, they didn't notice her until she tapped them on the shoulder.

"Mummy, Daddy!"

They turned and smiled, and she leant into them to give them a joint hug, feeling tears threaten as they returned her squeeze. They stepped away and she could see them looking behind her for Graham's tall figure.

"Where's our new son-in-law, darling?" asked Peter.

"Oh sorry, didn't I tell you, he's not coming." She smiled brightly.

"Whyever not?" asked her dad, looking puzzled.

"Oh, some emergency thing on his project. You know. Lots to catch up with." She smiled reassuringly.

Her parents looked relieved. "Oh well, if it's OK with you. And I must say it will be awfully nice to have you to ourselves for a change. You look super, darling. Marvellous in fact. All brown and shimmery," said her dad admiringly.

"Yes, you look rather exotic. Very tanned. I don't know where you get that skin from considering your father and I are so pale," chipped in Helen.

"Her Nana was dark you know. I won't say what they used to call her – not 'PC' these days. But as soon as she saw a bit of sun, she looked like this one," added Peter with a huge grin and wink at Charlotte. Charlotte grimaced at her mum. Her dad was awful sometimes.

"Stop teasing, Peter. Let's get going. I need to take the dog for a walk – she'll be crossing her legs."

"Good idea. I've got a bit of a headache and could do with a cup of tea and a sit down."

"Must be the jetlag, darling," Helen said soothingly as they walked swiftly to the car.

When they got back to the house, Charlotte was unhappy to discover that her parents had prepared the 'rose room' aka the best spare room, for the newly married couple. She was horrified – she didn't want to sleep there. She wanted to sleep in her own bedroom, located at the back of the house. The lovely little room that overlooked the paddock where her beloved pony Patches had spent many happy years rolling around and eating apples from the fruit trees that overhung the fence. Her parents hadn't changed the room since she'd left home at seventeen to go to the posh secretarial school they'd enrolled her in when they all realised A-levels and academia weren't for her. She was too tall for it really, but she still loved to sleep in the saggy single bed with its creaky springs and white metal bedstead.

"Mummy, can I sleep in my old room please?" She looked at her mum pleadingly.

"Oh, you silly girl. Why do you want to do that? You can sleep in the rose room, it's much bigger and more comfortable."

"But I want to sleep in my bed." Putting on her little girl voice to raise a smile from them, she wheedled, "I just like waking up in there and looking out the window. I love that view."

"Well, if you must. But Edna and I made up this room for you because we thought Graham would be with you and we know how funny he can get if there isn't an en suite," she finished with a roll of the eyes.

"Well, it's just me and I want to sleep in my old room if that's OK?"

Helen gave in. "Alright, if that's what you really want. There should be clean sheets in the airing cupboard, but you'll have to do it yourself because I'm taking that poor dog out for a walk. Unless you want to come?" she asked hopefully.

"Sorry Mummy, not now if you don't mind, I'm wiped out from the jetlag. I may make up my bed and have a short nap if that's OK with you both?" She looked at her parents who nodded. "Great, what time is dinner?"

"How about 7.00? It's just a casserole so we can have it whenever."

"7.00 is perfect; I'll come down before then."

Ten minutes later, Charlie was lying on clean but threadbare, pink cotton sheets that smelt of washing powder and fresh air and her headache had vanished. She read a few chapters of one of her favourite children's books harvested from the white wooden bookshelves, then drifted off into a refreshing snooze for an hour or so before her dad woke her up by knocking gently on the door.

"Charlie darling, it's time for dinner."

"OK, Daddy, coming now." She tidied herself up in the bathroom then came downstairs to find her parents in the kitchen, already tucking into the brimming plates of food in front of them. They'd put her at the head of the table and there was an empty plate put out so she could help herself to the casserole and veggies keeping warm on the Rayburn.

The first ten minutes of dinnertime were a little strained as she fenced off their questions about the honeymoon. Trying to keep the conversation on neutral subjects like restaurants, beaches and their new friends Marvel and Chad. She was massively relieved when the conversation turned away from her honeymoon and onto village life and she thoroughly enjoyed an hour of catching up on local gossip: who had a new dog, who'd been ill, who'd had babies and, most salaciously, who'd had their controversial plans for an extension (so they could open a Bed and Breakfast) turned down.

During the meal Charlotte and (mainly) her dad managed to get through the best part of two bottles of Waitrose Claret, Peter gleefully opening the second – despite Helen's urging him not to be so greedy. He gave his daughter a conspiratorial wink as he pulled the cork.

Just before nine o'clock she turned down their offer to watch the news and informed them she was going out for a drink.

"But it's so late Charlotte," said Helen. She was not going to be put off. "No Mummy, it's not too late. It's perfect timing. I've had a lovely dinner and catch-up with you two and now I can have a catch-up with Ali for a couple of hours. This the last chance I have before she goes back to Spain." She wasn't going to hurt their feelings by telling them that having the chance to talk to Ali was the reason she'd come home in such a hurry.

"Off you go out and enjoy yourself, darling," said Peter encouragingly, "and please give my love to Sammi," he added rather wistfully. He'd always had a soft spot for the leggy bartender but was limited to how many times he could visit the pub without Helen getting snippy.

"Do you want to come, Daddy?" Charlotte offered dutifully, "I know Ali would love to see you."

"And I would love to see her. But your mother is right as usual. It is late my darling. My nightcap is calling, and I guarantee the one I pour will be larger and significantly cheaper than the one they serve in the pub. I am sure you girls have lots to catch up on."

Charlie slipped out of the warm kitchen and into the chilly hall giving her parents a peck on the cheek. She reassured them that she knew where they kept the spare key, had a torch and would definitely be able to get back in.

She shrugged on her ancient padded gilet and pulled on her favourite scuffed Blundstones, which were always kept in the shoe cupboard for when she came home. Despite being June, (in theory summer in the UK) there was a definite chill in the air, especially as she had not acclimatised from the tropical heat.

The night sky was crystal clear and stars popped out to greet her as she strode off into the silky dark, heading left across the village green, towards the glowing orange lights of the village's 'public house' The Lamb. The pub sat bang in the middle of the village green and her parents' Queen Anne cottage was a scant three minutes' walk away if you cut across the springy grass – a few minutes more if you walked on the road.

Ali's parents' house was approximately the same distance in the opposite direction and as she couldn't see her friend walking on the moonlit green, she assumed she had already got to the pub and was waiting for her. She crunched up the gravel path, threw back the heavy wooden door and felt the unmistakable rush of hot air. She inhaled the tangy smell of hops, garlic and wood smoke – the experience was almost as familiar as arriving home. But then the pub was a home of sorts – she and Ali had spent an awful lot of time at The Lamb when they were teenagers, working as waitstaff to earn pocket money which they promptly spent on cider and crisps at the bar as soon as they were old enough to do so.

She waved and grinned at a shocked-to-see-her Sammi, who was busy serving a customer at the other end – then peered round the back of the trestle to see her best friend in all the world sitting at 'their' table in the corner, with two frosty halves of dry cider in front of her. She felt a huge grin take over her face and hurried over, avoiding bar stools and a grumpy fox terrier stretched out in front of the wood fire (there was nearly always a fire in the The Lamb – even in the summer). Ali stood up, grinned like a loon and opened her arms with a cry of "gimme some love" and the two girls hugged for a long time before Charlotte dropped her jacket onto the opposite seat, took a huge swig of cider and finally looked Ali in the eyes.

Ali looked at her quizzically; that was all that was needed.

"You are not going to believe what's happened …" started Charlie as it all burst out.

It took fifteen minutes to tell Ali the whole story from beginning to end. And during that time her friend didn't ask a single question; she just listened intently, eyes wide, making gratifying noises of support, shock and anger as Charlotte revealed everything that had happened to her from the start of the honeymoon. She skipped over the details of the hotel and the island and concentrated on Graham's moods and their arguments. She mentioned her new friends and revealed the sad story day by day. She was dry eyed throughout and stared at her drink for most of the time. When she reached the point where she revealed Graham's affair she finally looked up and was surprised to see sympathy in her friend's eyes rather than shock.

"You're not surprised?" she asked, reading her friend's expression correctly.

"Yes and no." Charlotte looked at her questioningly. "Yes, because why would you get married if you were gay like that. But no, because I just had a feeling about Graham – right from the beginning. Don't get me wrong I like him – still do. There was just something missing for me when I saw you together and now you've said this, it's all clicked into place."

"You didn't think he was right for me?"

"Oh god, that's hard to answer. It's difficult because I've been in Spain for most of the time you've been with him and, to be honest, I haven't spent much time around you both. You'd just met him when you came out to visit me for the weekend and all you did was show me pictures and say 'I can't believe someone this handsome likes me' and then you just told me about all the presents he'd bought you."

Charlotte winced; she'd forgotten about such shallow behaviour.

Ali reassured her with a wry smile, "Hey, that's OK. It was early days and you should have been gushing about him. Then I really didn't see you together much, of course. Remember when I came home for a visit you were both away on some weekend break to somewhere fancy and since then I've only really been around the two of you 'together' at the wedding. Like I said, I liked him, and I always felt you got on great – but maybe it felt a bit odd because it looked more like you were friends than boyfriend and girlfriend."

She made a parched sound. "I'm gasping. Let's get some more cider before last orders and dissect this."

"Oh Ali – 'dissect' it! That's the lawyer in you. How can I be that logical about something like this? It's just so ridiculous," she despaired to her friend's departing back.

"Any idea? – what do you want to do?" Ali asked as she returned with two dripping halves. "Let's be practical. Do you want to stay with him? Is it a phase? If he promised to give up the shagging around would you still want him? There's lots of women who live with this sort of thing you know."

"No way! it's definitely not a phase. We had a long talk about it. He's fairly sure what he wants I think." She finished sharply. "Bloody hell! It's me that's left with the mess to deal with really."

"He has got someone. The guy at the office?"

"No, I don't think that's going anywhere. I think he just wants to go out there and 'explore'. He said he's 'curious'."

Ali shook her head in dismay. "If Graham is gay – and wants to be gay – but for some reason hasn't had the confidence to come out of the closet, that's one thing. But just wanting to experiment and have the freedom to sleep with whoever he fancies and still be married to my best friend! NO way. That's just wrong. You want a divorce, right?"

"Yes, I think I do. Yes. I want to. Can you do it for me?" Charlie asked hopefully.

"No, sorry." She looked at Charlie's crushed expression. "Don't look like that, my lover. I'll help you find someone. I'm not the right type of lawyer but I will find you a good one that won't break the bank."

"OK good, and as long as you can help, I suppose there's no rush. I don't have any plans."

Ali reached out and grabbed her friend's hand and squeezed it. "What are you going to do now, though, love? Go back to London, I suppose? But where will you live? With him? No, you can't do that." Ali looked worried as she answered her own questions.

Charlotte's face brightened. She had one piece of positive news to tell her friend as well. "Leaving London, I had a bit of an epiphany – I don't know what I do want to do – but I do know what I don't want to do – if that makes sense."

Ali nodded encouragingly.

"I mentioned, that when I was in Zephyr, I met a really cool girl called Marvel. Talking to her about Graham and I, well, it made me realise that I don't like living in a city. It was more Graham's place. Not mine. I've made one decision. I'm not going back to London. I can't face him and the flat or our friends there. I want to be in the countryside, here or somewhere like here." Ali nodded encouragingly; once again she didn't seem surprised by what her friend was saying.

"I have to say that visiting that island was good for a lot of things – even if the honeymoon was shit. I wouldn't want to live there – I'd miss the seasons, it's hot all the time, too much sea and sand – not enough fields and trees – but I really liked being in a small community again, where people recognised you. You know, people called you by name after just one or two days? I think a smaller place is more me. In a village it's easy to make friends and you don't have to travel miles to hang out or make plans weeks and weeks in advance. You know, Graham and I had dinner parties planned three months in advance." She shook her head in disbelief, remembering their hectic social schedule.

"I don't think I'm cut out to be a big city girl – I don't think I ever was. I think I've only done it for so long because I thought it was the right thing to do for some reason."

"I agree. You are a country girl."

"And to be honest, I'm beginning to think that same thing about Graham – I mean I still love him, and I'm in shock now, but I already know I don't want him anymore."

Ali looked at her. "OK. Well, that's a positive. I'm glad you aren't pining for him so much you would take him back or try and make that funny arrangement work. But Charlie, what was it about him?"

"I'm beginning to forget after his behaviour on honeymoon. I don't know. You know I'm useless at making decisions sometimes. What do you think? You've always got a theory."

Ali looked a little embarrassed, but actually Charlotte was right, her friend did have a theory.

"Well, don't get mad at me – and this is pure conjecture. I think that you were always looking for something a little different and special. Remember when we were teenagers, I had a crush on a different boy every week and you never seemed to be interested in anyone? Well, apart from 'you know who', you always said you didn't have anything in common with the boys round here. Remember you called them 'The Wurzlemanglers'?" she finished in a broad West Country accent and they both laughed.

"That makes me sound horrible – like I'm some sort of snob – but in my defence they didn't like me either. They never asked me out."

"Rubbish, they liked you, but you just weren't interested in them and frankly I think they thought – you thought – you were a bit too good for them."

"Me? … thinking *I* was too good for *them*! You must be joking."

Ali nodded her head, and on a roll with her theory she continued, "I know that you are shy but I have to tell you that your shyness does not show on the outside. Sometimes you can just look a bit cool – not rude, just a bit cool," Ali added hastily as Charlotte looked stricken. "And you've never understood how great looking you are."

Again, Charlotte looked uncomfortable, but Ali ploughed on, "Honestly, you should look at yourself through my eyes – enviably tall and slim, with those great long legs, and straight hair you don't have to do anything to – like tonight – I bet you just put it up in a ponytail and 'voila' you swish it around and it looks great. Me on the other hand: I'm short, with no neck and a big bottom, got this thick curly hair that looks bad if it's cut too short and will not grow past my shoulders however hard I try. AND I can't ever seem to find jeans that make me look anything other than like I've got my mum's on!" she finished.

Charlotte had to respond. "No, Ali, no that's not you at all. You must see yourself through my eyes. You are sexy, *everyone* says so. You are curvaceous and cute, like a pocket Venus. And men love it that you are so short and have to look up at them! And then you're so bloody vivacious – you always know what to say and you always get noticed in a group, whereas I just clam up and disappear into the background."

Ali wasn't finished though, "Ah, but *you* don't see how all sorts of people are drawn to you. You stand out because you don't push yourself forward and you make people curious and intrigued and want to know you better. And then, of course, the moment anyone talks to you they know how special you are."

The love Ali felt for her friend and the frustration she felt that such an exceptional person didn't understand how great she was, made her desperate to get her point across. "Charlie, you have a gift for listening. You are beautiful inside and out, and you are a loyal and wonderful friend. I can see how you must have been the answer to Graham's dreams."

"Oh Ali, that's so sweet. You always make me feel better. But you know I struggle to see that."

"But that's everyone when they are feeling low. Even I, the mighty Ali, have my moments of insecurity." She pretended to be angry. "How do you think this little short thing felt walking around with a supermodel like you when we were growing up – no wonder I learnt to flirt, otherwise no one would have paid me any attention."

Charlotte snorted with laughter. "I suppose the grass is always greener on the other side. I think I probably fell in love with Graham because of how he made me feel. He made me feel beautiful … all those amazing clothes – he had such good taste – I knew that people thought I looked OK. He wouldn't have let me go out looking rubbish. How shallow is that?"

"Hey, don't be so tough on yourself. It was more than that. And you know what, Charlie? You did look stunning when you were all dressed up in your Gucci or Prada or whatever, but you look equally good tonight in your jeans and that awful old jacket, and much more comfortable."

"I know. I love my old Puffa. So glam!" They looked at the sorry looking lump on the chair and giggled.

Ali looked around and saw that the pub was nearly empty. She stood up and grabbed their empty glasses and turned to take them back to the bar to get washed.

"Look sharp. Sammi is trying to lock up and we don't want to keep her waiting. Let's meet up tomorrow and take the dogs for a walk and we can plan your survival strategy."

"Good idea. Thank god we got to talk. I feel much better. It's so wonderful to see you. I miss you so much now you live in Spain."

"I know, I miss you too." She paused, and then burst out excitedly, "But not for long!"

"Whatttttt???" Charlie raised her eyebrows.

"Well, …" Ali teased, "I didn't have the chance yet to tell you all my news – because tonight was all about you, girlfriend!" in her best-worst LA accent, "but … I'm delighted to say, I have been promoted and I'm coming back to join the firm's new practice in Bristol, and…"

"You're coming back to the West Country!? You said you would never live down here."

Ali had the good grace to look a little sheepish. "Well, you know me, never say never. Actually, it's a great opportunity and close to home – but not too close, if you know what I mean."

As the girls were walking to the door Sammi called Charlotte over. "Charlie, come here quick, love." Ali looked up, "You need me too?"

"No, just her highness."

Charlie kissed Ali on the cheek and walked back to the bar.

"Sorry I didn't get a chance to talk to you yet, Sammi. Ali and I had some serious catching up to do."

"I know that, love. I just wanted to say hi and hear how the wedding went?"

Charlie couldn't face going into it now. "I have lots to tell you." Sammi looked enquiringly. "But it's a long story and I'm tired and need to go to bed. I'll come and see you tomorrow."

"You do that, my lover, 'cos I've got some news for you too." And gave her a lascivious wink, which Charlie missed, as she hurried out the door.

CHAPTER 23
Charlotte

The next morning, bright and early, the girls and their respective pets met up on the village green to go for a walk: Charlie took Muffin the ancient, nearly toothless but still feisty, Jack Russell and Ali had Flopsy, a hyperactive Sprocker puppy, that needed to be kept on the lead in case she took off after rabbits or any other wildlife that crossed her path. Muffin didn't like Flopsy very much and kept as far away from her as possible – snarling gummily if the puppy came near. Flopsy loved everyone and everything but unfortunately didn't have the brains to work out when she was not welcome, so kept trying her luck and got nipped each time.

Setting off at a smart pace, Muffin trotted along by Charlie's ankles as the girls headed off on their favourite walk, a loop around the village, on secluded bridle paths. The lanes were dry, but long grass sprung lushly between the ruts and ridges created on the paths by farm vehicles. There was not a cloud in the sky, and the girls were soon pulling off their fleeces to ward off the early morning chill, tying them round their waists. The hedgerows were bosky and full of interesting rustles that tormented poor Flopsy, who pulled and pulled trying to get in them to explore. Muffin (who had gone a little deaf and was short-sighted to boot) ignored all but the most obvious signs of rabbits and other wildlife.

Charlotte couldn't think of a better place to get over her heartbreak. Her beloved village would ease her sorrows and help her focus on what she wanted for the future. The glorious Wiltshire countryside was a tapestry of golds and green spread all around. The waving grain fields and verdant hedgerows soothed her soul; the birdsong and sharp blue English summer sky filled her with hope. The snuffles, pants and padding sounds produced by the two happy hounds were music to her ears. She was at home. The friends walked and talked for an hour and by the time they looped back to where they started they had sketched out the bones of Charlie's 'three-point survival strategy' for post-Graham happy life, as Ali called it.

The first thing they agreed was that Charlotte should immediately 'fess up' to her parents about the marriage breaking down and ask if she could come home for a while. The second thing was that even though she didn't want to, she would have to go back to London to pack some stuff, talk to Danny about either resigning or taking an extended leave of absence from her job, and, of course, tell Graham she wanted a divorce. Then, thirdly, speak to the owners of The Lamb to see if there was any shift work available at the pub to give her some spending money and keep her out of her parents' hair until she decided what to do next.

Promising to keep in touch via Skype, they exchanged a brief, hard hug and Ali rushed back to her parents' to get a lift to the airport. As Charlotte watched her friend drag the still lively puppy back over the green, she felt a wave of unconditional love for her. At least my friends love me back and stay loyal, she thought. Ali was a Louise to her Thelma, and she couldn't wait for them both to be back in the same area.

Charlotte and a very tired Muffin slipped through the front door and made their way to the kitchen at the back of the house. The little dog went over to each of her humans to touch them in greeting with her wet nose and get a welcome home stroke before sighing deeply and collapsing in an exhausted hump on her tartan bean bag.

Walking to the other side of the kitchen to put the kettle on, Charlotte realised that now was as good a time as ever to tell her parents about Graham. Helen and Peter were sat at the large, distressed oak, kitchen table, reading The Telegraph (which they divided up) and drinking coffee from a cafetiere. Small plates, strewn with crumbs, had been pushed to one side and some soft-looking butter and a jar of her mum's homemade crab-apple jelly were languishing in the middle of the table. Family tradition had it that everyone took their time over the papers in the morning – especially on a Sunday. Charlotte could tell that many rounds of toast and at least two cups of coffee had been consumed while her parents read and reported the most interesting stories to each other. Breakfast was Charlotte's favourite time with her parents – an opportunity to share news and gossip. Graham had never 'got it', always in a hurry to get out of the house and 'do something'.

Stirring her coffee, she took a deep breath, "Mummy, Daddy, I have something rather disappointing to tell you …" and launched into it before she chickened out.

Once again, she told her story. It was the toughest conversation she'd ever had with her parents – who winced with pain when she revealed Graham's affair. She saw their faces sag and age before her eyes, as they absorbed what their only daughter had been through.

She felt terrible. They were completely unprepared and had swallowed the lie she'd told them the day before – that Graham was working – because, she realised resentfully, that was what he always did. Charlotte was glad she'd had the chance to practice the story on Ali first – who'd just let her talk until she got to the end. But her parents kept interrupting, stopping her to ask questions that she hated having to answer but knew she had to. She didn't want to break down and cry herself and add to their pain. It was terrible to see the distress and disappointment on their faces. Her own hurt was one thing, she could learn to live with that, but to see them so devastated made her hate Graham all over again.

The conversation dragged on. They had lots of questions and she answered them honestly. They were shocked and hadn't had a clue that Graham 'was like that'. It was incomprehensible to them that the man they thought loved their precious daughter had treated her so badly. Peter kept shaking his head and saying, "but I don't understand – why did he marry you?" and Helen went on and on about what an incredible day they had all had and what a perfect-looking couple they made. After a while, her mum stopped talking and started crying softly so Charlotte just pulled a chair up and hugged her for a while.

Charlotte's head was killing her, she felt overheated and sick. Her parents kept the Rayburn going all year round – even in summer – and the kitchen was hot and stuffy.

She got up and ran the tap until the water got cool, poured herself a big glass of water and gulped it down, then she poured one for each of her parents.

It was nearly lunch time, but the breakfast cups and plates were still on the table. Charlie wearily started tidying up. She realised that she'd got more used to what had happened now. Maybe she actually felt worse about the marriage breakup for her parents' sake than she did for her own. Given their reaction she could tell it was going to be difficult for them to accept. And to add insult to injury, the bloody wedding had cost them so much money – even though Graham had paid for a lot of it, her parents had insisted on contributing a hefty whack for the dress and party. She shuddered when she remembered Peter handing over a huge cheque and saying with a teasing smile, "We've been saving up since you were born for this day and you'll only get married once, darling. It's an investment to guarantee us some grandchildren."

And then an awful thought suddenly occurred to her – what if Mum and Dad didn't want her to come back and stay with them? What if they were too embarrassed? There would be so many questions asked, and she knew how important village life was to them.

"But what are you going to do, darling?" asked Helen, right on time. "Where are you going to stay? Will Graham let you have the flat? Oh, that lovely flat, I did love going to visit you there," and her eyes threatened to fill with tears again.

"No. That flat is definitely his. He bought it before we decided to get married. I don't want to be there anyway, Mummy." She looked between both parents anxiously and said,

"I've decided I don't really like London all that much anyway. I think that I would like to move back to the country, and I wondered … if it's not too much trouble … I mean if it wouldn't be too uncomfortable for you, if I could stay with you for a while until I get straight?"

She needn't have worried because at the exact same time Peter said, "Of course that's OK, darling, you must come."

Helen said, "Well, your home is here and we would love it if you came and stayed with us."

"Thank you, that's such a relief ... but ... are you sure? Won't it be a bit embarrassing for you to have me here?"

Peter snorted. "Of course not! And what business is it of anyone else's anyway? Your marriage didn't work out. That's it. You decided it wasn't what you wanted. No one needs to know anything else. Anyway, at the moment I want to kill Graham because he's hurt you so badly, but he's still family in a way and I definitely don't need a witch hunt against him."

Charlie thought she might cry. Her dad really was an amazing man, he was always surprising her. His wife looked at him proudly.

"Oh, you are so good, Peter. You pretend to be such an old conservative, but you really are quite the modern man."

"Well, it's not like we don't know it happens. Gay people are all over the TV and in the Daily Telegraph. We've even got a married couple at the golf club! I quite like them actually – bloody good golfers and always very smart. I just wish that bloody idiot had decided he preferred boys before he married my beautiful daughter."

CHAPTER 24
Tracy

"Hi Honey, I'm home!" Tracy joked as she unlocked the door. It was a grey old day outside which only made her lovely salon even more colourful and welcoming.

The familiar rich smell crept up her nostrils: the unmistakable combination of fresh flowers, the salon's signature shampoos with just the faintest whiff of something chemical layered underneath. Manipulating the dimmer switch so that the artful lighting kicked in, she looked at the room with pride. The salon was her creation and it mixed the industrial with the extravagant, the pretty with the practical and it was a wonderful place to behold.

She loved the décor. Roughly finished concrete walls, distressed oak floorboards and floor-to-ceiling antique gold-framed mirrors mixed in with glittering crystal sconces and sixties-style salon chairs covered in cherry faux leather. Towards the back, there was a lounge area with a long, black leather high-sided couch, flanked by armchairs covered in a rich cherry velvet. A low, glass-topped coffee table was covered in a towering collection of glossy magazines. She'd had the back wall completely mirrored in antiqued smoky glass and placed a cocktail bar made out of glossy black wood in front of it. An enormous glass vase filled with white tea roses adorned the right-hand side of the bar and a shiny, state-of-the-art coffee machine stood on the left. One bar shelf was groaning with flavoured vodkas and unusual liquors, the other with a collection of coloured martini glasses and antique cocktail shakers – the final one with pastel-coloured hair products and vibrant nail varnish.

Tracy checked her reflection in the mirror behind the bar and was pleased to see she looked better than she felt, her skin glowed, her hair curled prettily, and her eyes looked unnaturally large and luminous. She even had cheekbones if she tilted her head and pouted.

At least misery agrees with me, she thought glumly, then blew a kiss at her reflection.

She didn't kid herself – she was aware that the reason she looked so good was that the light in the salon was extremely flattering. This ensured that all her clients felt they looked their best when they were there. The very high ceiling was painted black and was dripping with her precious collection of chandeliers. She'd acquired them over many years from antiques shops and charity stores, as well as car boot and house clearance sales. She was always on the lookout for more but was very selective over what she bought and could only fit in a couple more before she reached capacity. By hanging them at various heights and using low voltage light bulbs the ceiling resembled a shimmering, sparkly star-filled night sky.

Opening the hidden door to the right of the bar she entered the employees only area, a large open-plan space that doubled as an office, store cupboard and staff rest room. She turned on the lights, hung up her coat and put her handbag on her desk. Grabbing her iPad, she walked back into the salon and turned the coffee machine on. It had been a major expense, but the clients loved the fancy coffees they served – and she was sure that was an important component in getting the above average prices she charged for cuts and colours. Same with the martini bar. All customers were offered complimentary coffee during the day and complimentary martinis from the afternoon into the evening – it had proved very popular.

After making herself a rich and delicious, caramel flavoured cappuccino with a double espresso and plenty of froth, she sat down on her favourite cherry velvet armchair and logged onto Facebook. She was normally a Facebook fiend but she hadn't visited the social media site since she left the UK – and she realised she hadn't missed it at all – because she had been so happy experiencing the 'real world' in Zephyr.

Every day there she had spent most of the time outside: breathing clean air, relaxing on the beach, walking and swimming, drawing, dancing, chatting, eating, exploring – just hanging out and loving everything she encountered. *Liming*, she thought sadly. Liming – that's what they call it – I like liming a lot.

Here, in the UK, everything is about work and being inside. Or checking my phone or iPad every five minutes. *And it's no one's fault other than mine.* I've made it that way and I can unmake it. I can change the not-going-outdoors thing easily. I'll make the effort to go walking in the park or swimming more often.

But for now, sitting indoors and checking her social media was a necessary evil. The salon had its own Facebook page, so she logged onto that first. Cheryl had been doing the updates, and she was pleased to see they'd gained a whole bunch more 'likes' and that the competition they'd been running for a free pamper afternoon had proven popular. Facebook was great for the salon – it let her keep in touch with her clients and really build loyalty. She featured them (if they let her) on the site in her 'Hairdo of the Month' competition – which was really popular and got them loads of likes and shares. Facebook was free marketing – and anyone who didn't take advantage was an idiot. She couldn't understand (but was glad they didn't) why her competitors didn't use it much.

Satisfied that everything was OK on her business page, she logged onto her personal page and saw that she had three new friend requests. Curious she clicked on the icon and scanned the list and felt a rush of happiness, they were all from Zephyr friends. One from Cheeky Bugger, one from Shelliqua and one from Barb – one part of the American tourist couple she'd made friends with at the hotel. She quickly accepted them all and checked out each of their pages.

Practising self-discipline, she forced herself to check the other two first before clicking on CB's. Her stomach was in knots as she scanned his page for a post about, or photos of, Diver. There was nothing. Then she went into his friend list and scanned that – nothing. Finally, she dropped him a private message.

> Hiyah, sorry I didn't get to see your cheeky face in person again before I left. Thanks for the rum and the jokes 😊 Miss T

She felt herself choking up a bit so took a swig of coffee and one deep breath before getting back to the screen. From CB's personal page she linked to the Treasure Island fan page and 'liked' it. It was good – similar to the one she had set up for her salon. It was filled with photos of happy guests enjoying drinks or raising a glass. She smiled to see that he had a photo competition for best sunset selfie – the prize being shots of his lethal rum.

Scrolling down the page transported her back to the colourful friendly bar and the evening she met and made friends with CB. She missed him too. *It's rubbish that I didn't even get to say goodbye, it's rubbish that I won't get to see him anymore.* Her eyes filled up again. It's not right to miss someone and someplace this much, she thought, I was happy before I went to that sodding island. Before I met that bloody man.

She put down the iPad and went to the bathroom to check her face out, not wanting Cheryl or any of the other girls to come in and find her with mascara running down her face. She had an image to keep up. They never saw her looking dejected and they never would.

Standing in front of the mirror, she splashed her face and began the tidying up process. She could hear faint clattering noises in the salon and surmised someone had come in. The next thing she heard was the low throb of music filtering under the door. Usher, Cheryl's favourite.

"Tracy! You old slapper – where are you? Get out of the bog – I want to see your white bits!"

Cheryl's Essex accent was easily loud enough to carry through the two doors separating them. Tracy grinned as she patted her face dry with the hand towel.

"Give me a chance, you cheeky cow! Don't forget you're not in charge anymore," she shouted. "Make me a coffee," and for added emphasis, "The bitch is back!"

"Cheeky bloody cow back. OK, this time I will be your skivvy – but only because I want to hear all the 'goss' before the others come in. Did you notice I came in a whole half an hour early despite being worked to the bone for the last two weeks? – just so you could spill the beans."

Tracy smiled into the mirror – the woman was hilarious. "OK, OK! Give me a minute. I'm washing my hands. I'll be with you in just a sec."

After checking her reflection to make sure her eyes were not too red, she joined her friend in the salon. Cheryl's long, lean figure was propped against the bar and she had a look of lascivious anticipation on her immaculately made up face.

"Awwwww, look at you babe, all gorgeous, all golden brown and blondey hair and shiny eyes. How was it?"

She assessed Tracy thoroughly, making a point of looking her up and down, then put her head to one side. Confident she was onto something.

"Did you get some? I reckon you got some. You look too good not to have bloody got some," she teased.

Tracy hesitated before she answered. Not sure what to do. She couldn't tell her the truth about Diver, it was far too hurtful. She considered lying for a split second. *But she knows something went down – she'll never stop going at me, so I'll just have to give her what she wants to hear.* She smiled weakly, trying to match Cheryl's jokey tone, but feeling sick to the stomach that she was trivialising someone so important to her.

"You know I shouldn't tell you because they say a lady doesn't kiss and tell – but yes, yes indeed – I did get some."

Cheryl had straightened up and was literally quivering with excitement – like a greyhound at the start of a race, "And?"

"And … it was great, I had my little holiday fling and it was wonderful. Job done. And now it's just a distant memory. Story over. Finito."

Cheryl hooted with disbelief, "Are you mad? You got some, then say it was wonderful, but you don't want to give any details? No way, you stop at that? No way."

She ticked her off with her finger, "You have to spill. Who was he? Was he any good? Did he have a big one? Was there room in the suitcase for him?" With each question her big green eyes with their supersized lash extensions got wider and wider.

Tracy couldn't help but laugh. Maybe it would be good to joke about it a bit. And Cheryl was loving it, especially when she, with a wicked gleam in her eyes, held her hands apart like a fisherman describing his catch. She was rewarded with a squeal of excitement.

"Ohhhhhh lucky you … but did he know how to use it?" Her eyebrows wiggled suggestively.

"Cheryl, you have a one-track mind. I'm not telling you – it's none of your business." But then she took pity on her friend and threw her a bone, nodding her head theatrically.

"Oh, yes."

Cheryl's eyes bugged and she begged for more detail.

But something felt wrong. She'd already said too much. It felt disloyal. I don't want to talk about it – *I didn't even bloody well sleep with him in the end.*

She put her hands up in mock surrender, "That's it – that's all you are getting. There's nothing to tell. I had a little fun in the sun, and there is no need to discuss it anymore."

Cheryl tried to interject.

"No. I don't want to talk about it. Understand?"

Cheryl knew her friend well enough to gauge when Tracy had had enough. "OK I will stop with the interrogation for now. But, to paraphrase the famous bard, 'I think the lady doth protest too much'."

Cheryl picked up her coffee and took a big swig before changing the subject, "So what about the other stuff … how was the hotel – the rest of the holiday?"

Relaxed now the spotlight had been taken off her love life, she could at least speak freely about Zephyr. "I loved the hotel and the island. It's a special place – I made some great friends actually."

"OK, what was so good about it apart from the men?"

"It had all the normal things, palm trees, tropical flowers, sunshine, white beaches and amazing blue sea. As advertised – but you know how photos are always better than the real place in holiday brochures? Well, the beach where I stayed was ten times better than it was in the pictures …" she trailed off, struggling to find a way to describe what she'd experienced rather than sound like a travel brochure describing any tropical paradise.

"The best thing about it … was how it made me feel about myself."

Cheryl looked puzzled. "What do you mean?"

"You know I've been off my game a bit. Sad about Dad. Well, I don't know if it was the climate or something funny in the air – but almost as soon as I got there, I was happier, I literally didn't think about work."

Cheryl made a shocked noise.

"I've been a bit antisocial recently but found I was open to meeting new people, like I made friends with this girl Shelliqua – she worked at the hotel. Then there was CB, a real cutie – he ran a bar."

Cheryl raised her eyebrows.

"I was at home from the moment I got there – well, after I'd left the airport and met my taxi driver," she smiled as she thought about her funny little friend Morris. "In a way I felt more myself there than I ever feel in the UK … I don't know … it just sort of felt right to be there …" she was rambling on a bit. Cheryl looked confused by the touchy-feely direction of the conversation.

"This CB fella – is that who you had a fling with, then?" she interrupted, back on a topic she could relate to: men.

Tracy laughed and shook her head. "No, no, he was just a friend. But he was a really nice guy." She knew Cheryl didn't believe her and decided not to try to change her mind. Let her believe what she wanted to.

"Well, the holiday obviously did you good – you've got your sparkle back, but I'm not sure I want you going back there again, we may not get you home."

They both turned as they heard the front door rattle. Anne, one of the stylists, tried the key in the door.

Flipping into work mode Cheryl said, "Anyway, if you're not going to tell me the juicy stuff, I better fill you in on what's gone down here. We've been fine – but I need to tell you some stuff before everyone gets here and starts bugging you."

"Good, you do that," said Tracy, relieved to change the subject. And within minutes she was all business again.

CHAPTER 25
Charlotte

After Charlotte's emotional revelation in the kitchen, the Pierces were far too exhausted to do anything else that day, so Charlie didn't manage to get to the pub and catch up on the local gossip her friend Sammi had been so keen to share.

Instead, the little family stayed in and licked their wounds. Charlotte made a couple of phone calls: the first to Graham – who, to her relief, didn't answer, so she left a short message on his mobile phone explaining that she was staying in Wiltshire for a bit longer and that he shouldn't bother calling back – she'd be in touch when she was ready. She called him on his mobile, avoiding the landline because hearing the funny message they'd recorded together just before the wedding would be hard to stomach.

The second call was to her boss, Daniel, and it had taken much longer. She was hoping to avoid a difficult conversation she'd started by telling him that she wouldn't be coming back to work on Monday. The story went along the lines of: due to an obscure Caribbean stomach bug her doctor had advised her not to come into contact with anyone and had signed her off work for another week (she crossed her fingers as she recounted the whopping fib). The pointed silence at the end of the line was proof that he hadn't swallowed the feeble excuse for one second.

He questioned her in his trademark toff accent. "Bullshit, Charlie, tell me what really happened, I saw Graham at the weekend and I know something smells fishy."

Daniel went on to describe how he'd bumped into her husband at a wine bar in Clapham Old Town on Saturday evening. Graham was drunk and hanging out with a bunch of guys from his office and he thought he looked 'shifty' since he wouldn't answer any of his questions about the honeymoon. He was further convinced something was wrong when Graham told him that she had gone back to Wiltshire for the weekend.

"What's really happening, girl? You two having a lover's tiff?" Charlie gave in gracefully – and gave her boss the 'less scandalous version' of the breakup story she'd devised with her parents the previous day: that they both got carried away planning the wedding, and …

"We really shouldn't have got married, as we want different things. Basically, I want to move to the country and have kids – and Graham doesn't."

It wasn't a lie, but Charlie could tell that Danny wasn't one hundred percent convinced. He was clearly sceptical and kept asking questions, smelling the proverbial rat, and fishing for more 'dirt'. But she held firm. She had decided she wasn't going to say anything to anyone (apart from Ali and her parents, obviously) about Graham's sexual ambiguity – because it was no one else's business.

Over the time she'd worked for Danny, he had morphed from boss to something much more. Older than her by eight years, he'd taken on the self-appointed role of older brother and was extremely fond and protective of her. She'd ended the call twenty rather painful minutes later – feeling a little like she'd been mauled by a friendly bear – Daniel loved to dish out 'tough love'. He was pragmatic about her situation, and said that although he loved her and was sympathetic with her plight he wouldn't accept her resignation, sensibly opining – that she was "being ridiculous, it was far too early to make such a big decision like leaving London" and he would just hold onto the temp for a bit longer.

She didn't argue back, grateful for his kindness but, for once, knowing her own mind would not be changed. Although she'd made good friends and had some fun times working at the Chartered Surveyor practise in Kensington, she knew already she would never go back to the daily commute to an office job or the packed city lifestyle she'd had before she went to the Caribbean. She felt at home in the country.

She spent the evening slumped on the sofa, stroking Muffin's shiny soft ears, absorbed in a recording of Crufts Dog Show that her parents had saved for her.

Oh, the glamour! If my friends in the Caribbean could see me now. From mega-yacht to sharing Mum's Mini – this wasn't supposed to happen. I feel like Bridget Jones waking up boyfriendless at her parents' house every Christmas. What a failure I am.

But then a happy thought popped into her consciousness.

"Perhaps I can get my own dog now. Mum, Dad, what do you think?" Getting a pet had been an ongoing bone of contention between Graham and herself.

"I don't see why not, darling."

They discussed the qualities of the different breeds on the show, but it was a one-sided discussion because for all three of them, there was only one dog that counted – the magnificent and mighty Jack Russell.

The next day no one felt like cooking, so Charlie invited her parents to have lunch at The Lamb. They chatted companionably as they strolled towards the picturesque building. Noting that the car park was full, Charlie wished she'd thought to ring ahead to book – the pub had become ridiculously popular since a glowing review in the Sunday Times made Sammi, the bartender, and the owners, Bob and Dale, minor celebrities in the area.

The 16th century building was a warren of small cosy rooms – all of which had different characters. The family Pierce preferred the public bar but could see from the door that it was standing room only, so they turned right and headed towards the more formal dining room. Sammi was busy with a customer at the far end of the bar, so Charlie didn't attempt to speak with her and get the news – she would wait and catch up in a more leisurely fashion after lunch.

Entering the room, they asked the charming but slightly harassed teenage girl whose job it was to seat guests, for a table for three. The girl, Sarah – who her parents recognised but she didn't – was the daughter of one of Peter and Helen's friends from the village and was serving the usual 'village girl apprenticeship' of working in the pub for the summer before going off to uni, or on a gap year, or wherever she was transitioning to. She flicked her messy ponytail over her shoulder, smiled and asked them very politely to wait a couple of minutes and she would find a table for them as soon as possible. Good as her word, a few minutes later she told them they could sit at the little round table at the window. As they squeezed through the packed room, it became obvious that Peter and Helen, who were walking in front of her, obscuring her view, knew the guests at the neighbouring table.

"Hellooooooo!"

"Isn't this nice having lunch at the pub with our children?"

Charlotte peered around her dad's solid frame and saw that it was Penny and Charles, Ali's parents. They were having lunch with a younger couple who had their backs to the room. Charlie smiled and waved enthusiastically – she was always happy to see the older couple, their house had been a second home growing up and Penny often referred to Charlie as "the other daughter".

There was a big kerfuffle as everyone at the table got up to greet them. She headed directly to Charles who wrapped her in a big bear hug and then passed her over to his sweet-faced wife. Penny held her for a long hug then pulled back and looked at her seriously – her kind brown eyes seemed to say, "So sorry, my love" and Charlotte realised Ali must have said something to her mum. She didn't mind. They loved her and she knew it wouldn't go any further. It also meant one less person to explain the situation to.

She mouthed, "I'm fine" and disengaged from Penny with a squeeze on her shoulder and a reassuring kiss on the cheek – then turned round to see who was behind her. It was a tall, heavyset man in his late twenties, with dark-blonde hair and grey eyes – that were examining her with frank curiosity. He looked familiar, very familiar indeed. His face crinkled in amusement when he noticed her frown then take a small step back in self-defence. Undeterred he stepped forward and greeted her with a light kiss on the cheek.

"Charlie Girl, how nice to see you … and looking decidedly tanned and tasty too." His warm eyes teased, clearly enjoying her discomfort. "I can tell you're terribly pleased to see me too."

Too surprised to return the kiss, she looked around wildly, trying to avoid the concerned glances the rest of the group were sending her way – clearly baffled by her behaviour. The silence lengthened and she still couldn't find the polite words of greeting she knew she should speak to appear normal. Her thoughts deafened her. *What's HE doing here? This is a bloody nightmare. I can't believe it. This is just too much on top of everything else.*

"Hello, Simon," she finally croaked, "what a surprise."

"Why are you surprised pet? Didn't Ali tell you Simon was back? Didn't she tell you our wonderful news?" Penny was bubbling with excitement as the words gushed out of her.

Charlotte shook her head dumbly – *this* must have been the news Sammi was trying to tell her, the news Ali had forgotten to share, and that she had been too self-absorbed to ask for.

Penny persisted, "You didn't know, then? That Simon's coming back to live in England?"

No, I bloody well didn't, she thought.

Charlie tried to smile for Penny's sake; she knew what this must mean for her.

"No, no, she didn't. We didn't talk about Simon at all. We had lots of important stuff to catch up on."

Trying too hard to come up with an excuse, she had just made it worse by implying, much to Simon's obvious amusement, that catching Ali up on her honeymoon was far more important than asking about the return of the prodigal son after many long years in Australia.

"Getting an update on your white bits never fails to enthral, Charlie Girl," deadpanned Simon.

"Now you two," chuckled Charles, "don't start bickering already. Five years since you went away, Simon, but you're already winding each other up. Play nice children. What will Sandra think of you?" and turned to include the girl standing quietly behind Simon in the conversation.

"Sandra, this is Peter and Helen, our good friends, and their daughter, Charlotte, who you may have gathered from that conversation is our Ali's best friend. All of you, this is Sandra, Simon's lovely girlfriend."

Sandra stepped forward into a circle of golden light thrown by the room's stained-glass window. She glittered and shined, lighting up the room like

Tinkerbell. The 'lovely girlfriend' was petite, with glossy, multi-hued, long blonde layered hair and a perfectly even, wide white smile. She wore a simple white shirt with a pair of faded jeans – and looked effortlessly 'put together' with lightly tanned dewy skin and a slick of shiny pink lip gloss her only makeup.

She's so small and perfectly formed she could get work as a Kylie Minogue look alike. Charlotte thought, I feel like a cart horse looming over a Shetland pony.

"G'day," chirped Sandra, completely at home as she gazed around her circle of new admirers. Her dad, in particular, seemed entranced. Charlie noted his soppy smile. Peter loved pretty ladies.

"Nice to meet you all," she said perkily, tilting her head in an engaging way. As Simon looked on, filled with manly pride, Charlotte decided she wanted to slap him across his big smug mug and punch Sandra on her perfectly freckle-dusted nose.

Introductions complete, the family Pierce finally dragged themselves away to order lunch. They all agreed the pub deserved its recent accolades, as everyone's lunch was delicious. But Charlotte found it difficult to enjoy as much as she should, because annoying Simon was putting her off her food. Every time she looked up, she could see him studying her, a sardonic smile on his face. Fed up with his staring, she poked her tongue out – but was caught in the act by Helen.

"Don't be so childish, Charlotte," she said sotto voce as she waved her friends goodbye. "I don't know why you and Simon always have to fight."

"Mummy, it's not my fault – it's his. He's always winding me up. He's just so bloody annoying. He's spoilt to death. His mum dotes on him. He always gets away with murder."

"Charlie, you exaggerate."

"I don't ... You all think butter wouldn't melt, but he's really naughty. When we were teenagers, he was always playing tricks on me and Ali. He winds us up, then we'd retaliate and because he's a cunning bastard, we were the ones that would get into trouble – never him," Charlie whined.

Helen and Peter exchanged looks as their daughter worked herself up further.

"You know I used to hate it in the summer holidays when he was always hanging around and being annoying. He was always teasing us and taking the piss out of what we wanted to do. But, if he couldn't get any of his stupid friends to come over *then* he'd want to hang out with us, and make everything about *him,* and change everything, and take up far too much of Ali's time. And then when he went off to uni – Oh … My … God … he was so full of himself, you'd think no one in Wiltshire had ever got into Cambridge before. Rubbing it in how clever he was, showing off about what a good time he had."

Helen smiled tightly; she'd heard it all before. "Well darling, he's not an annoying schoolboy now. He's a highly respected veterinarian and he's come back to Wiltshire to work in his own practice. His mum and dad are over the moon and *we* are extremely happy for them too. If you are going to live with us for a bit, I want you to be nice to him *and* Sandra. She's moved from Australia to be with him and doesn't know anyone. It would be kind of you to make friends with her."

Charlotte pulled a sulky face. Simon really brought out the worst in her and she'd taken an immediate dislike to his girlfriend.

"I'll try," she said grudgingly, "but I doubt he's improved with age."

After lunch, Helen and Peter went home to make some coffee and Charlotte went to the bar to pay the bill and catch up with Sammi. Her friend was now on her own, loading a huge row of glasses into the dishwasher.

"Why didn't you or Ali warn me *he* was here?" she hissed, looking around to check no one was around.

Her friend shrugged. "I tried to! You said you were coming in yesterday lunchtime. I was going to tell you then. It was too late when you got here. So, how was it?"

Charlie slumped against the bar and leaned her head in her hands. "Oh, he's just as insufferable as ever. Not helped by having bloody Kylie Minogue on his arm."

"I know, she looks good. And she's got brains as well as beauty … I think she's a vet or something posh."

"I suspect she must also be a saint, to put up with him," Charlie said glumly.

Sammi giggled, "Don't be so bitchy, it doesn't suit you. Simon's turned out lovely. I always thought he was a good-looking boy, but Australia's made him a very handsome man." She paused for effect ... "I think there was a time you thought he was quite the looker too?" she teased.

Charlie snapped back, "Stop it. Don't go there – I was young." Her friend raised her eyebrows, making her point effectively without saying a word. "And I'd drunk far too much cider – which I was probably drinking underage and will tell people you supplied if you ever breathe a word about it to anyone."

She paused and looked around the room again, double checking no one was listening to them. "It was a moment of madness – and a moment that only you and Ali know about."

"Well, I haven't forgotten. And I doubt he has either. I swear he's still got a soft spot for you even if he doesn't show it. But that's all academic anyway – I'm just winding you up. You are married now ..."

"Hold on, partner." Charlie had to stop her friend from rabbiting on – it was time to spill her beans. "I've got some news of my own. I'm going to help you to tidy up so you can finish your shift and then I have something important to tell you."

SEPTEMBER 2014

CHAPTER 26
Tracy

Three months had passed since she got back from the island – and not even a successful salon, plenty of money in the bank, robust health, some enjoyable sex with an ex and a busy social life could mend the tear in her heart and replace the colour, light and laughter that had seeped slowly, but surely, out of Tracy's life from the day she left the Caribbean.

And today has been a particularly horrible day. Quite frankly, she thought, it's been a joyless week – the culmination of a number of highly dispiriting months.

Depressed, perched on the toilet, head in hands, she tried to analyse what made this particular day so bad, and concluded it was not so much about the things that had happened – it was more to do with what was wrong with her.

Somewhere along the line she had lost her ability, and the patience, to deal with the silly, petty, annoying, distracting, inconvenient things that were a normal part of everyday life. Silly little 'things' that in theory she should easily be able to cope with. 'Stuff' that in the past she would have been able to knock off her list with efficiency and even good humour.

When she'd first got home she was numb – her loss hadn't really sunk in. Catching up with work and friends kept her busy and distracted. When, after a few weeks, her funk hadn't shifted, she went into survival mode, determined to eradicate negative thoughts from her mind: thoughts of Diver and his rejection of her and the idea that somewhere, out there, she had a half sibling.

She'd been soldiering on for three months now – trying not to let anyone see how much she was hurting – but today stupid 'things' and raging hormones were conspiring against her. She had never felt as depressed as this in her life. She'd reached an all-time low.

She looked back at her day: first thing in the morning – over their normally companionable coffee, she'd had a rare disagreement with Cheryl who had reprimanded her because she'd become irritated with and was rude to one of the salon's best clients, feeling a bit miffed she decided that Cheryl could "be the bloody boss, then" and she went out to do some chores. A terrible idea – because once she hit the grey streets of Reading, she realised the weather was abysmal. She got chilled to the bone doing a round robin of mind-numbingly boring and annoying chores, getting stuck in queues she didn't want to be in – basically getting wet and freezing her ass off despite it only being early autumn.

Having missed the opportunity for lunch because she was stuck in a bloody queue, and with no evening plans to look forward to, she went to the bookshop on the way home for a cup of hot chocolate and a biscuit. This was a half-hearted attempt to cheer herself up – the hot chocolate was cold. She trudged home determined to have a hot bath then call the Chinese takeaway to deliver a big feast – even though the last thing she needed to do was put on any more weight, and, as she turned onto her street, she managed to tread in a big, sloppy pile of dog shit that the pet's owners had wisely (on their part) not attempted to clean up. She then had to walk through the lobby, past the supercilious doorman of her apartment block and into the pristine lift, bringing the noxious stuff with her. Once inside, she stubbed her toe on a hideous, cast iron frog door stop (a gift from her favourite auntie that she felt too guilty to give away). Then she went to run a bath and the water was cold. She'd turned something off and it would take an hour to warm up. She called her favourite Chinese to find out they were closed that night. Finally, she'd sat down on the toilet, did a wee and only then realised the loo roll had run out.

Such silly, silly things. But they added up – until it was all too much. She didn't want to cry but she couldn't help herself. *How pathetic to be sat on the toilet blubbing like a baby!*

She stared blurrily at the cover of the novel she'd just bought –

inappropriately named 'In The Company of Cheerful Ladies'– hoping it might brighten her day up.

She had seen and loved the *No. 1 Ladies Detective Agency* TV series first and was now romping through the books.

"If I could only ask Mma Precious Ramotswe, everyone's favourite traditionally built heroine, to investigate Mum's story and find my half brother, then intervene between Diver and me, – maybe all would be right in the world again," she said to the novel's brightly coloured cover.

But she couldn't. She wasn't in Alexander McCall Smith's fictional Botswana – she was in bloody Reading. She grabbed the innocent book and threw it full force towards the door.

The paperback skidded and thudded across her polished wooden floorboards then crumpled, as it slammed against the door frame. "GOOD. Good shot, Tracy." Then added, childishly, "I hope it bloody well hurts," before giving herself up to a bout of piteous and pathetic crying.

But she couldn't sustain her tears for long. The petulant book-throwing had calmed her, probably because it made her feel silly. She snorted. *You are being pathetic – pull yourself together, Tracy,* at the same time as thinking that finding some loo roll would be a good start. She shuffled over to the bathroom cupboard to find something to wipe her bum and blow her nose with, then decided to run a nice soothing bath.

Grabbing her favourite coconut bubble bath, she poured nearly half the container under the hot tap. The sweet, tropical smell immediately made her heart ache – *but in a good way,* she decided. The way your heart aches when you think about someone you love very much or when you watch a classic film that makes you laugh and cry. As she eased into the water, a sigh of utter pleasure escaped her. She leant back onto her bath pillow and allowed her mind to flood and fill with memories. She looked down at her boobs floating like white balloons on top of the water – there was only a tiny shade of difference in skin colour from where her bikini top had been now.

Her tan faded quickly despite coming back to what was called summertime in England. She missed her golden brown skin and blonde curls. For some inexplicable reason, she had dyed her hair to a very sensible mid-brown, with the subtlest of highlights, a few days after her return. Then immediately regretted her decision. She hated it but wouldn't admit that to anyone – especially as her annoying, know it all friend Cheryl kept telling her she'd made a mistake.

I don't recognise myself at the moment. I'm not me! Tracy realised. I don't like the way I'm acting or feeling, and I certainly don't like the way I look … I don't look like the woman that went to Zephyr … the one that floated contentedly in the sea for hours and hours and thought great, big interesting thoughts … a woman on a quest … a woman that danced a lot and didn't mind who watched her … a woman that was confident in her body, a woman who felt enticing and irresistible. The woman Diver wanted but wouldn't recognise today.

Gazing out her steamed-up window, she calculated the English 'summer' had offered up approximately nine days of sun since she came home. Once again August bank holiday had been a complete wash out – with floods spoiling family and friends' plans and forcing most people to stay at home for the long weekend. Autumn was already here and just around the corner another long, depressing dark grey winter. She nearly started crying again at the thought.

Grey, I hate BLOODY grey – it's my worst colour. I don't mind cold weather, but it's the greyness I can't stand, she thought. "I don't know if I can get through another British winter, with those days that end so early, with hardly any blue sky, with everyone wearing black or grey or navy or brown, with no leaves on the trees – just horrid grey twigs, with no sun or flowers 'til after Christmas, with no bloody light … Guess that book was never going to work with me – Fifty Shades of Grey? – Fifty Shades of dull more like."

In a stream of consciousness moment, she pondered the multi-million-selling erotic novel, which had failed to stir her senses. She thought about the two young and genetically gifted protagonists, and their complicated, painful, courtship filled with expensive gifts, mind games, rules and regulations. Then compared it to her sweetly sensual memories and the impulsive instinct that had brought her together with Diver in the sea. She relived the affectionate courtship: the chatting, kissing, giggling, dancing and anticipation of what was to come. Her stomach knotted sharply like it always did when she thought of him.

The water had cooled, and her fingers and toes had turned to prunes. She had to get out of the bath.

*

Sometimes you must visit the deepest darkest depths of rock bottom before you can float back up to the sparkling surface. After the previous night's mini-meltdown, Tracy woke, stretched, counted her blessings, and decided to *Stop moping around – and do stuff!*

First off, she 'spring cleaned' her apartment then arranged the delivery of some flowers – spiky red ginger flowers, tropical bird-of-paradise flowers and loads of lush orange tiger lilies with deep red stamens. The brightly coloured blooms immediately brightened up the neutral décor of her city-view lounge and bedroom.

She sorted all her old magazines and put them in her recycling bins. Then she cleaned out a really annoying drawer in her study, getting rid of endless credit card receipts, never-looked-at-again business cards, perished rubber bands and a whole bunch of dried up pens.

Next she sat down at her pristine desk and made a list:

1: Book a holiday (learn to paint)
2: Chase up Isilma?
3. Research salon idea (take a week off?)
4: Talk to Mum AGAIN.

That evening she declined a night out 'with the girls' at an eighties-themed nightclub and instead feasted on a delicious Thai takeaway – eating half and leaving the rest for Sunday night. Her brain had finally quietened – tired out by the day's activities and she spent the evening contentedly curled up on the sofa watching telly (she still couldn't face her book).

On Sunday she made a decadent pile of eggs benedict for brunch and then spent an enjoyable hour online researching artistic retreat holidays. Discovering an extremely promising looking one on a spectacular organic coffee farm in Costa Rica. Just looking at the views of waterfalls and lush green mountains cheered her up. She could picture herself in the cabin shown on the website – sketching the views from the wooden deck, gazing at the tropical flowers and the rolling terrain – miles away from everyone and everything.

Convinced it would be the perfect getaway, she spent another half an hour or so looking at flights to Costa Rica, then when she realised that she would have to fly over Zephyr to get to Costa Rica, she started looking at how much it would cost to tag on a stay on the island after the artistic retreat. Excited, she danced into the kitchen to make some more coffee and grab a pad and pen to write down the different quotes she'd got – and realised that even thinking about booking an airplane ticket to the Caribbean made her feel happy.

Later that evening, she went into her dressing room and pulled out her travel bag. It smelt of Mango Bay – sunscreen and the slightly musty air conditioning unit – and felt a rush of affection for her cosy room at the friendly hotel. She went through the pockets until she found Isilma's business card then hurried back to the study and fired off a very quick 'remember me' email then picked up her mobile and called Cheryl.

"Babe. I got a BIG favour to ask".

*

A week later, dressed in her favourite black trouser suit, spike-heeled, super-soft suede ankle boots and leopard print mac, she drove into work. Ready for anything life might throw at her.

Her old energy was finally returning. During her week off she'd realised that although life at the salon was still good, she just wasn't as passionate about it anymore. The island had helped her realise that. It was time to make some changes, to stop beating up on herself and admit that life had been tough for a while.

Her dad's death had been awful, she missed him so much, but she'd hardly had time to grieve for him because she was so worried about her mum – and then she had to deal with the whole bombshell about her mum's secret life.

And, in the last few months, it had struck home that she – Tracy Maria Smith – was no spring chicken. *I may have felt like a teenager on Zephyr, but I'm already forty-three!* My clock's ticking and it's ticking fast.

She liked kids but had never been particularly maternal. She wasn't one of those people who cooed over babies and didn't feel the overwhelming desire to reproduce that many of her friends experienced. If she'd met the right man, no doubt she would have given it a go, but she hadn't, and wasn't interested in 'making it happen' and doing it on her own. It wasn't a conscious choice; she had never said to anyone 'I don't want kids'. The reality was her busy, mostly-happy life had sped by. And it was unlikely she would ever be a mother now.

There *had* been a moment where the thought had entered her mind that Diver would make a lovely dad. It was that night, at his house, just before their big argument. As she gazed at him, eating up every inch with her eyes, the image of a cheeky little chap with a gap-toothed smile had flashed into her mind – and she realised she would have loved a child that looked just like him.

There was so much promise in the air that night, so much to look forward to. Driving through the Reading traffic toward the salon, she was transported back to his home. She could feel the warmth of the evening air, smell the light, citrussy cologne he used, recall the exact impression of his arms, as she pressed her face against his chest and he rested his chin on the crown of her head. And although it still caused her pain to think about him – because she'd blown it, and they wouldn't ever be together again – she knew as clearly as she'd ever known anything in her life that she not only loved him, but also needed to go back to the Caribbean.

Entering the salon twenty minutes later bought her back to earth. The salon was a successful, stylish and sustainable enterprise (business was booming – it wasn't the salon's fault, she just wasn't excited by it anymore) something she had created from scratch and was immensely proud of. But these days Cheryl and 'the girls' were the beating heart of it.

Her ability to take a week off with zero notice proved that Cheryl had the business running like clockwork. Tracy was redundant – apart from doing the marketing and as a figurehead. And that wasn't enough for her. She wasn't the sort of person that could just sit back and watch others work – she needed to challenge herself and that was why she'd decided she was going to diversify the services the salon could offer.

She spent her week off researching an idea that had been bubbling around in her brain for the last few months. An idea whose genesis was sparked on the day she visited the busy salon in Zephyr with Shelliqua. Despite her misery on the day in question, she had been impressed by how much business the island salon was doing. The room was packed with local girls – many of whom didn't earn that much (she'd checked with Shelliqua afterwards what the average daily wage was) spending hours and hours getting weaves, relaxers and other expensive treatments. She talked to a friend of Shelliqua's called Tamika, who explained what she had done to her hair on a regular basis. She explained that she was unusual in that she changed her hair monthly (because she liked to go to the beach), whereas her friends would change theirs less often – and guard the style carefully. Tamika confirmed what Tracy had suspected – most of the Zephyr women made a significant investment. She concluded that they spent equally as much money, if not more, than her Reading clients.

Tracy spent time doing research on the internet, making appointments and visiting hairdressers in and around London. She tried to find salons that offered services for Caucasian, biracial and Afro hair, confirming her suspicions: there were very few.

One day she sat in a coffee shop in the local shopping centre, a high-traffic area, and approached and talked to a few women about her idea – picking out people she thought would be her potential customers. She quickly realised – given the culturally diverse nature of the area her salon was in – that there was a demand for a more diverse hair salon. In particular, Tracy noted a gap in the market for mixed-heritage children.

Her research showed that white and even Black mothers of mixed-heritage children sometimes didn't have a clue what to do with their kid's hair. Tracy called up her friend Mavis, went for a coffee and presented her idea. Mavis was biracial and confirmed that her long curly hair needed different products and procedures to pure Afro hair. Apparently, her Black mother had unwittingly over-processed it from an early age. It was only when she did some research and started paying for her own trips to the salon that she was able to realise and unlock the potential of her softly curling tresses.

The final stage of the research was to talk to Cheryl before she went any further and she did so over their regular Monday night martini at the salon.

Her friend was uncharacteristically quiet as she listened to Tracy's idea. She paid attention, asked a few intelligent questions, then with a big gulp of her appletini, nodded her shiny head and said, "Good thinking Batman – I reckon it could be a money maker *if* we can find the right stylists."

Tracy nodded in agreement, "Glad you like the idea, and I agree – the stylists are key." She felt so proud of her friend. "You're amazing, you know. I've had months to get my head around the idea – you 'got it' immediately. No wonder we make such an excellent team."

She grabbed Cheryl's empty glass and went behind the bar to mix them both another one.

"Of course, there would be no point in doing it if we can't do it as well as we do everything else. What do you think? Would you be interested in cross-training?" Tracy asked hopefully.

Cheryl said emphatically, "No, not at all. I'm too set in my ways and have more clients than I need as it is. But we can ask the girls. I'm sure they'll jump at the opportunity. In terms of quality, I think it would be best if we could get them on some courses and then also recruit someone specifically. We should see how it works and then get her to head up that section."

Tracy found herself looking forward to the next few days – they'd agreed to tell the girls tomorrow and see if any of them had suggestions or input on courses, and then look for an experienced stylist who would fit into their friendly team. Exactly the kind of challenge she relished.

And so began the recruitment process. First off, Tracy messaged Shelliqua who had the brilliant idea of posting a 'stylist wanted ad' on her own personal Facebook page, asking her extensive friends and family in the UK to share it. The ad asked anyone who was qualified to work Afro and mixed-heritage hair and was looking for work in the Reading area to be in contact with Tracy at the salon. After that she tagged CB and asked him to share the ad with his friends and family too.

The quest started well – there was a healthy response and they set up a few interviews. Unfortunately, Tracy hadn't been particularly impressed by the two girls and one male stylist they'd seen so far – they were nice enough, but not the right fit – basically not dynamic enough to deal with Cheryl and crew.

But today, … well, she was more than a little excited about the girl that was coming in later that day. Her name was Jazmin and she was twenty-eight with ten years' experience (including some in New York). According to her CV, Jazmin had just moved back to London and was keen to start work ASAP. But even better than that was the fact she'd seen the ad on CB's Facebook – and had already told Tracy she was CB's (and of course Diver's) cousin.

Good news also, was that her mum had cheered up and was getting back to normal – even if she was steadfastly uninterested in learning more about her trip. Rosemary had finally taken an interest in her garden again and was even putting on lipstick and going out for the odd drink with the neighbours. It was such a relief that she was getting back to some sort of normal.

But it wasn't normal-normal. *Before we were able to talk about everything – and now there is an elephant in the room: Zephyr.* They never talked about Diver because she'd never told her mum that she too had met and had a relationship with someone on the island. And that made her sad because it should have brought them closer together.

She really wanted to talk about him but although Tracy had loads of friends who would love to listen to her, she just couldn't do it. It was too complicated, there were so many strands. She was ashamed about their argument too and what a terrible light it cast her in. And then there was the difference in age and culture. Though she knew their attraction wasn't sordid, she was worried anyone listening would stereotype their affair: Her, the middle aged, unmarried, English woman looking for a bit of uncomplicated fun in the sun and him, the unscrupulous, island gigolo.

It didn't help that there had been loads in the media about desperate ladies of a certain age, falling hopelessly in love with younger, poorer men on holiday in places like Jamaica or the Dominican Republic. Men who were sometimes looking for a passport or money for their families and saw their North American or European girlfriends as a meal ticket – even though many of those women didn't have much themselves, having saved up hard for their visit to 'paradise'.

Diver wasn't a man like that. He had a good job, was well travelled and highly educated. Occasionally, though, at her lowest ebb, she asked herself what he had seen in her. Had he sensed she was wealthy? Because, true, she was quite well off. She had a portfolio of rental properties, plenty of money in savings, as well as stocks and shares. She just chose not to splash it around.

The visit to Zephyr felt like a lifetime ago and she hadn't so much as spoken his name to anyone in months, but he was still the first person she thought of in the morning and the only person she fantasised about at night. She should have forgotten him by now, but she hadn't, and it wasn't for lack of trying. She'd been out on some dates and had even had sex – spending a pleasant weekend with an ex who'd moved back home to Greece but happened to be in London on a flying family visit. They'd had a nice time, dinner and a trip to the theatre followed by a night in a hotel. He was attentive and sweet, being with him felt reassuringly familiar but, if she was honest with herself, she was really just going through the motions. She'd even felt guilty about cheating on Diver afterwards.

It probably didn't help that she had daily reminders of island life through Facebook and Instagram. She checked CB and Shelliqua's photos and pages religiously, as well as the 'Zephyr Fans Facebook Group' – scanning the screen for mentions or photos of 'him', even though she knew she shouldn't. It was bitter-sweet having ongoing access to glorious photos of beaches and people enjoying the wonderful island vibe. And, in fairness, Diver wasn't the only reason she checked in with them all so often. She missed the island so much too.

And, of course, she'd Googled Dr Clinton Derrick. Trawling hyperspace, she'd discovered lots of stuff: that the museum didn't have much of a website; that he had two published dissertations – one of which she had downloaded (but didn't read because it was a bit long); that although he wasn't on

Facebook he was on Linkedin. (She had a Linkedin profile herself, but she wasn't brave enough to request a connection). She even found some photos of him online in the local newspaper archives. They were saved in a folder on her desktop even though they were terrible quality. But, tonight, she promised herself, tonight, when she got home from the studio, she would delete them. It was time to move on.

CHAPTER 27
Charlotte

Charlotte couldn't believe how quickly summer had sped by. Autumn was already halfway through and it was three months since she had 'officially' moved back into her parents' house and she still hadn't made any plans to go anywhere else. Her split from Graham had been public knowledge for some time, and the flood of pitying looks and questions on his whereabouts from nosy neighbours, had diminished to a trickle. Life was actually alright and she was surprised by how much she'd enjoyed being at home and being looked after by her parents, who –after the initial shock – were delighted to have their only child back under their roof.

As hoped for, she had managed to find quite a few hours' work at The Lamb, and she enjoyed working alongside her friend Sammi, gossiping and giggling like teenagers whenever they got the chance. She'd landed the job of waiting food and drinks out to the beer garden, so she spent most of her time balancing trays filled with brimming pints of cider, beer and 'Henrys' (orange juice and lemonade in local parlance). She shuttled trays out of the bar and into the picnic-table-filled walled garden to the hardy customers who were determined to sit outside, even if the leaves had begun to fall off the trees. She felt a bit embarrassed to admit it, but she loved sleeping in her old bed, getting her favourite meals cooked for her (and cooking the occasional one herself) and apparently her mum and dad loved having her 'back home' because they hadn't asked her to leave yet.

Muffin was looking as sleek and fit as a two-year-old: she had never had so many walks before, getting taken out morning, noon and night by both mother and daughter. The summer weather hadn't been that great and her Caribbean tan had faded a long time ago but it didn't really matter. She looked healthy, felt relaxed and was totally happy about being able to spend lots of time outside in the fresh air. She'd watched the emerald-green bridal paths fringed with frilly white cow parsley get covered with blackberries. And seen the sloes and the bosky wood tunnels begin to thin out to show more sky as the leaves began to fall. Country walks were tempting in any kind of weather and she wondered time and time again how she had been content living an indoor city life for so long. Her previous life with Graham seemed almost to belong to someone else. She missed his company, because back in the day they'd had some wonderful laughs together, and did think fondly of her London circle of friends, but she didn't miss their life together – which was sad and telling in its own right.

Back in July she made one swift trip 'up to' London, arriving around ten in the morning. She grabbed a coffee with Daniel and formally handed in her notice before heading off to Clapham to confront the demon of her old flat. Looking around for the last time, she thought that there was extraordinarily little she wanted, that hardly any of the things in the apartment truly belonged to, or had been chosen by, her. As quickly as she could, she grabbed some of her more casual clothes, her two favourite 'dressy' dresses, added the few knick knacks she'd been allowed to contribute to the décor, altogether barely enough stuff to fill her suitcase, and was back in Wiltshire by teatime. She decided to leave her 'city' clothes behind for Graham to give to Oxfam.

They had spoken only twice in the past four months – both times on the phone as she still didn't want to see him in person: once to arrange the trip up to the flat to get her things and then a few weeks ago when they discussed, quite amicably, beginning divorce proceedings. The conversation was tough for both of them and they were stilted to start with. However, after a stiff round of "how are you?" and "how are your parents?" type of questions, they got stuck into the real conversation and it became clear that they both wanted it over and done with as soon as possible. They'd both talked to lawyers and had independently come to the same conclusion – it would be best to proceed with a 'no fault' divorce so that the reason for their separation would not need to be cited. Charlie was hopeful that it could all be settled out of court.

Although they had only been married for a few days, Graham indicated that he still felt a financial obligation to her and wanted to give her a one-off payment as a settlement – which was a big relief. He had always provided the bulk of the money for their luxurious, joint-lifestyle but she had contributed most of her much more meagre wage to the pot also and so she had no savings to fall back on and was basically skint.

The hours she worked at The Lamb really amounted to pin money and her parents wouldn't take anything off her for rent. She also wanted to pay them back some of the costs they had incurred because of her ridiculously extravagant wedding. The current situation was that Graham and his lawyers were coming up with a figure and would get back to her shortly with an offer – then fingers crossed – it would all be fairly straightforward. She'd been dreading talking to him but felt OK when she put the phone down, and, although she didn't ask or want to know what was going on in his life, she was glad that he sounded quite upbeat. She did want him to be OK – he'd been a great friend for too long to just not care anymore.

She was OK being single and rarely thought about the things that had been so important to her when she was in a couple. She had created a simple yet satisfactory routine that was about working a few hours a day, playing tennis or golf most days with a group of her old school friends who were delighted she was back home, walking the dog and enjoying leisurely coffee/shopping/ladies lunch outings with her mum to the local market town or garden centre. It wasn't a long-term plan, but it suited her just fine for now. Best of all, Ali was moving back to the West Country this week and she was going to go to Bristol at the weekend to help her move into the new flat and unpack. In return, Charlie expected Ali to give her a good kick up the arse and help her get focused on 'what next'.

The only thorn in her side was the constant and annoying presence of Simon and his too-good-to-be-true Aussie girlfriend, Sandra – Sandy – who turned out to be as irritating as she looked on introduction. The lovebirds were living in the village with Penny and Charles in their enormous 16th century farmhouse. Sandy insisted on telling her they were "nice and cosy in the guest cottage", which was really a converted barn at the bottom of their immaculately landscaped two-acre garden. But that it was just a temporary solution while Simon got his teeth into his new job and until she found their 'dream cottage'.

Charlie managed to avoid Simon most of the time. However, his proud mother couldn't help talking about him constantly, especially when she came over for her daily coffee with Helen. Despite not being interested in the slightest, Charlie now knew everything, inside out, about his relationship with Sandy, his new job and the story behind his homecoming.

Penny explained that Simon was buying into an existing practice in the 'horsey' village of Kimble, about ten minutes' drive away. He had a summer job there when he was at school and, because of that experience, he made the decision to study to be a vet rather than become the doctor his parents and teachers aspired for him to be. Kimble Veterinary Practice was a family business that three generations of Browns had built into a thriving practice – but Mr Brown Junior was now fifty-nine and his only child had declined to follow in family tradition (having witnessed first-hand the terrible hours and occasional heartbreak associated with caring for animals) and had opted to do a BSC in Computer Games Development at the University of East London instead.

Edmund, Eddie, Brown and Simon had bonded when the young man worked for him, having a similar dry sense of humour and a passion for rugby. Eddie had encouraged him to be a vet and followed Simon's career with a paternal interest, giving him a crisp one hundred-pound note to celebrate with when he won a place at Cambridge. Then he sent him a Bath Rugby sweater and a teasing note to not take up Aussie rules football when he landed a top job with a great relocation package at a veterinary practice in Australia.

Apparently, according to Penny, one day when Eddie was saying how he would probably have to sell the practice to some 'townie' – the ultimate betrayal in his book – his wife Kitty suggested he ask Simon to join them, before he put it on the market. Eddie thought it was a wonderful idea but hadn't held out much hope as Simon already had a satisfying job and apparently loved his life 'down under'. Egged on by Kitty, Eddie emailed

Simon to see if he was interested in discussing a partnership with him in the practice and was pleasantly surprised when his young friend wrote back from Australia with a swift and emphatic yes. Simon, it transpired, had learnt what he could from his existing job, was not particularly fond of sheep (and he did an awful lot of sheep work) and was missing Bath Rugby Club, his family and the gentle Wiltshire climate. He also mentioned that he would prefer that his children (although still yet a twinkle in his eye) be educated in England.

Eddie's offer came at just the right time. He'd been in the process of selling his 'bachelor pad' to upgrade to a bigger, family-style house (for all the upcoming children and on Sandy's request) and, as he got a great price for said pad, he had the cash to invest in the business.

Penny's only concern, now the prodigal had returned (and one that was voiced on a daily basis), was getting them into a house of their own so that they could hurry up and marry and have babies and she would get her longed-for grandchildren.

The small but mighty Sandy (she reminded Charlotte of the film *Beverly Hills Chihuahua* every time she saw her) was broody and putting pressure on Simon to get a move on with impregnating her, and finding their new dream home. Reading between the lines, it seemed that Sandy wasn't quite as charming and easy-going as everyone had first thought. Penny was far too kind-hearted to openly bitch about her beloved son's future wife, but Charlie had known her for a long time, and knew her 'tells' as well as she knew her own parents'. The strain of having the Australian minx poking around their charming but slightly old-fashioned house, making 'constructive' suggestions on how the guest accommodations could be 'brought up to date', was beginning to show.

Charlie could tell Penny was slightly intimidated by the lovely Sandy – who was a qualified practice manager and had run the highly successful, state-of-the-art veterinary hospital that Simon had worked at in Hunter Valley, New South Wales – and despite her small stature and seemingly fragile charms – was a Titan in the office. Penny indicated that she was highly efficient, extremely professional, conversant in the latest technological innovations in practice management and not very forgiving of people that weren't 'on the same page' as her.

When Simon and Eddie discussed the partnership by videoconference from opposite sides of the world, Simon made a job for his girlfriend one of the conditions of his returning to Wiltshire. But there was now trouble in paradise. Once she got stuck into work at the practice, it became abundantly clear that the job wasn't suited to her. There was plenty to do – but it wasn't the sort of work she wanted to do.

Brown's was a general family practice that did some equestrian, so although there was some glamour from the middle-tier trainers and owners coming into the practice, more than fifty percent of the business came from tending to local livestock farmers and domestic animals. Kitty also ran a boarding kennel for cats and dogs in the garden behind their house (which was adjacent to the practice). This enterprise shared their office and, to add insult to injury, the practice also had responsibility for looking after a Shetland pony sanctuary. These two sidelines meant that the communal areas were more often than not pure mayhem: clients bringing in their animals for medical attention, boarders being dropped off and the occasional visitor for the sanctuary – all having to be looked after in the same space.

The sanctuary was a bequest from a wealthy villager, Lady Clarissa Hodge, who loved horses and had a pet peeve about 'the wrong sort of people' buying small horses: "Don't know how to look after them – think they've bought a bloody dog!" She had left a few acres of prime village land, a row of purpose-built, luxurious Shetland pony stables and the bulk of her significant fortune (in trust) to ensure that "those dear little characters get a decent shot at life, by damn."

The practice received a fat administration fee for looking after the health of the little critters, and, in return, gave up a desk in the crowded office to a revolving cadre of ageing volunteers, who handled the finding and rescuing of the animals and – in theory – did the visitor tours. However, as the volunteers were exactly that, they often didn't show up for 'work', and the veterinary receptionist often had to handle the Shetland pony business as well as their regular duties.

Charlie had just learnt, much to her hidden amusement, that Sandy only managed a week at Brown's before being asked to leave. On the first day, she threw a fit when she found out that the client records were still kept in paper files in the ancient grey filing cabinets that flanked one wall, and that their supplier database was an ancient, sellotape-enhanced Rolodex. On the second day, she snapped at Kitty when she got scratched by a nervous Siamese, whose owner was going to Marbella for three weeks and was running so late that she literally threw the poor pussy into a shocked Sandy's arms. On day three, she had a huge row with Eddie who had made a rather clever joke about said pussy which Sandy just didn't get. On the fourth day, she bit the head off the nicest of the Shetland pony volunteers and made her cry. (She'd made the mistake of asking Sandy very politely if she would mind listening out for the phone for a few minutes while she popped out to the village store for some cough sweets). On day five, a stern faced Eddie took Simon to one side and said firmly that he didn't think Sandy would work out, and that he had a friend with an opening at a posh equestrian practice in Lambourn that would suit her better.

Apparently, the job in Lambourn did suit her a little better but was a good forty-five minutes' drive away and quite challenging hours, and, apparently, between Simon's schedule at Kimble and her new job, they were hardly seeing each other. Penny worried constantly that if Sandy was unhappy Simon would be too – and would go back to Australia.

Charlotte tried to look sympathetic when Penny discussed her son's less-than-satisfactory domestic situation, but inside she was rejoicing, hoping they wouldn't stay either. She didn't want to see Simon because, well, she just didn't like having him around. And she found Sandy highly irritating. On the rare occasions the couple deigned to visit the pub and she had to serve them, she found herself wanting to 'accidentally' trip and spill drinks over them.

Sandy was a self-proclaimed food and wine expert, and couldn't visit The Lamb without complaining that they didn't have any "really good Aussie red" on the wine list. She loved to see Charlie running back and forth to the bar, normally because the wine was corked, or to get extra glasses – and then leave an insultingly small tip – which Simon would surreptitiously overcompensate for, by sneaking into the bar and handing over a ten pound note to Sammi. But, worse of all, were the sickening public displays of affection. Sandy always seemed to be mauling him, stroking her boyfriend's thigh or nestling into his side and looking up at him like a baby otter – then asking Charlie to take a photo of them. It made her want to gag.

She had tried to get on with Sandy, even if she would never like her, for Ali and Penny's sake. She had even made a friendly gesture and invited her (after being nagged to death by her mum) for a game of golf. She had been warned that the diminutive Aussie was a brilliant golfer – with an eight handicap to her eighteen – but she thought that maybe they could still have a good game.

No such luck. The four hours had been depressingly hard work and she didn't enjoy her game at all. Sandy had put her off by lecturing her on her swing; 'helpfully' providing tips on how to improve her putting; comparing Charlie's beloved North Wilts to some fancy championship course back home (and finding it wanting) all while bitching and complaining about 'those people' at the Kimble practice. By the end of the morning it was clear the two women didn't have anything in common – and, despite Sandy's obvious good looks and blatant adoration of her boyfriend, Charlie could not understand what Simon saw in her. She figured he must have had a personality bypass in Australia to be able to spend so much time with someone who didn't find Eddie Brown's famous jokes funny.

Simon was funny. He didn't hold forth in pubs cracking jokes or telling stories, but he was always looking for the comedy in situations, he didn't take himself too seriously (normally) and had a great sense of the ridiculous. Although he teased the old ladies wickedly and made wisecracks about the pets and their owners, he was never malicious. He had turned into an undeniably cool guy, and Charlie was finding it increasingly hard to be around him without thinking about the old days – and she didn't want to do that. She didn't want her long-buried feelings for him to surface. Because, once upon a time, she thought the world revolved around him, and there had been a moment when she thought that *he* thought the same about her.

From the moment they met, Simon had taken the mickey out of Charlotte. She was his little sister's best friend so he'd teased her just like he teased his sibling. She'd been a lanky eleven-year-old who could pass for a boy with her straight up and down figure, short hair and tomboy tendencies. Ali was a tomboy too and they both thought they were as good as any boy. The two of them challenged Simon on everything: biking, tennis, swimming, climbing trees, playing video games and real games like football and cricket. He called her 'Charlie Girl' because she looked so much like a boy and he said at least that way there would be no confusion. She didn't mind the name then. But when she reached fifteen, she started thinking more and more about the birds and the bees (by that age Ali was obsessed with boys and sex), and about the thrilling possibility of being someone's girlfriend one day. And then, self-conscious teenager that she was, she decided that Charlie Girl was a lame name and decided to ask him to stop calling her that and call her Charlotte instead.

By then Simon was eighteen – tall, good-looking, the most popular boy at school, a real young gun. He spent a lot more time with his school friends and rarely spent time with the two girls anymore. One day, when he was teasing her by the school tennis courts, she sulkily asked him to stop calling her "that stupid name".

Simon just raised his eyebrows laconically and said, "Whatever, Charlotte." and walked off.

In the weeks afterwards, Simon strode past Charlie without saying anything. She felt snubbed and foolish. Charlie kicked herself for mentioning it. Before, at least he'd been teasing her, and after, well, he just stopped talking to her – not calling her anything at all. It was doubly painful because, as Simon had apparently forgotten that Charlie existed, she found herself thinking about him more and more. It didn't help that the other girls in her class kept talking about how good-looking he was, and how lucky she was to get to hang out with him. She was best friends with the sister of the coolest boy in school.

That summer she made the decision to try to look more like a girl. Enduring the gentle teasing of her parents and her classmates, she literally 'grew up' overnight, reaching her final height of 5ft 10 by the time she was sixteen. She had her hair cut into a more feminine style, enhanced her little boobs with a tiny padded bra, applied heavy black eyeliner on the inside of her lids and was never seen without lip gloss – all the while suffering the agonies of a major teenage crush she was too embarrassed to say anything about to anyone – especially Ali.

The object of her desire didn't notice her transition from little girl to young woman, but she couldn't blame him – it was an amazing time in his life. He'd been accepted at Cambridge to study veterinary medicine and his life was about to change forever. He was young, fun, with loads of friends, and he didn't have time for silly games with Ali and Charlie. He had more exciting things to do than tease two girls three years his junior.

Simon had passed his driving test a few days after his seventeenth birthday, and a few months later, as a gift for getting into Cambridge, his parents gave him some money for a car. He and his friends spent that golden summer roaring around in his battered jeep, experiencing the heady joys of total freedom for the first time. They would load up the car and drive down to Cornwall to camp and surf, or go to house parties in London and attend festivals all over the country. Even Ali would only see him fleetingly as he came home for a sleep and a change of clothes. Charlotte died inside as Simon's father would gently boast over drinks about how there was a different girl calling for his son each week. At the end of that summer, Simon went off to university. Charlie missed him terribly, but would never have admitted it – knowing that her crush was unrequited. She knew the whole thing was ridiculous and that Ali would laugh her knickers off that her best friend had a crush on her 'super-stud brother', as she now called him.

Simon got so caught up in his new life at Cambridge that he rarely came back to Wiltshire and when he did, Charlie hardly saw him. He would spend his days being fussed over and cooked for by his mum and helping his dad in the garden. In the evenings, he would rush into the local town to hook up with his old school friends and in the long holidays he would travel – seemingly visiting one exotic location after another – staying in the impossibly glamorous-sounding homes of his Cambridge friends' parents: ski lodges in the French Alps, villas in Barbados and even a trip to Singapore with an exotic girlfriend.

Charles and Penny never said a word in criticism when Simon didn't come home to see them in the holidays, seemingly happy that he had the opportunity to do such lovely things. And according to them, although he partied hard, he was studying harder, so all was well with the world. Ali grudgingly said she missed him too, they'd always been close, but, like her parents, she understood what a great opportunity Cambridge was for him. And anyway, Ali was busy with her own life – studying for uni, discovering sex with her various and changing boyfriends and, of course, hanging out with Charlie.

The summer Charlotte turned eighteen she'd completed a secretarial course and was spending July and August hanging around the village, doing a part-time job at the local nursery, kicking her heels so she could keep Ali company as her clever friend waited for her exam results. Ali had got her results letter two days before, and, as Charlie had anticipated, had aced them all: her friend was now excitedly preparing to go to University College London to study law.

Charlotte was not so focused or excited. In fact, she was filled with doubt and fear, because she had no idea – at all – about what job she should do. But as she had to do something, Ali had decided she should come to London too and share a flat with her (Ali's parents were renting her a nice flat in Bloomsbury) and had even got her an office junior position lined up with a Chartered Surveyor called Danny, the son of some old family friends. Even though she didn't really want to move to live in a city, there was nothing to keep her in Wiltshire: no boyfriend, no job and soon – no Ali. So Charlie decided she might as well go too.

Charles and Penny – delighted with Ali's excellent exam results – decided to throw a last-minute party to celebrate. Ali called all her school friends and her parents invited all their friends from the village. Money talks, and despite the late notice (and it being summer wedding time), Charles made some calls and a marquee had miraculously appeared in their huge back garden. That afternoon the house's driveway had been jammed with cars and vans arriving and dropping off stuff, including an impressive looking sound system for the DJ and a large white pig, which had been roasting on a spit for the best part of the day. The Hobson family loved fancy dress, so they had decided that costumes were a necessary element. However, as the invites were issued at such late notice, they opted for something simple – Penny decided it would have to be a toga party "because everyone had a sheet, darling!".

Ali had come over to Charlie's house for a cup of tea and some peace and quiet, while Penny did what she did best: organised food and drink for a guest list of over a hundred.

"Well, your family certainly doesn't do anything by halves," said Charlie as the girls watched a large silver van belch out hundreds of purple and green helium balloons that transformed into huge, floating iridescent bunches of grapes before their eyes.

"Indeed. She's gone completely crazy over this Greek theme – she's wiped out Sainsbury's entire stock of hummus, feta and olives within a hundred mile radius, I think. I had to stop her from ordering ouzo and retsina – I told her it's rank. And yesterday she somehow conjured up a Vestal Virgin outfit for us both – who's she kidding?"

Charlie giggled. "She'll start calling the portaloo the vomitorium if you're not careful," and the girls cracked up.

The party was scheduled to start at 6.30pm to make the most of the glorious August evening. And because people liked things to start on time in Puddlington, there were plenty of cars parked outside the house by 6.15. As Charlie was getting ready, she watched a steady trail of guests arriving – most by foot, as those that lived close enough, left their cars at home and walked to the party, knowing how generous their host's hospitality was and that they would want to imbibe freely.

Charlie didn't like dressing up that much, but she thought toga parties were good fun. There was something about the plain silliness of a bunch of adults walking around in sheets that appealed to her sense of the ridiculous. That night she was pleased with her costume. She made a decent Roman. Her simple outfit comprised an old headband that she'd attached some leaves to and sprayed gold, and her mum had helped her to make a short white, cotton toga that left one shoulder bare. She didn't have anything on underneath apart from a pair of flesh-colour 'granny knickers'. She couldn't wear a bra without it showing, and luckily her small boobs didn't need one. Earlier that day, figuring she might look a little too plain, she'd rushed up into town and fortuitously found some gold strappy sandals in one charity shop and some huge gold ear hoops and a swathe of jingly gold bracelets in another. When she looked at herself in the mirror, she was happy with her appearance and wished there was someone going to the party that she fancied because for once she looked pretty and might stand a chance with him. Her long legs were tanned, the skin on her exposed shoulder glowed and the heavy eye makeup Helen had insisted on putting on for her, made her dark eyes look huge and exotically alluring.

When Charlotte walked downstairs, her dad gasped, his eyes glistening with proud tears. He told her how beautiful she looked and warned her to watch out for any naughty Neros that might want to make her their next conquest.

The party was in full swing by the time the Pierce family arrived at 7.00pm. They immediately splintered off, Peter to do his duty – getting Helen and the lady vicar (a close family friend) a drink – and Charlotte to find Ali. She pushed her way through the crowd at the entrance and strode off towards the DJ booth, assuming that her friend would be supervising the tunes – DJ Marky was her latest squeeze. Rushing, she didn't notice the tall gladiator backing out of the crowded bar area with a full pint in his hand; Charlie nearly knocked herself out from the force of bumping into him. He was so big and so solid that she barely caused a ripple in the surface of his drink.

"Sorry," they both said at the same time and Charlie looked up to see a shocked-looking Simon staring back at her.

"Hello, Charlie Girl," he said with a smile. "I might've known it was you rushing around not looking where you're going."

"Hi, Simon, what a surprise. I didn't know you were coming." She hadn't seen him for ages, hadn't thought about him for a few weeks at least, and she hoped she was over him, but here he was and her heart still leapt about crazily at the sight of him. He looked absolutely stunning in his gladiator costume – like Russell Crowe – but better.

"I thought I'd better surprise my bratty but brilliant little sister. You know I wouldn't have missed it for the world."

Charlie looked sceptical. He'd blotted his copy book a few months ago when he'd missed their joint eighteenth birthday party despite his mother's pleas. Ali's anger and disappointment were acute (but, of course, she couldn't show this).

They stared at each other assessing the changes since the last time they'd met – nearly two years ago.

Simon broke the silence. "I have to say, Charlie Girl, you scrub up well. You look really good in that toga. Do you think you might have been Greek in a former life?" His eyes teased, and then his face hardened and became serious as he looked her up and down, boldly checking out her long legs and her pretty, flushed face, framed by glossy dark hair and the wreath of golden leaves.

He looked puzzled. "Did you do something? You look so different. Really beautiful. Has your hair changed or something?"

Oh my god! She screamed inside. *He said I look beautiful.*

Rather than show her excitement, Charlie lowered her lids and smiled shyly at the ground before slowly looking up (Princess Di style), to see if what she hoped she would see in his sparkling blue eyes, was there. She nearly jumped with joy. It was. He was looking at her in a completely different way to normal. He was gazing at her, admiring her as a woman, not a little girl. She smiled triumphantly. It was intoxicating and wonderful. She felt amazing, filled with confidence, powerful, sexy … like a goddess. She loved her toga!

Charlie pouted a little and gave him a wicked grin. "I guess I just grew up, Simon – but you wouldn't know – because you haven't been around."

Simon shook his head in wonderment. "No, I haven't. And I think I may have made a mistake not coming home more often. I should have been keeping an eye on you – lord knows how much trouble you've been getting yourself into."

She flirted back, "Well, that's classified, Simon."

Charlie was on cloud nine – she couldn't believe that Simon, *her Simon*, the Simon she'd had a crush on forever but who had ignored her for all these years, was actually flirting with her! She was so excited she couldn't be cool any longer. Joy radiated out of her. She beamed at him, and he beamed right back, clearly as enchanted by her as she was by him.

The party raging around them receded, relegated to a theatrical backdrop for the main event – rediscovering each other. *I could look at him forever!* But someone had to say something.

"Well, ..." she posed, head to one side.

"Well what?"

"Well, don't you think we should go and find Ali? I don't want to be responsible for her mood if we don't get on that dance floor soon."

"You are wise for your years, Charlie Girl. Let me grab you a drink too and you can come with me – I need safe escort through all these Puddlington Romans. I'm scared one them is going to send me to the Coliseum."

She giggled. "I wouldn't blame them. It's a wonderful gladiator costume. You look really manly – even in the skirt."

He pulled his sword out and struck a warrior pose. "Glad you like it." Then spoilt the macho moment by lisping, "I did wonder if the gold tassels were a teeny-weeny bit over the top – but the man in the costume shop said I looked *fabulous!*"

Charlie cracked up. "It certainly shows off your manly thighs," she gave them a long appreciative gaze before a look of concern crossed her face.

"Erm, Simon, ... don't mean to be rude but, do you have anything on under that skirt? It's a bit short and there's a bit of a wind at that end of the garden. I wouldn't want you to embarrass yourself."

Simon looked mildly affronted. "Yes! I have my gladiator cod piece on, would you like to see it?"

He walked towards her with a dopey grin, flapping his 'skirt'. Charlie squeaked in panic and stepped back, putting her hands in front of her eyes.

"Don't make me look," she pleaded.

He bent down and tugged the bottom of her sheet. "How about you, Aphrodite? This toga doesn't leave much to the imagination."

"Don't worry mortal, I'm wearing my trusty golden merkin – you're safe," she deadpanned and they both exploded into peals of laughter.

It was a magical night. From that moment, Simon never left her side. They grabbed a tray of drinks then went looking for Ali who spent the rest of the evening either hanging out with them or necking with her DJ boyfriend. They took the piss out of everyone's costume, danced like crazy people, feasted on 'wild boar and vittles' and drank far too much 'nectar of the gods'.

Eventually the crowds left, DJ Marky wearily packed up and drove off in his van, leaving the last three standing – Simon, Ali and Charlie. They lolled drunkenly on top of each other, salvaging the last dregs out of the cool boxes, dissecting the party. Ali, slurring her words, made her excuses and left them for her bed and for the first time ever in the history of their friendship Charlie was pleased to see her go – because she was dying to be alone with Simon.

The atmosphere changed as soon as Ali left. Anticipation raged in Charlie's tummy. They sat side by side – she had been casually leaning against him for a while and the place where they touched burnt hot. Simon reached for her hand and covered it. She studied his big hand stroking her smaller one. His thumb rubbed up the back of each finger, smoothing over her nails, and then rubbing back down. It was a simple gesture, but easily, the most exciting sensory experience of her life to date.

She had to remind herself to breathe, because every cell in her body was excited and on anticipatory alert. Charlie knew that after all those years of wanting him to, Simon was going to turn and kiss her and that she should relax and enjoy it – because it really was going to happen … any minute now. She felt him shift and finally looked up to meet his eyes, only a few inches away. He smiled his familiar smile, the one he'd shared with her for years, but somehow different now, then inclined his head a few inches so that he could lay his mouth against hers. At that first touch of his lips, her stomach hit the floor and she let out a tiny moan of excitement, she couldn't help herself, and she felt his mouth curve in a smile as he recognised the sound of absolute surrender. Charlie thought his lips were everything a girl could dream of: soft yet firm and tasting sweetly of passion fruit wine cooler.

When she looked back on that evening, she couldn't remember how they had moved from the marquee area to the quiet grassy area under the apple trees. But that was where they ended up and that was where they undressed with clumsy haste. And then it all happened so fast, and before she knew it, it was over.

Afterwards he pulled her close, snuggling her head onto his broad chest, one arm underneath her – chivalrously trying to keep her off the grass – and the other over the top to keep her warm. Then Simon immediately fell asleep.

Charlotte remembered how she didn't want to sleep; she didn't want to waste a minute of their time together. Despite the chill of the ground, she didn't feel any discomfort – she could have been lying on a bed of nails, and still would not have moved from that spot.

With her head nestled between the crook of his arm and his shoulder, his downy chest hair tickling her nose, she was blissfully content. All she could hear was the steady beat of his heart and the gentle sound of his breathing as he slept soundly.

How indescribably wonderful that he has finally fallen in love with me … this is the most amazing moment of my life. Their joint future played out in her imagination. They would be lying together like this for the rest of their lives. To start with she would visit him in Cambridge, meet his friends, and support him in his studies while he finished his degree. Then once he was qualified, she would follow him to wherever he got a job and then of course a house, children, dogs … Charlie finally dropped off to sleep.

An hour or so later, the sun rose. Simon woke and shook her awake. He was embarrassed that they were both naked and rushed to cover her up. Gentle with her, helping her reassemble her toga, but not laughing. He dressed quickly, shrugging off her joking offers of assistance and told her he would walk her home – all without looking her in the eye once. Grabbing Charlie by the hand, he marched her quickly across the green, almost pulling her behind him. She mucked around trying to get him to slow down but he became impatient and dropped her hand. When they reached the tall box hedge in front of her parents' house, he paused and looked down at her.

"Well, I'll be off then."

She put her face forward, expecting a goodbye kiss, but he ignored her. She understood then that something wasn't right.

"Simon, why won't you kiss me?"

In the future, she'd wince when she recalled the range of emotions that passed over his handsome face when she asked that. First shame, then guilt and finally anger. She reached out to touch him, and he pushed her hand away.

As he stepped back, he blurted, "Look, Charlie, I don't want you to go getting the wrong idea. We had a great night. Tremendous fun. Don't get all serious on me now and start thinking it's more than it was."

It was a nightmare. She felt sick to her stomach. That he regretted what they had done was written all over his face. He was making what had happened between them seem cheap and shoddy and to add insult to injury he obviously wanted to get away from her and stop talking about it as soon as possible. He was backing away, desperately trying to leave before she made a scene.

Last night he had looked at her as though he loved her – but he was just a big phony. She loved him, she probably always would, but at this moment she hated him too. She wasn't going to let him see how much he'd hurt her. And she wasn't going to let him spoil anything else, like make things awkward for her and Ali – or with his parents. She could be a phony too.

Charlie shrugged her shoulders and looked at Simon pityingly.

"You're the one that's overreacting and making things awkward. I was drunk and I can't really remember much about it, to be honest. Went by in a flash," she laughed and said, almost as an afterthought, "probably more fun for you than for me – given your poor performance – so I wouldn't want to repeat the exercise anyway."

And that was that for Charlotte and Simon, a night to remember but one never to be repeated. She remembered how she had crawled into her bed and cried herself to sleep that morning and vowed *never* to speak to him again.

A few months after that event, following a particularly drunken night out on the tiles, early days in London, she confessed what she'd done to Ali and cried again. Her best friend rolled her eyes, gave her a hug, told her she was a "fucking idiot", and pointed out that even though she loved him to bits, her brother was a "man-whore" and wasn't ready to settle down. Ali advised Charlotte to sleep with someone else as soon as possible – which she did when they went to Greece on holiday.

Simon went back to Cambridge and, when he graduated, moved to

Australia. Charlie moved to London and met Graham. But now he was back in her life, back in her village, drinking in her pub, and he was back in her thoughts, big time.

CHAPTER 28
Tracy

Tracy hummed "Hot, Hot, Hot" as she glided around her home straightening furniture and tidying up the last little bits and pieces from the previous night's party. She was as happy as a clam. Mentally patting herself on the back, she smiled as she thought about her newest recruit. Bringing Jazmin into the team had been a huge success.

The girl was *tal-en-ted* with hair and was a natural born teacher to boot. She already had two of the apprentices hanging on her every word – eager to learn as much as she would teach – even staying late to watch her with some clients. Jazmin was a strong personality, for sure, and there had been, and were likely to be, more fireworks between Cheryl and the new girl, but she could sense that would even out. The two women were quite similar: opinionated, intelligent, driven and creative – they even had a similar, bawdy sense of humour. The salon was a lively spot at the moment for sure.

The party was a thank you gift to all her girls and their partners for their hard work. It seemed fitting to do a Caribbean-themed night, and so she'd employed a local caterer to create a feast of tasty West Indian food. A smiling lady of Zephyrian extraction, who lived in nearby Slough, turned up with seemingly endless, enormous silver trays filled with fall-off-the-bone barbeque ribs, glossy with rich, dark sauce. Alongside this came lightly spiced, coconut-crusted fish fillets, fragrant curried chicken, peas 'n' rice, scalloped potatoes, salad and a colourful coleslaw. For dessert there was coconut tart and homemade rum and raisin ice cream. Tracy had hired a party planner who scoured the shops for fresh limes, juices and different flavoured rums to make a potent punch and make sure the barman was well stocked with Carib and Red Stripe beer. Jazmin had helped her with the music for the party – bringing along a special playlist packed with reggae, soca and calypso.

By the end of the evening, everyone was completely sloshed and in the mood to dance, so Tracy and Jazmin demonstrated how to 'wine', a Caribbean dance style that was based on winding and grinding the pelvic area in rhythm to soca music - much to the onlookers' entertainment. Then they made everyone get up and join in with the 'electric slide' dance, which was a huge hit, especially with Cheryl who kept making them play it again and again, 'til she got it down perfectly, finally collapsing, flushed and cheerfully exhausted.

Jazmin had opted to stay over at Tracy's that night as her temporary home, a twenty minute drive away, was with a cousin who'd just had a baby and she didn't want to wake her up going home so late. Tracy was glad to have some alone time with the younger woman. After clearing up the worst of the mess, and picking some more at the leftovers, they sat down with a big glass of Bailey's and ice apiece in Tracy's living room. Tracy sighed with pleasure as she put her feet up on the coffee table. She closed her eyes for a moment, pleasurably reliving the party, but Jazmin had something on her mind.

"Tracy, can I ask you something personal?"

"Depends on what it is," said Tracy, warily but with enough of a smile to encourage the girl to go on.

"What's going on with you and my cousin?"

Tracy wished she'd never responded. She should have kept her eyes and mouth closed.

"With CB? I mean Jimmy?" she feigned. "Nothing – you know that we're just friends."

Jazmin shook her head. "No, not him, my other cousin ... Diver." She paused then looked at Tracy curiously, before blurting out, "Jimmy says you're in love with each other, is that true?"

She is certainly direct. Tracy took her time to answer, "In love with Diver? I wonder why he would say that?"

Jazmin eyed Tracy speculatively, "Well, he told me it was really obvious."

"Go on."

"You want me to tell you what he told me?"

Tracy knew she was on dangerous ground and that she should try to change the subject, especially as she was determined to forget him, but she couldn't resist hearing what CB had said. Dying to hear what made it 'obvious' that they were in love.

"Well, I messaged him about you. After he placed the ad for the stylist on his Facebook page, I wanted to know why he was so friendly with some white woman from England." Jazmin sounded a little defensive, she shrugged her shoulders and looked sheepish. "I was suspicious about why he has helping you out, I suppose. I know him well – we spent a lot of time together – most summer holidays when I was growing up. I know what he used to be like."

Tracy nodded, she could see the sense in that, CB was good-looking and very flirtatious. He must have been a real heartbreaker back in the day.

Jazmin continued, "He's good these days, settled down, but when he was younger he used to be a big player and I suppose I wanted to make sure I wasn't coming to see some woman who was making up a job just because she'd got the hots for my wicked cousin. It's amazing what lengths some women will go to, to get a man, you know."

"Anyway, he told me how you'd met at the bar and that he really liked you ... you had great chats. And then he started laughing and said that even if he'd wanted to try it on, you only had eyes for one man, and that was his brother," she finished with a smile, "to be honest I was surprised when I heard that."

"Why?"

"Because D, that's what I call him, was – is – quite different from his brother. He's not a player, in fact he's very cool around women, and – as far as I was aware – never dates tourists. But Jimmy said that night D walked into the bar, took one look at you, and it was like POW and the two of you were inseparable ever since."

Tracy nodded, remembering him leading her by the hand to the deck and then just getting absorbed in each other. It probably did look like that.

"Spill the beans then! I'm dying of curiosity. I want to know *exactly* what happened. Jimmy said one minute the two of you were loved up – he'd never seen his brother like it before, cooking for you, ignoring work – and the next minute you had rushed off the island without saying goodbye to him. Apparently, after you left, D disappeared from the radar for a while, said he was working on some research and wouldn't come out liming at all. He even stopped fishing for a bit, which pissed Jimmy off, because he relies on him for the restaurant. And when he finally surfaces, Jimmy asks him about you and all he would say was that it hadn't worked out."

Jasmin paused for breath for a moment and Tracy took the opportunity to ask,

"Wow. That was some chat you and CB had."

Jazmin looked a bit sheepish. "Yeah. We did have a really long conversation about you. Sorry. But Jimmy really likes you and he's intrigued. He thinks there's more to it than meets the eye. And, that your silence speaks volumes. He says that you never ask about D directly, but you're always asking funny little questions that make him feel you're still interested in each other. And apparently, D is doing the same. He's started coming back into the bar and the other day he even asked Jimmy if he ever heard from you."

Tracy's heart was racing. Could it be that Diver was still thinking about her, still cared for her? She didn't want to get her hopes up but the fact he was asking about her sounded positive.

"What exactly happened? I don't want to pry, Tracy, and I guess you might think I'm overstepping here, but it seems to me that you could do with talking about it."

"Jazmin, honestly, I would love to," she said with a sigh, "but it's not professional. It's your family and I don't want to spoil our friendship or compromise our working relationship. You know I'm so happy to have you at the salon."

"I promise it's OK for you to talk to me, and if you're worried that I will hear something I don't like and I'm going to get vexed and leave, don't be. I'm not going anywhere. I love this job, love working with those heifers, and nothing that happened, or didn't happen, between you and D is going to change that. I like and respect you and, *trust me*, I know those two guys. D is a fine, educated man but he is also one hundred percent West Indian, and they play by their own rules. I think you may need some advice from a woman who knows how Caribbean men really think."

I do. I bloody do, she thought and, giving in to her long-suppressed desire to reminisce, Tracy told Jazmin everything (well not quite everything – she didn't go into graphic detail). She told her about her mum's big secret – the shock of finding out she had a half brother and how that had driven her to visit the island in the first place. About meeting Diver at the bar and how much fun they had hanging out and how she'd assumed that he was 'just' a fisherman and that in doing that had missed all the clues and had failed in her quest.

Jazmin was the perfect listener – hanging on her every word. She felt nervous when she described their final argument, worried about what Jazmin would think of her and watched the younger woman's face carefully. But apart from one impatient shake of her head when hearing about how Diver had spoken to Tracy, plus another at the fact that Diver hadn't responded to her note – Jazmin didn't seem to find what Tracy had said anything other than fascinating.

She was clearly captivated, and, in keeping with the subject matter, broke into pure West Indian, "Lawd, what-a-ting!"

The two women giggled, and Tracy, needing a break from the storytelling took a watery slug of Bailey's and melted ice before replying.

"I know, it's the biggest drama in my life to date."

"When are you going back to the island? – seems like you got plenty unfinished business over there."

Tracy sighed and shrugged. "I wish – I want to. But it's difficult – what with Diver hating me so much and with Isilma not getting back to me yet. I don't even have any leads."

"Girl, your head is so messed up by my dumb-ass cousin, you ain't thinking straight." (Jazmin had now segued into the pure Brooklyn accent she used when she got riled up in the salon, and which Cheryl teased her about unmercifully).

"What do you mean?"

"Well, firstly, it was just an argument. Don't go taking it serious. Sure, it was a big-ass argument, but that's all it was. Do you argue much in your family?"

"No, we don't. When I come to think about it, this whole thing about Zephyr is the most I've ever argued with her." A childhood memory sprang immediately to mind. "Once Mum and Dad were in a bad mood with each other for weeks and the atmosphere was horrible, but I never knew what it was about. I don't think I ever saw them argue. Mum doesn't like to argue at all. If she was angry about something, she would give us the silent treatment. Dad and I would tiptoe around trying to work out what we had done wrong until she started talking to us again!"

Jazmin nodded her head like she had learnt something important.

"Thought so. It sounds to me like you completely overreacted to the argument."

"What?"

"You're not used to arguing. You were not supposed to take it that seriously, girl. Yes! You hurt his pride big time when you mistook him for a fisherman, and that made him so angry he didn't hear anything else and lashed out. It's what people do. You hit a sore spot. One thing about D, he's really proud of his education and his profession. That you hadn't noticed he was different, more upper class you would call it I guess, would have made him really mad."

"But I tried to apologise."

"Maybe you didn't try enough. You should never have gone back to the hotel that night – you should have stood your ground. Don't you know you never go to bed on an argument, Tracy? A few hours later he woulda been madder that you gave up on him so quickly, and didn't get in touch, than about whatever you argued about in the first place."

Jazmin paused for effect. "The way I see it is that your differences are not that you're white and he's Black. It's that you are an "uptight" British woman and he's a "cool out" Caribbean man. Basically, you're from different cultures, been brought up different. It's like you're playing different games. You want to play his game but you don't know the rules yet. That makes it hard to sort out any arguments."

Jazmin looked pleased as punch with her theory, but although Tracy had heard the words, they did not compute.

"What about the note? I tried to be in touch."

"I think it was probably too little too late. Should have been a grand gesture. Or maybe the receptionist never delivered it?"

"I did think that, but she has no reason not to, I thought I was just grabbing at straws."

"Was that it? Did you try any other way to get in touch?" she probed.

"No, I thought he'd never want to talk to me again."

Jazmin threw herself back into her armchair, and said firmly, "Tracy! That's the problem. He's probably *real* confused. He would have been expecting you to try to make up. The fact that you two were all in love and then you just upped and left the island without contacting him, well, … you've damaged that big ole male ego. He probably thinks you're just not that into him."

"You're kidding me? You really think he might still want to hear from me?"

"I think so. Look, listening to what you said, you're both equally to blame. You were swept along in your little holiday romance – you didn't take the time to get to know each other and neither of you wanted to ask too many questions. Sure, what you said was bad – but so is what he said. And, to be honest – knowing where he comes from and now getting to know you – I think it's likely the prejudices, even if they are unconscious, are on both sides."

"So why do you think that?"

"Well, did he ever tell you much about his mother?"

"No. Not really, but then I know so little about him. He told me his dad had taught him fishing – but that he died when he was eight, and he and CB were brought up by his grandmother – who he loves to bits. I got the feeling his mother wasn't around much either, but apart from that …"

"Well, I heard his dad, my Uncle Franklin, was a sweetheart. But his mother, Shandice, is a real piece of work. Super smart and good-looking too, but not a mothering type. She was always more interested in getting to America than in spending time with her kids. She had them young and then left them with her mother-in-law as soon as she had the opportunity."

"That's rubbish. To lose your dad and have your mum leave you like that." Tracy was indignant on their behalf.

"Well, it's fairly common in the Caribbean to be brought up by your grandmother. Anyway, it did not work out for her up there for some reason or other and she had to come back to Zephyr – she's got a huge chip on her shoulder. Now the sons support her."

"That's so nice."

"Yep. It is. Especially considering her relationship with Jimmy is strained at the moment."

"In what way?"

"She threw a fit when Jimmy married 'out' – Mia is East Indian. She told him he should stick to his culture, which I think is hypocritical considering she would have married a US citizen in a second – if she could have got a green card. Anyway, she will make it clear to anyone that will listen that she doesn't approve of biracial marriages – so maybe some of that has rubbed off on D. He's very into the island's history and culture as you probably know."

It was fascinating to hear Diver's family history, she wanted to know everything about him. "You know I can't blame her, she's exactly the same as my mum – or how I thought my mum was until a few months ago. I think a lot of mothers don't want their children to date or marry someone from a different culture – they're worried it's going to be difficult for them."

"But it sucks, Tracy. People need to get over it. Seems like it's up to people like us to make a new generation, it's got to happen sometime – look at me I'm a Black woman who loves Asian men, must run in the family!" and winked naughtily.

Tracy smiled playfully, "Oh really?" she said in a fruity growl.

"*Really*! I had the most amazing-looking Japanese boyfriend for a while." She sighed and fanned her face furiously as if she were suddenly hot.

"He had these smooth arms covered with a bunch of crazy tattoos, man I loved to stroke them … mmm … he was delicious." Jazmin gazed into space dreamily, lost in pleasurable memories.

Tracy cleared her throat dramatically, attempting to get Jazmin's attention back to their conversation, the girl reluctantly shrugged off her daydream and continued.

"Seriously, I believe it's all about the guy and how he makes you feel. For me, it's all about the individual. Sure, culture plays a part, but you can learn about someone's culture and be respectful of it, I'm not saying it's easy, but it can be done. Finding someone you have a real connection with, that's the hard part."

Tracy nodded in agreement. She loved Jazmin's idealism. The girl had wisdom beyond her years and a great perspective on life, the universe and everything. Tracy decided she wanted her take on her other burning issue.

"As we are talking about a diverse generation, that conveniently leads into my next question … do you think I should continue to look for my half brother?"

"Of course! It would be cool for you to have a 'brother' for a brother. Brother for a brother! Get it?"

Tracy grinned. "I got it, funny girl."

"Seriously, he's got to be easy to find. I think you're just not looking in the right place."

"What do you mean?"

"I think there's plenty you can do by yourself. You don't need D or that ice cream lady to help you."

Tracy giggled. "Ice cream? You mean Isilma, you silly sod. Go on."

"You need to go back to the source. Talk to the people your Ma was staying with in the Caribbean when she fell pregnant. I'm sure they would know what she got up to then and with who."

"But how would I find them? She doesn't talk to them anymore."

"So what? Just because *she* isn't in contact, there is no reason *you* shouldn't be. You have every right to try to find your brother – and get to know him. You need to get that name out of your Ma and track her down. Assuming she is still alive. Yep. That's the place to start."

Tracy felt like a complete bloody idiot. *Of course!* The best and simplest solution had been staring her in the face. Her mum kept everything. There was bound to be something in the house that would identify the mysterious friends. If that failed, she would shake it out of her. Jazmin was correct. It was her right to get to know her brother if she wanted to.

*

First thing next morning she drove to her mum's. Rosemary was surprised but pleased to see her. After a companionable cuppa, Tracy decided she couldn't face sneaking around in the attic and just came out with it.

"I know I said I wouldn't interfere. That it's your story. But it's not. It's not *just* your story, it's *mine* too – and the situation is doing my head in! I want to know more about the baby. I need to try to find him. Please, Mum, I know you don't want to know anything about him. But *I do* – I need to. Please help me out here. Why did you go to Zephyr? Who did you stay with? When was it exactly? What else can you tell me?" Rosemary tightened her lips stubbornly.

Stupid idea Tracy, you should have known she wasn't going to say anything.

Sighing heavily, she shoved her chair back from the table sharply in frustration and was just about to stomp off and start ransacking drawers for who knows what – when Rosemary croaked out a name.

"Hyacinth."

"What?"

"Hyacinth, H, that's the name of my friend."

Tracy, sat down and leant over the table, almost too nervous to breathe in case it put her off,

"OK, thank you. And who is Hyacinth?"

Rosemary went on to say, in a stiff little voice, that her friend Hyacinth was married to an architect called Jonathan Bowles (Tracy double checked and wrote down the spelling), friends from London who had gone to live in Zephyr and that she'd travelled out there in the late sixties.

And then, just as abruptly as she started, she stopped. When Tracy pressed she said she didn't talk to Hyacinth anymore and she had no idea where she lived and 'that was that and if you don't mind, I need to go water my tomato plants'.

It wasn't much, but it was enough for Tracy. She raced home, sat at her computer, and took exactly three minutes to discover that Jonathan Bowles was indeed alive. In fact, Jonathan was doing extremely well for himself.

All she had to do was Google 'Jonathan Bowles Architect', and she was directed to the website of the Royal Institute of British Architects, where she found three recent articles about him – one of them about a lifetime achievement award that he had received the previous year. From there she was able to find his practice website and easily extract a telephone number. She called immediately, and was told that he wasn't in today, but to leave a message and he would call her back. She declined to do so, saying she would call back the following day – preferring to explain in person rather than be introduced via a call back message.

The following day she called twice before she got through. Mr Bowles was a busy man apparently. She was dry mouthed and uncharacteristically nervous by the time he answered the phone.

"Jonathan Bowles," he said in a deep, fruity, English accent.

"Hello, Mr Bowles, sorry to bother you, my name is Tracy Smith."

"Yes, Miss Smith, how can I help you?" he asked politely, and with no hint of recognition.

Tracy felt sick, she said quietly, "I'm the daughter of Mrs Rosemary Smith …"

"Rosemary Smith? Afraid it doesn't ring any bells my dear."

Tracy's heart sunk, then she kicked herself – foolish girl – he would know her mum by her maiden name.

"How about Rosemary Davis?"

Bingo!

"Rosie? Rosie Posie? Hyacinth's old friend?" The man sounded quite excited; Tracy smiled at the nickname he had for her mum.

"Yes, that will be the one, although I've never heard her called that."

"Well, how marvellous, how absolutely marvellous. Um … how is your mother? We haven't seen her since …" he trailed off.

Yes, exactly, thought Tracy – best not to go into that yet, she wanted to see the Bowleses face to face to discuss the situation.

"Anyway, Mr Bowles I know you don't know me, but I was wondering …

would it be possible to meet? I'd love to chat to you about mum's time in the Caribbean, I know you lost touch but I am trying to find out something very important, and I think you may be able to help me."

There was a long silence. Tracy held her breath and crossed her fingers and toes.

"Well, I would be happy to talk to you my dear – but I will have to run it past my wife first. I should explain, she was terribly upset when Rosie stopped writing to her, and I don't like to assume, she's a bit tetchy these days."

Tracy let out a breath. *What a nice man.* He sounded a bit cautious, but she felt fairly sure he'd try for her.

"Thank you, I understand completely, and I appreciate that you need to ask. I really hope we can all talk. Like I said, it's very important to me."

"Yes, I'm sure it is, dear. Now I must be getting on." He sounded distracted, like someone else was talking to him.

"Of course. Can I give you my number and perhaps you could call me back?"

"Certainly, now hold on while I grab a pen." He rustled around.

To fill in time while he searched for something to write with, Tracy said, "I went to the island, you know. It's incredible. I fell in love with it. Apparently, it hasn't changed that much since you were there."

He stopped rustling and said in a dreamy voice, "That was my first major commission you know. Just qualified and I get the opportunity to design an airport. Be unheard of now. They'd have to hold a bloody competition." And he chuckled.

He took down her number and said goodbye. He seemed nice, but Tracy still worried he wouldn't call her back, so it was a pleasant surprise when he called the very next morning and invited her over to their Hammersmith home for coffee on Sunday.

Driving to their appointment, Tracy wondered if she'd been wrong in not telling her mum about the meeting. She hadn't because she wanted to see what these people were like before she put her through any more painful experiences.

The Bowleses lived on a tree-lined street, in a largish Victorian terraced house close to the River Thames. She struggled to find parking but eventually squeezed her small car into a spot between an A-Class Jag and a brand-new Audi. It was clearly a very 'nice' area. Number 14's small front garden was immaculate, filled with lime-green acers and a spectacular camellia in a huge, grey pot. Tracy walked the short path covered with Victorian ceramic tiles to the front door, which also looked original with its stained-glass panels featuring an artfully stylised tulip design. It was painted a sleekly traditional British racing green with a huge, heavy brass doorknob, which she raised and dropped three times, each time making a very satisfactory 'thunk'.

After a longish while, Mr Bowles opened the door. He was a tall, thin, grey-haired man, wearing a sloppy, navy-blue woollen V-neck jumper with a pale blue and white checked shirt collar peeping out of the jumper on one side – tucked in on the other. Less traditionally, he wore a pair of soft, faded jeans that were slightly too short for his long spindly legs. He had come to the door in his bare feet which she noticed were rather nice: tanned and not at all hairy, with neat, clean, toenails. His hair was off-white, plentiful, and rather flyaway; he reminded Tracy of the gentleman with the thistle-down hair from the book, Jonathan Strange and Mr Norrell. Unlike that gentleman, this gentleman looked kind, because he had very twinkly, warm brown eyes which creased in pleasure as he took her hand in both of his and pressed it warmly between them.

"You must be Tracy. How lovely to meet you, I must say you are the spitting image of your mother, I would have known you anywhere."

Tracy smiled and felt her neck and shoulders relax at the genuine welcome. It was funny, when she was a teenager, she *hated* being told she looked like her mum, just didn't seem right, but now she felt happy that she looked like her pretty mother.

"So they say! It's so nice of you to invite me."

"It's our pleasure, please come on in, my wife is dying to meet you."

The inside of the house was the opposite of the traditional I. They had taken down most of the interior walls and the downstairs was one huge room that transitioned from living room to kitchen-dining area to a huge glass-roofed conservatory. The views over the garden led down to the gleaming

Thames. It was the most exquisite room she had ever seen, filled with light and, despite being mainly white, incredibly warm and welcoming. Large, blue paintings lined one wall and there were several lush, dark green, human-sized ferns dotted around.

At the end of the room, looming over a kitchen island, was a black-haired woman in an extremely capacious turquoise nehru-style top, pouring coffee from a filter jug into three slender white mugs. She was tall like her husband, at least six feet, but more heavyset, her sharp, bobbed hairstyle displayed a distinctive white stripe running over her right eye. She was wearing black 'Andy Warhol' glasses which added to her bohemian look.

As Tracy got closer, she noticed that the turquoise blouse had silver and white embroidery at the sleeves and around the neck, cleverly depicting dolphins playing and jumping through waves. It reminded her of something she had seen before, and a picture flashed into her mind then disappeared before she could properly recall it. Under the tunic top the woman wore white cotton leggings (that were baggy at the knee) and on her large feet white Crocs with silver stars strewn randomly on them. She was quite impressive.

She looked up at Tracy and gasped out something that sounded like, "Is that you, Rosie?"

"No darling, it's not Rosie, it's her daughter *Tracy* come to see us," said Jonathan very slowly and clearly, then he leant down close to Tracy's ear and stage whispered, "Don't worry, she gets a little confused sometimes. I did tell her you were coming, and she got excited, but she's in the early stages of senile dementia – please be patient."

Tracy felt terrible, the poor lady – then looked up sharply, when she heard a loud snort, to see the woman smiling wryly at her husband and shaking her finger from side to side.

She gave him a slap on his non-existent bottom and said, "Bad boy! Tracy do not listen to him. Jonathan, don't be such a twit!"

After stage-frowning at him some more, she turned and beamed at Tracy.

"Ignore him, darling, that's the silly bugger's idea of a joke. Goodness, you do look very much like her."

Tracy tittered nervously. *What a pair of nutters!* Thank god it was a joke, she thought, the conversation was going to be tough enough already. These two were eccentric, but very funny and seemed nice.

"How do you drink your coffee, dear – do you have sugar, milk?"

Tracy, who normally took both, said no, she was feeling a bit overwhelmed and not thinking straight. She grabbed her coffee and followed them over to a round white table with high, ladder backed chairs close to wall-to-wall French doors that led onto the garden. The glossy surface reflected the weak autumn sun and was perfectly positioned to take advantage of the view down to the river.

She took a deep breath, looked at them both and suddenly felt much calmer. They were looking at her intently, waiting for her to say something. Despite the big woman's imposing presence, Tracy could see that she had kind eyes behind the scary glasses, and that gave her the confidence to speak.

"First of all, thanks very much for agreeing to see me."

"Nonsense, we are delighted to see you, we were hoping you might make an appearance one day."

Really? Tracy thought, surprised they even knew she existed and looked at the woman quizzically.

"Yes. I was very fond of your mother you know, and I hoped she would see sense and get back in touch. Silly bloody moo. It's entirely her fault we don't see each other," Hyacinth said breaking the ice.

"Yes, I sort of gathered that."

"Now my dear, what did you want to talk to me about?"

Tracy briefly explained.

"Why isn't she here too?"

"She doesn't want to find him. She seems to want to forget it ever happened. She was angry with herself she let it out."

Hyacinth nodded and muttered something under her breath, that sounded distinctly like "always was a bloody coward".

The older woman looked at her intently. "How well do you know your mother, Tracy? Has she told you much about her early life?"

Tracy said wryly, "Well, up until about nine months ago I would have said I knew everything about her, but now, I wonder if I know her at all. I know she had me in her thirties, that her and Dad didn't meet until she was twenty-nine and she'd given up on meeting anyone. But he came along and was the love of her life. He was older than her by quite a bit and she was older than my friends' mums. I knew she must have had a life before Dad and me, but I suppose I was too self-absorbed to ask much about it. I was the only one and a bit spoilt, to be honest, and it took this happening for me to realise I knew very little about her. Like the fact you called her Rosie, Dad always called her Rosemary, you see …" she trailed off.

Hyacinth stepped in, seemingly keen to reminisce. "Well, I met Rosie at Liberty's Department Store. We started working there on the same day. I was there to learn about buying merchandise – handbags, scarfs, hats, that sort of thing and Rosie was a secretary for the head of that department. I didn't really need to work to be honest, Mummy and Daddy weren't keen, my type of 'gal' didn't normally work, but I wanted to do something, and so they had a word with one of their friends, and got me the job. Your mother needed to work, because her dad had died when she was young, and she had become the main breadwinner in the family. I was terribly impressed by that.

"Rosie graduated top of her class from secretarial school, was as bright as a button and had her boss and I wrapped around her little finger within days. I thought she was the most adorable thing, so chirpy, with a unique sense of style and although she didn't have money to burn, she was always immaculately put together. And she had this great sense of humour, God she could make me laugh! Anyway, we soon became best friends – we would meet up out of work and go to the Hammersmith Palais most weekends to dance and flirt – until I met beloved, of course."

Hyacinth gestured towards Jonathan.

"Then we would go out as a foursome with whoever had asked her out that week. All Jonathan's friends wanted to go steady with her, but she just was not interested in settling down. Eventually, Jonathan and I got married and he got the airport commission and we moved to the Caribbean, and then, a few months later, she came out to see us. We had invited her – I was a little lonely for female company, and I'd sent a bit of money along for the ticket – and although I wanted her to, I hadn't really expected her to come. You cannot imagine what a long and difficult journey that was for a young woman on her own to make in those days. Especially someone who had never travelled further than Whitstable before! She was always a spunky one, but we were terribly impressed when she said she was coming.

"When Rosie got to the island, she caused a bit of a stir. We went down to the dock to meet her and she jumped off this smelly old cargo boat they used as a passenger ferry in those days, in a primrose yellow sundress, looking fresh as a daisy and I swear every man at the seaport fell in love with her on the spot. News travels fast on that island and within hours we had people turning up to say hello to our guest."

Hyacinth was a compelling storyteller; her beautifully modulated voice reminded Tracy of Judy Dench playing Q. As she spoke, she would gesticulate with long, red-tipped fingers covered with chunky silver and turquoise rings, to add emphasis.

"We had the most wonderful time, Rosie was such fun to be around. We explored the island, had picnics and parties, sometimes we would go off for the day on a fishing boat to Prickly Pear or some deserted beach you couldn't get to by road. In those days, there were hardly any hotels or restaurants, so we had to make our own entertainment and we were all in and out of each other's houses. You could count the number of white people on two hands, so most of our friends were locals, and we were welcomed into the community."

She smiled widely, "Rosie had the most marvellous time you know. She was the belle of the ball with her blonde curls, wearing pretty dresses that showed off her tiny waist. Everyone noticed her and half the island was in love with her. It seemed like a different chap was turning up at the house every week trying to take her 'for a walk on the beach'. Bobby was the most persistent of all her beaux. He was very good looking and had the gift of the gab. She liked flirting with him but wasn't in love with him. She *thought* that she was in love with someone else, an older, professional man called Remington. Super chap, an important figure in local politics, a big fish. Remington had been most helpful to us when we arrived, and we became close friends. Rosie met him at one of our house parties, there was an immediate connection between them, they talked all evening – I think it was love at first sight don't you, Jonny?"

Tracy dragged her eyes away from Hyacinth and her spellbinding story to look at her husband. He nodded his head in agreement.

"… but nothing untoward ever happened. They just gravitated together. Remington was enchanted by her and she by him. He was charming and charismatic and, like many West Indians, a bit of a flirt, but he was a good Christian man. He was married, with children, and he made that abundantly clear to her. Sometimes, at parties, they would dance together – but that was as close as they got. I would look at her face and could read it like a book – I had never seen her look at anyone that way before. And then something happened, I was never sure what, I think that maybe she pushed Remington for more than he could give, or maybe his wife got wind of their friendship – and he started to avoid her, didn't come to the house anymore.

"Well, Rosie was devastated and … well, she went a bit wild for the last few days of her trip. Bobby, like I said earlier, had been terribly persistent and clearly adored your mum, so she gave in and went out with him. I believe it was to distract herself and maybe make Remington jealous. Bobby was not a bad person, and he was terribly good-looking, just a bit wild and unreliable. Everyone knew he was what they call a 'rummer' there. He drank too much and there was talk that he had women up and down the islands – a typical young buck really."

Hyacinth tightened her lips and shook her head sadly. Tracy was flabbergasted, struggling to process the story and unable to relate the woman in H's story to the woman who had raised her. *Mum flirting with a married man and playing one man off against another? It was inconceivable.*

The shock must have shown on her face because Jonathan gave his wife a tap on the arm and a hard stare. Hyacinth backtracked a bit.

"I probably shouldn't have but I encouraged her to go out with Bobby on her own and have some fun, who was judging? I certainly wasn't. I think all the attention and the pure excitement went to her head. It was the most extraordinary and exciting time in her life. Even in the sixties, young women were still supposed to act a certain way and their choices were extremely limited.

It was her first holiday and she was experiencing freedom for the first time in her life – it was heady stuff. Rosie had a tough time of it growing up – she'd lost her dad and she'd been brought up in the shadow of the war with its rationing and curfews. Everyone had to 'make do' because there was no money, or anything nice to buy in the shops, and – apart from the occasional dance – there was nowhere exciting to go. Of course, this holiday experience all went to her head. I wanted her to have a wonderful time, I wanted her to forget about Remington – clearly, no good could come of that. She was being a little racy, but who would guess she'd do anything as stupid as getting pregnant! – bloody little idiot." Hyacinth shook her head sadly and went quiet.

Tracy was on the edge of her seat. She needed to know more.

"The baby was Bobby's?"

"Yes. Definitely. She went back to England and a few months later wrote to me and said she was pregnant and that Bobby was the father and she didn't know what to do."

Hyacinth sighed and shook her head sadly. "I felt so responsible. I didn't think she would have been so foolish as to have slept with him. Jonathan and I tracked him down – he'd left the island by then and was working on an airport project in Turks. We found out that with a little financial incentive – which we were happy to supply – Bobby could have been persuaded to marry Rosie. But Rosie said no. She didn't want to marry him. She didn't love him. She was sensible enough to realise that it wouldn't work out with Bobby. There would have been some challenges with a mixed marriage in those days – even if they *had* been madly in love with each other.

"Sadly, she also felt there was also no way she could live in the UK as an unmarried mother. It was just too hard back in the day. We sent a ticket for her to come out and stay with us before the baby started showing, by this time we had moved to Trinidad. She was with us until the baby was born. She decided adoption would be the best choice and, to be honest, she made a good job of looking like she was OK about it. I have to say, your mother certainly pulled the wool over our eyes. She put on this tough act, telling me that after the baby was born, she didn't want to know anything about where it went – who adopted it – nothing at all!"

"I can imagine that. Sounds just like her." Tracy empathised. She'd learnt that her mum was very good at pulling the wool over everyone's eyes where it came to her feelings. What a burden Rosemary had shouldered all this time. "Are you OK Mrs Bowles? Do you need to take a break?" Hyacinth shook her head no and took a long gulp of her water. She looked tired and sad but seemed determined to press on with the story.

"What she didn't know was that when we talked to Bobby he said even if they didn't get married, he wanted the baby to come to his family. So we quietly arranged for one of his aunts to come and get the baby. We gave them some cash – and that was that. Neither Jonathan nor I could bear to know any more details, and we did feel a bit guilty about not taking the baby ourselves, but we were young and trying to make a go of our lives together, there wasn't room for someone else's baby. I convinced myself the child would be OK with his father's family and that we should stay out of it.

"It was an awful situation. After the baby, Rosie changed, she got all brittle and hard, acting like it had never happened. She only stayed with us for a few days before she flew back to the UK. I tried to stay in touch, I wrote to her for ages, but since I never got any response I just stopped trying. To be honest, the whole thing had upset us so much, we decided to just forget about Rosie and move on."

Jonathan, who had kept quiet during the story telling, was watching his wife with tender concern. He grabbed her hands and gave them a loving squeeze then moved closer to whisper something in her ear, which Tracy couldn't hear but assumed were words of comfort. He softly kissed her on the cheek before reclining back in his chair with an unreadable expression on his face. Hyacinth got up abruptly, cleared her throat, made her excuses to Tracy and left the room, moving stiffly and looking much older than she had earlier. Tracy had spotted the tell-tale gleam of tears as she walked past.

Tracy sat, stunned, for what seemed like ages but was, in reality, only a few moments. She didn't know what to say to either of them, so was grateful when Jonathan cleared the coffee cups away and moved over to the sink and started washing up quietly. She gazed at, without seeing, the garden and the river beyond. It was so terribly sad. Tracy couldn't imagine what her mum,

Rosie (!), had gone through, and once again, chastised herself about how little she really knew her.

It was hard to imagine her mother, travelling the oceans in a cargo boat, captivating an island with her charm and beauty, falling in love with the island's JFK, then sleeping with a young stud to get back at him. It was fantastical. How could it be that her lovely, but very sensible mum, with her comfortable shoes and Mark's and Spencer's blouses, her mum who loved to have the same routine, week in week out, and who panicked if Tracy offered to take her anywhere out of the norm, could have experienced this secret life? This was the woman who could never be persuaded to go on holiday anymore, and who she would have sworn had only ever slept with her dad.

Tracy looked up to see her hosts had returned to their seats and seemed to have recovered their composure. They were staring at her, obviously concerned about the effect the tale had had on her. She smiled weakly to reassure them it was OK. She was in shock, but she was OK, and, if they were up to it, she needed more information from them.

"Hyacinth and Jonathan, thank you, I can't tell you how much it means that you have told me all this. It is so good to know. But I need to know more, I know it's a lot to ask and it must be painful for you, but I can't give up without finding out more about him, my brother, so if you could bear to, I was hoping you could tell me the name of the hospital and maybe the date when the adoption happened to see if I can track the baby down?"

The couple looked at each other and smiled, which was not the reaction Tracy was expecting.

Then Hyacinth burst out excitedly, "We can do much, much better than that, my dear. We can tell you where 'the baby' is. In fact, we can even give you his email address if you want it!" and looked a little smug.

"What the Fuck! Sorry, don't mean to swear ... but ..." You could have knocked Tracy down with a feather. *Email address? These two were certifiably bonkers.*

The Bowleses took her swearing in their stride.

"Yes, he lives on the island," Jonathan chimed in, eyes twinkling, clearly enjoying revealing this bit of news. "In fact you may even have met him when you were there – he has a business – a bar."

"What's his name?" *What the bloody hell*, she thought, it couldn't be CB could it? What would that make Diver to her? No! – he's too young.

Hyacinth continued with a chuckle, "His real name is Charles, Charles Claxton, but he has a nickname, like everyone else there it seems – Chix, and he goes by that. He owns the beach bar called D'wine. I expect you went? Everybody does at some stage or another."

What a relief! Tracy shook her head numbly. *Chix!* She could not believe it. Everyone went to D'wine except her. Everyone knew Chix except her. Just imagine. She'd meant to go –was supposed to go – and if she *had* gone, she would already have met her brother.

"So how do you know it's him? Did you track him down? How did you find him?" Tracy pleaded.

"We didn't, he found us, actually. Johnny darling, do you mind filling Tracy in? I'm exhausted from all this talking. I think I'll open a bottle of wine to soothe our throats." And she promptly got up from the table and walked swiftly to the wine fridge, where she pulled out a few different bottles, before finding something to her satisfaction.

Jonathan beamed, delighted to take over the tale; Tracy imagined he didn't often get a word in when his wife was in full flow.

"Well, I will have to give you a bit of background first. Our association with the island didn't stop when the airport was completed. By that time, we had fallen in love with the place, made lots of friends, and so we decided to buy some land there. We didn't do anything with it for a while – I worked around the Caribbean for a few years – in Trinidad and a little bit in St Martin and St Barth's, then finally came back to the UK to work on a big commission. But it was winter when we came back home, and we hated it! Long story short – we decided to get on with building a house on our land in Zephyr, so we could escape to the sun whenever we wanted. We built a house – which we still have – and then a few years later got involved in a hotel project there, Paradise Point?"

He looked at Tracy. She nodded her head, yes – she knew it. She and Diver had popped in during their boat trip round the island.

As Jonathan carried on with his story, Tracy realised why Hyacinth's turquoise top had rung such a loud bell. It was part of a line of designer island clothing that was sold in the posh hotel's overpriced gift shop. She had considered buying one for her mum but thought it would be too colourful for her. Little did she know. And now looking around the bright, airy reception rooms she realised that what she thought were big, blue, paintings lining the walls, were photographs. Close-ups of crystal clear, sparkling turquoise sea and powdery white sands, adorned with tiny, perfectly patterned shells and sculptural pieces of pink and white coral. No wonder she loved the room. He watched her looking at the artworks with dawning recognition.

"As you can probably tell, we still love the place. In fact, we live there for about five or six months every year and will be heading back over soon – we normally go just as the weather gets unbearable here."

He looked up and smiled at his approaching wife.

"Best of both worlds, eh darling?"

Hyacinth nodded enthusiastically as she put a silver tray in front of them, laden with wine, tall navy-blue wine glasses and some nibbles in shell shaped bowls.

"Oh, you lucky things – I envy you. I really loved it there." She pointed at the walls. "I've just realised that those photos are of the sea there. Unmistakable once you realise. It was the most amazing colour. Endless turquoise."

"Indeed, well spotted." Jonathan nodded approvingly at her.

Hyacinth had poured each of them a glass of rosé, and laid out some olives stuffed with almonds, alongside a bowl of crispy, cheesy biscuits. They sipped and nibbled for a while in comfortable silence before Tracy had to ask.

"Would you mind explaining your connection to Chix?"

"Yes, I need to get to that. Well, we knew Chix for ages before we worked out who he was. He grew up on another island, but he came to Zephyr in the early eighties looking for work. He joined our construction crew, the original team, in fact, that built Paradise Point. By the time the hotel opened, he had impressed us all and he got taken on as a water sports assistant. He was popular with the guests, hardworking and ended up overseeing the whole department. Then, when he got the money together, he decided to open the bar and then a few years later his own water sports centre."

"When he first arrived on the island, he'd asked around to see if he had any other family here. I think a family member had told him a little bit about his background – that he was half white – so he made some enquiries but drew a blank, probably asking the wrong people to start with.

"We weren't around much in those early days either because we were basically dealing with the money side of things and he was just a young labourer sweating over the soil, so he wouldn't probably have the nerve or even thought to approach us. He asked the other builders in the community about his father, though, and found an old drinking partner of Bobby's. He was closed-mouthed, but eventually told him, probably after a bottle of rum was procured, that Bobby had only been on the island for a few months and he didn't think he had a local girlfriend – probably because he'd been more interested in drinking himself silly.

"The man said he did not know anything about a white girlfriend either, so Bobby had obviously kept his crush on your mother a secret. I think Chix would have left it at that, because he wasn't really that interested in a mother that had clearly abandoned him and he'd found out he had no other family here. But a few years later, his business partners, a very nice American couple who'd met him as a young man working at the hotel and have a villa on the island, encouraged him to try again to find out something about his mother. Anyway, another long story short, he went back to the old drinking pal, this time he found out that his dad was working with me around the time he was born. Chix came and spoke to me and asked if I knew what had happened and – after Hyacinth and I discussed it – we told him about your mother."

"And …"

Jonathan paused, looked briefly at his wife for support before continuing softly, "And, then he asked me if we were still in contact with her, and if she'd ever tried to find him. And we had to tell him, that no, we had not kept in contact and we didn't know where she was. We were both worried, but he took it well, and I think he was almost relieved. He said he would make some enquiries in the UK, we even talked about him coming to stay with us here for a bit to try to find her, but it all ran out of steam. And then I think he decided to just leave it be – let sleeping dogs lie, I suppose. He knew who he was, what he had achieved, and that he had been successful in his own right, and my guess is that he decided that if his own mother didn't want to be in touch, he wasn't going to chase her down. Hyacinth thinks he didn't want to be rejected if he reached out. I think he's just being pragmatic."

Tracy nodded. *What a ridiculous coincidence – who would believe it?* She had spent all those weeks worrying and fretting. She had gone off on a stupid 'quest' to find her long-lost brother, only to find out she'd literally walked past him one afternoon, and not had a clue who he was. She'd wasted all that time and money going to the island, and instead, if her mum had played ball earlier, she could have made a couple of phone calls, and solved the mystery in a few hours. It was too much to take in. Tracy suddenly felt a bit faint. She was overwhelmed. it was far too much to process.

Jonathan and Hyacinth looked at each other in concern. Their guest had gone awfully pale and was staring blankly at her empty wine glass.

"Are you alright, dear? Can I get you something? Would you like a glass of water? Or would you prefer something stronger than the wine."

"No thanks, I don't drink much, so that would probably finish me off," she joked, half-heartedly. "To be honest, I think I'm a bit shell shocked."

"I'm sure. Look why don't you sit quietly and we won't talk to you for a minute, you need time to digest all this, and by the way, there's no need to rush off, we'd love it if you could stay for lunch, wouldn't we Jonathan?"

He nodded his head vigorously in agreement.

"And then when you're feeling a bit brighter, we can have a chat about what to do next."

Tracy was happy to comply and grateful that she didn't have to drive for a bit. As the couple busied around the kitchen, banging pots and plates, opening doors, and chopping things up, she looked vacantly at her own reflection in the glass doors, lost in her own damning thoughts.

How could I have been so stupid? And how could I have been so wrong about my little mum? ... Rosie Posie, pudding and pie kissed the boys and made them cry ... who would have thought it ... my mum, falling for a married man, having a rebound boyfriend … well, they say never judge a book by its cover … and my poor old dad. He did not have a clue. He was married to a vastly different person to the girl Hyacinth described. And then to find out that the famous Chix, is my half brother! For fuck's sake, he's my friend on Facebook. Well, if he's not I definitely 'liked' the D'wine page and I've seen loads of photos of him … not sure if we look alike but I can tell he's really cute … *arrghhh* – what if I'd gone to his bar and flirted with him and something had happened … yuck …

She shuddered at what could have been and distracted herself from that horrible train of thought by standing up abruptly and asking where the loo was.

Two hours and two bottles of rosé later, (which Tracy had hardly touched because she was driving) the threesome had examined the situation from top to bottom and also spent a pleasurable time talking about the island and what a special place it was. H (as she preferred to be known) – "too many syllables in Hyacinth, darling" – had gone in search of old photo albums. The two remaining sipped coffee and chatted.

"What I cannot get over, Jonathan, is the coincidence. How you two could have known Chix for so long, independent to your relationship with my mother, and he ends up being her son? How come, even though I have only been to the island once, I'd heard of him, and he ends up being the one I'm looking for? That does not happen in real life, surely? That only happens in the movies." Tracy made some air quotation marks to emphasise her point. Jonathan smiled knowingly.

"It seems far-fetched, but it's the sort of bizarre thing that happens in the Caribbean. It's my experience that in the islands, the whole 'six degrees of separation' concept averages out at about two or three degrees. Especially on small islands like Zephyr, where everyone knows everyone. For example, only a few thousand people live there all year round, but there are thousands more out there in the diaspora, talking about 'home'. And most importantly, on top of that, there are hundreds of thousands of tourists coming to visit every year. And because it's a popular holiday destination, a special place where visitors have a wonderful time and create abiding memories of the charming people they met there – they hold it close to their heart. They have photos taken with their favourite waiter or waitress, or barman or beach butler, as if they were film stars or pop idols, and they keep in touch with them and look forward to seeing them every time they return."

"And a person like Chix, working with tourists, being interviewed by all the travel journalists that come and stay because he runs the best beach bar on the island, I would estimate, conservatively, that he will meet hundreds of thousands of people over his career, many of whom think he is the best thing ever, and who will remember his name and count him as a friend. As I said – he's a local celebrity. It's a similar sort of thing with the expats like us. Although lots of people dream about it, only a small percentage fall in love with the lifestyle to the extent where they move to somewhere like the Caribbean to live and work full time. That circle is pretty small, as is, for example, individual professions like architecture or clothing design. So over on Zephyr people like H and me are relatively well known in our communities as well – better known than you ever would be in a large community like London. We are biggish fish in a smallish pond," he said self-deprecatingly.

Then Jonathan turned and looked at Tracy, his face gentle with concern.

"So how are you feeling about all this now? It's rather a lot for you to take in."

She nodded and explained what she was feeling – totally at ease, because she felt she could say anything to this lovely man, and not sound stupid, even though they had only just met.

"It *is* a lot to take in, but it's fascinating. I'm feeling OK about it now, really. I'm so glad I met you two, and even as it turns out I didn't need to go to the island at all to find my brother, I'm still glad I went there. And now there is an even better reason for me to go back. And maybe even spend lots of time there. I feel like my visit earlier in the year started a process. The process of re-evaluating my life, and what I want out of it, and I know now, that although my life is good, it could be better, and I think it would be better there."

Jonathan nodded thoughtfully. He was just about to respond when H made a big entrance, interrupting them with a shout of "look what I found" and triumphantly waving a black album with a gold tassel. It was helpfully labelled 'Photographs'. They huddled up and flicked through stiff pages, crammed with small black and white pictures that showed Jonathan and H's life on the island in the sixties. There were pictures of the two of them standing outside a small West Indian cottage, one of Jonathan and a whole bunch of construction workers standing around a big hole (not a hard hat to be seen) and, most thrillingly for Tracy, a picture of a small, ugly ferry boat with a young woman with stiff, blonde curls leaning over the side of the boat and waving at the camera – her mum looking remarkably like a young Marilyn Monroe!

There weren't any pictures of Bobby but there were lots of wonderful shots of Rosie: one in a fabulous high waisted bikini that made her look like a movie star, and one of the two friends that depicted her mum with H looking very stylish in a tight, stripy Breton style top with short white shorts and a long glossy black ponytail. Rosie was a good eight inches shorter, in a white, broderie anglaise sun dress that showed off her tiny waist. Hyacinth had one arm draped over Rosie's shoulders and they were both smiling happily into the camera.

"Oh look, I love that photo," said H wistfully.

"You look smashing, old girl," said Jonathan, "look at those legs," and he reached over and gave her thigh a squeeze. Tracy had an idea.

"H, Jonathan, could I borrow this album? I promise to bring it back … I'd like to show it to Mum … Rosie … because another tragic thing about this whole tragic situation is that she gave up her friendship with you two when she gave up that baby. And I think in doing that she gave up a bit of herself too, the side I have not had a chance to experience and that I really want to meet. Maybe this will remind her."

CHAPTER 29
Charlotte

Charlie's highly anticipated weekend in Bristol was turning out to be the best time she'd had *forever*! Ali was on top, top form – excited about her new job and thrilled to bits with the glamorous flat her company had rented for her. It was a huge, luxuriously appointed penthouse, with a fabulous open-plan kitchen-dining-living area. It sat on the top of a stunning old, architect-renovated building in one of Bristol's newly trendy areas. There were panoramic views of the city and the Clifton Suspension Bridge from the floor-to-ceiling windows, and on the doorstep a range of funky bars, interesting restaurants and quaint shops. Her friend, as she kept saying, 'had arrived'.

As it was a company flat, Ali had been advised that she would have to share the place with another lawyer, a thirty-something year old guy who was visiting from the States, for a few months. But as the flat had three en suite bedrooms and he was "a fucking god" she was quite happy to do so.

"He is soooooo good looking. I really don't mind bumping into him as he makes his morning coffee in his underpants. In fact, I might make underpant-wearing coffee preparation part of the home-sharer's agreement contract," she postulated. Ali was more than a little drunk already as they'd had a couple of rounds of two-for-one margaritas at happy hour, then moved on to toasting Ali's new job with passion fruit tequila shots, at the lively Tex Mex restaurant they'd chosen for their celebratory dinner.

Charlie had to concur. She'd made a cup of tea for Dwayne that afternoon and they'd had a nice little chat. The American lawyer was drop-dead gorgeous, a heavier set Leonardo de Caprio type, as well as being friendly and nice.

"I may have to fight you for him, Ali," she warned her friend.

"S'OK sweetie, you can have him. I am not allowed to fraternise with team members. Anyway, I think you're more his type, he definitely fancies you. And it is about time you … emm, what's the term for it … got back in the saddle. And his saddle looks mighty fine, I'm sure you would get a good ride – ha!" and cracked up at her own hilariousness.

Charlie smiled proudly, "Well, I don't mean to boast, but he did slip me his contact details." She waved her phone at her friend to underline her point, Dwayne's WhatsApp profile plain to see.

"You sneaky bitch! When were you going to tell me? Well, good, I hope you use it." Ali wagged her finger at Charlie in a schoolmarm way.

Charlotte smiled. She already had. She had messaged him to say hi and he'd already responded.

Now she was content that Charlie's love life was sorted out (at least temporarily), Ali's agile mind moved on to the next big thing: finding a job for her friend. Looking a lot more sober than she was, she asked what her plans were.

Charlie's shoulders slumped. *What a downer, I was having so much fun – Ali should know I hate being asked that question.*

"Oh Ali, I don't know," she whined. "You know I never know what I should do." She gave her friend a pathetic shrug. "I've always been particularly useless about a career – no direction at all. I think that's what got me into trouble, why I grabbed hold of Graham so hard. I didn't have to think what to do. I knew he would support me."

"Stop whining. Look, I know you are not particularly career-minded, but you cannot expect someone just to look after you all your life. You must do *something*. I know you are going to get money from Graham but it won't be that much, I'm sure. And anyway, you are far too young and have too much to offer to be a lady of leisure."

Charlie looked at her friend in despair. *Nightmare!* Her mind was blank. She shrugged her shoulders and looked pathetic again.

"I don't *know*. I never know what I want to do!"

Ali sighed, "OK let us break this down. You're not stupid, right?"

Charlie responded in a silly robot voice "No-I-am-not-stupid."

"You can read and write?"

Robot voice again, "Yes-I-can-read-and-write-you-cheeky-minx."

"You know how to type and use one of those things ... what are they called?" Ali pretended to wrack her brains, "Oh yes – a computer?"

Charlotte laughed and stuck her finger up, "Fuck you, Ali."

"OK seriously, I've got it. How about becoming a high-class call girl? You're not bad looking, some men might fancy you. We could rescue your old clothes from Graham's flat and I could be your madam. Bristol's booming, I'm sure you could do well here. What do you think?"

And with a dopey smile on her face, Ali put her head to one side and looked at Charlie expectantly.

"Will you stop it?" Charlie was laughing so hard she thought she might wet herself.

"All right. OK. Really, serious now. Let us go back to basics. What do you like to do? In an ideal world, describe your day. Exactly what you would like to do from getting up in the morning to going to bed. It's a really good exercise."

Charlie thought for a minute and then recited in a singsong, little girl voice, "In an ideal world I would get up in the morning and walk to work or cycle or, if I had to drive, drive for maybe ten minutes max. I'd like to start work early so I could finish early and be able to go for a nice walk or play tennis or do something outdoors in the evening ..."

Getting into the swing of it, her tone changed and the words came out fast, furious and increasingly decisively.

"I want to wear my jeans into work and not have to put on an uncomfortable suit or high heels. I should spend my day helping nice, kind, people – not arrogant city slickers. I don't mind making tea and coffee for my boss if *I* can stop for a cup of tea *too*. I'd like to work with animals and definitely be able to go outside for at least part of the day. What else ... oh, I'd like to work for a charity actually, because at least I would feel like I was doing something useful ..."

She trailed off because Ali was howling with laughter, literally rolling around and holding her sides, and at the same time muttering, "She's got it, by George she's got it!"

What on earth was her crazy friend doing? She was causing a scene – all the rest of the drunk people were looking!

"What are you laughing about, lunatic girl?"

Ali gasped through her laughter, "You know the job you're describing, don't you?"

"No. What job? Tell me. Don't be so mental! Stop laughing, I can hardly understand you."

"You're describing ... working at the vet's."

She was laughing so hard she could hardly gasp the next words out.

"Working ... for ... my ... brother."

Charlotte gawped at her. *Bloody Hell, she's right.* When Penny described the job that Sandy despised, she'd thought it sounded like great fun (apart from the fact that she could NEVER EVER work with Simon of course) – especially the bit about the dear little Shetland ponies and helping with the kennels.

"Bloody hell, you're right." She felt excited, "I *could* get excited about a job like that!"

And then reality bit. It was hopeless, it could never happen. They hated each other, didn't they?

"But wouldn't we kill each other, Simon and I?"

"Probably, but you would love everyone else in the office, and they'd love you. It will be a struggle. You'll have to learn how to be in the same room with each other without wanting to hit him over the head with a saddle or something. But it's got to be worth it ... because believe me, it's the perfect job for you." She did a fist pump of victory. "Get on! I'm a bloody genius."

"Let me think about it a bit more," pleaded Charlotte.

In her drunken imagination, she pictured herself arriving at the practice wearing a smart red Puffa jacket and shiny riding boots, carrying a glorious homemade Victoria sandwich, and getting a round of delighted applause from all the old ladies. Then she imagined graciously cutting and serving a slice of said cake to Simon, who would be so impressed by her ladylike manner and light touch with a sponge that he would have no choice but to behave charmingly to her. She could also imagine pouring the accompanying cup of tea over his head as he made some snarky remark about putting the milk in last.

Charlie shook her negative thoughts away. *I would rise above it. I am better than him. And I would be perfect for the job, so I should not let a silly little thing like our shared past come between me and my dream career.* "OK, let's call him tomorrow," she croaked

But, determined to act, confident (as always) that she was right, Ali had already got out her phone and dialled Simon's number. She was trying to tell him their plan but was struggling to make any sense. Shaking her head in frustration, she thrust the phone into Charlie's hand, hissing, "I can't make him understand. You talk to him."

Charlotte gulped. *It was now or never – Ali was right, she had to do this. Margaritas gave you wings.*

"Simon, hi, it's Charlie ... Yes, I know it's Ali's phone but it's Charlie speaking ... Yes, she's fine. Yes, I'm fine ... No, nothing to panic about ... No, we are not that drunk ... Well, maybe a little but not too much. Two margaritas, half a bottle of wine, some passion fruit tequila thingies ... how many? Maybe two...or three ... No, she has not danced on the tables ... yet ... No, she has not snogged anyone ... Yes, we will be careful ... No need for a taxi, the flat's literally next door – don't panic!" She looked at Ali, shook her head impatiently as she held the phone at a distance and spoke pointedly.

"Your pain-in-the-arse brother is worried about us being drunk in big, bad Bristol."

Then bringing the phone back to her mouth, "Hey, Simon, listen. Much though we appreciate your concern, I didn't call you to tell you about our evening ... I would like to make you an offer. No, delete that, I got that wrong, I meant to say ... I have a suggestion for you ... I think I am what you want ... No that came out wrong too ... will you *stop* laughing ... No not like that, you twat. Listen, Ali had a great idea, she thinks, I should be ... your office manager ... I would like to do it and think I could just about bear you. What do you think? Could you bear being around me?"

She looked at Ali for encouragement and crossed her fingers. Ali crossed hers back in support and waved them at her.

Charlotte listened intently and seconds later a big grin split her face.

"You like the idea? You want me? Great, great! I'll call you next week to sort out the details. Yes, I will..." She looked at her friend and put her thumbs up. "He sends his love to you, Ali ... Yes. OK, goodnight, same to you ... Yes, we will be careful, and Simon, thanks. No really, thank you!"

CHAPTER 30
Tracy

In the days following her visit to the Bowleses, Tracy did some research on Chix. According to everything she read online, he was respectable, successful and, as far as she could see, an all-round nice guy – albeit exceedingly popular with the ladies. That is, if the Trip Advisor reports were anything to go by, which were filed almost entirely by women.

She looked up his water sports company "Wet 'n' Wild" and got his personal email, chix@wetnwildfun.com. She composed a long email, explaining who she was, and telling him a little about how she'd found out about him. But when she went to press send, she could not do it. She needed to tell her mum what she was doing first.

The next day was a Sunday, and she went, as usual, to her mum's house for their regular roast dinner, popping the photo album into her shoulder bag before she left. When she got there, she discovered that Reggie had been invited too, so she could not say anything just yet. They enjoyed delicious roast beef with yummy gravy, and then snoozed in the lounge, as they digested it. Reggie eventually went home, and Tracy asked her mum if she wanted a cup of tea. When she said that would be lovely, she told her to sit at the table, and have a look at something she'd brought to show her. Tracy pulled the photo album out of her bag, placed it in front of her mum then turned away, busying herself with making the tea.

She could hear the stiff pages of the album being turned over, and the sound of the tissue paper that protected the first page crackling as it was gently pushed aside. She could hardly breathe she was listening so hard. Her mum drew in a sharp breath as she started looking at the photos, and then carried on turning the pages – but said nothing. Tracy had her back to her, looking over the sink and out at the garden, listening intently because she could not bear to look. The turning-page noises had stopped: she must have reached the end of the album. Then she heard the saddest sound she could imagine, her mum crying very, very quietly. She turned round and wrapped her arms round her narrow shoulders and nestled her head against hers, cheek to cheek as she spoke.

"Mum, Mum I'm sorry, please don't cry. I didn't want to upset you. I just wanted you to see it. I went to see the Bowleses and they were so nice to me. I loved them. I just wanted you to … I'm sorry I didn't mean to bring up bad memories and make you cry."

Rosie peeled her daughter's arms off her and patted the chair next to her, indicating she should sit down.

"Tracy love, it's alright, I'm glad you brought it. I am crying but I'm not sad. Honestly. I'm happy. Really, really, happy to see those photos. That was such a wonderful time, maybe it was the happiest time of my life. I feel so disloyal to you and your dad saying it, but oh, what fun it was. Look, I want to show you something."

And with that she opened up the album again, and Tracy leaned in close. They flipped through the album together and Rosemary showed her daughter all the things she'd done, and all the people she'd met. She stopped at one picture, and looked at it for a long, long time. In it, she was dancing with a tall man in a dark suit. She was quite a lot smaller, but she looked comfortable dancing with him, and her smile was radiant. The man's head was turned away, and slightly in the shadow, he was unrecognisable, but you could make out that he had a wide smile on his face. Tracy sighed: she had a feeling she knew who the man was.

"You look really pretty, Mum, and so happy. Who was that you were dancing with?"

"Oh, I don't remember his name. Just some man that H and Jonny knew. He was in politics or something."

Tracy didn't press, if her mum wanted to tell her about him one day, fine, if not, well that was her business. After they had looked at the album, Tracy felt brave enough to tell her mum the news about Chix. Rosemary cried some more and asked a lot of questions which Tracy answered as best she could. After a while Tracy asked her if she wanted to see a picture of him and she said that she did, so they got out Tracy's iPad and she showed her mum some pictures from the internet and a magazine article about the island that featured Chix's bar. Leaving her mum with the device, Tracy made up some excuse about a phone call and went to her room for a while, to give her some time to look on her own.

When she came back her mum had stopped crying and had a big glass of wine in front of her. She thanked Tracy, then told her to put the iPad away, she had seen enough for now.

Tracy told her that she was going to write to her brother, if Rosemary was OK with it. Her mum gave her blessing and said that she would like to write to him too, but she wasn't quite ready – she would write in her own good time.

PART FOUR
THE CARIBBEAN

NOVEMBER 2014

CHAPTER 31
Tracy

God it's good to feel the sun on my face and smell the ocean breeze again. And, sitting on the front of a James Bond-style speedboat with a rum punch in hand was an infinitely preferable way to arrive in Zephyr than by 'death plane'.

The small seaport was approaching rapidly and, before Tracy knew it, she had been helped off the boat and was pointing out her red shiny case to the porter. Clearing customs and retrieving her bag this time took but a blink of an eye – she had filled out her form in anticipation.

"Taxi for you, Miss?" a tall handsome young man asked with a twinkle in his eye as she walked into the arrivals area.

"No thank you, someone's coming for me."

She twinkled back as she scanned the sunny room for a familiar face. He wasn't there yet. There were lots of people coming and going. Even a herd of goats had wandered near, intent on entering the departure area. She found a cool spot with a good view of the road. Her ride was late but she didn't mind, she knew he wouldn't let her down and it was wonderful to soak in the atmosphere. Everything smelt, felt and looked just right. Unmistakably Caribbean. She was 'home' and she loved everyone and everything at the little port and couldn't, if she tried, wipe the delighted grin off her face.

A flatbed truck, with a tower of lobster pots in the back, roared down the road and pulled up sharply. Dr Clinton Derrick BA, MSc, rolled down his window and grinned at her.

"Hey, Miss T. Want to go diving?"

It was amazing how easy it had all been in the end. A week after she had met H and Jonny and found out about her brother, Diver emailed her out of the blue.

It was a long, carefully composed missive, detailing the research he had done and the people he'd talked to, in an attempt to find her brother for her. He was writing to tell her he had been successful: he'd found out who he was, Charles Claxton, aka Chix.

The email did not refer to their argument. Or to her note to him. He did not apologise for what he'd said to her either – but by doing this amazing and thoughtful thing for her, his actions did that job. She was incredibly moved that he had spent so much time and effort tracking down her brother and had presented Chix to her, like a knight presents a favour to his lady. She read the email greedily, stomach in knots with tears pouring down her face. Touched beyond measure, relieved that he had not forgotten her, delighted he'd forgiven her.

Immediately afterwards she called him on his Museum Man phone, the number burnt into her memory. He answered after three rings, and in his usual relaxed way seemed unsurprised to hear from her. There was no awkwardness. They talked and talked until her phone battery died.

Later that day they video-called, which was even better. Looking at his face, hearing his voice, laughing at his jokes was both familiar and exciting. From then on, they settled into daily, sometimes hourly, communication.

Tracy decided not to tell him yet that she had already known who her brother was before she received his email. She'd taken on board what Jazmin had said and learnt some valuable lessons about the male ego in the process, and she thought this was a little white lie that could only do good. Diver's timing was perfect as she hadn't yet reached out to Chix yet. One day she told him she had written to him and he confirmed he'd never received the note. A few days later he mentioned that he 'took a pass by Mango Bay' and talked to Desiree who swore that she had posted it and blamed the inadequacies of the Zephyr postal service. Tracy had a strong suspicion the note never got posted but was prepared to be generous and let sleeping dogs lie, seeing as it had all worked out in the end.

Of course, as soon as the floodgates of communication opened between them they were desperate to see each other, and so, with Cheryl and Jazmin and the rest of the girls' permission, she'd taken a three month sabbatical from the salon, and here she was, watching Diver put her red shiny case in his flatbed truck, before taking her in his arms, kissing her thoroughly and taking her home.

FEBRUARY 2015

CHAPTER 32
Charlotte

Charlotte sat on her favourite bar stool at D'wine and admired Chix 'working the crowd', marvelling how much had happened since the first time she came here.

Her honeymoon, the night she met Marvel and Chad was only seven months ago. Unlike Graham, the American girl had proved to be a true and faithful friend, and had kept in touch religiously, sharing news and demanding updates about Charlotte's life on a weekly basis, via email and occasional chats on Facetime. A few weeks ago she'd invited her to come and stay at the family house for a little bit of winter sun – Chad was too busy to leave work but Marvel was in need of a break from the cold NYC winter. Marvel needed some sun and wanted a buddy to hang out with – so she invited Charlie, strangely confident that her response to coming back to the place where her marriage had failed would be positive. Marvel's instincts were right, Charlie didn't blame the island at all. She was delighted to be invited and booked a ticket immediately.

She had the money. Quite a lot of money. She had a decent salary from her job at the vet's, as well as some savings in the bank, because Graham had recently transferred over the settlement from the divorce. And she had the time: she was allowed four weeks off a year, so she decided to treat herself to a couple of weeks in the sun away from Britain's horrid winter weather.

Peter and Helen had been rather concerned about her going back to the place where Graham and she had split up, but she explained that the island, although it had some bad memories, had almost taken on a mythical importance to her.

ENDLESS TURQUOISE

As she explained to Ali, "Where else in the world could you go on honeymoon, split with your husband and still have fond memories of the place?"

She'd found that when she thought about the island, it was mainly good things: how she'd met Marvel, how lovely Chix had been to her, how much she'd enjoyed sunning herself on the stunning beaches, how much she'd loved the music and the rum drinks, the friendly bars. Also, it was curious how much her life had changed since visiting there – for the better. It had been a catalyst in helping her find a new life and a new attitude that was so much more suited to her.

The fact that the British January weather was getting everyone down and Charlie was desperate for some sun and a little change of scenery meant that her friend's offer could not have come at a better time.

Marvel had left Charlie to go talk to some older people on the other side of the bar. Charlie was being lazy and didn't want to give up their prime positions. The couple were friends of Marvel's parents, and even if she had not known who they were, she would have noticed them – they made a striking pair. The woman was even taller than Charlie and had the most extraordinarily flamboyant style of dress, a bit like the British fashion designer Zandra Rhodes. Charlie thought she looked fabulous. Graham would have shuddered in distaste at the patterned caftan, layered ethnic jewellery, funky eyewear and flowing headscarf. The lady's husband was very tall too, extremely slender and rather elegant in a collared white linen shirt and khaki shorts. She thought they looked like a lovely couple, and nearly got off her stool to say hi, but once again thought she was just too comfy to move. They had come to meet a younger couple who looked vaguely familiar to her – a chubby white woman, who she guessed would be in her early forties with slightly mad blonde curls and an engaging smile, and a heavyset, short haired local guy, who looked a few years younger. The man had his arm draped heavily over his girlfriend's shoulder, his splayed hand lay flat on her chest and his middle finger was lazily stroking the top of her prominently displayed breasts. She seemed perfectly content with the public display of affection.

As the blonde woman turned to say something to her boyfriend, Charlie saw her in profile, her retrousse nose and rounded cheeks struck a chord and she remembered where she had seen her before. She was the woman she had enviously watched dancing, with more enthusiasm than rhythm, at Shell Cay. That was the day she had met Chix and Graham had ignored her. That day, Charlie assumed it was just a holiday romance. She remembered clearly how jealous she had felt of the chemistry sizzling between them. *I got it wrong, it must have been much more, because there they are, all these months later, looking incredibly happy to be in each other's company.*

Charlotte was not jealous watching them this time. She was happy for them. Back then, she now realised, there was so much wrong with her own life that it was tough to see people that were happy in theirs. Now, her life was every bit as happy as theirs appeared to be.

As usual, Ali knew what was right for Charlotte, better than she did. The job at Kimble veterinary practice, with its daily roundabout of animals and their humans was the best job she had *ever* had. She loved going to work, because she loved working with Eddie and Kitty and the two student vets.

She adored the little old ladies (well, most of them) who made up 'the posse', as Eddie had christened them. These volunteers for the Shetland pony rescue facility spent more time drinking tea (that she had made) and chatting, than actually volunteering. She'd been told she was great with the pet owners – sensitive to their stress over leaving their beloveds at the boarding kennel, reassuring them by being kind, and getting their names right. And working with Simon, well, Simon was Simon, but that was OK too. She had been nervous and uptight around him to start with but had soon mellowed. He still teased her constantly, and still drove her crazy, but he also made her laugh all the time. And he was good at his job – so thoughtful and kind with the owners and animals that Charlie had discovered a new level of respect for him. And, because she did such a good job with the office, the animals and the volunteers, swiftly becoming an important part of his team, Simon was treating her with a level of respect she'd never experienced from him before. He constantly told her she was doing a great job.

Simon and Charlotte were getting on well. More than well. They even spent a little time outside of work together, bumping into each other walking their dogs on two occasions. Last time he had suggested that they go for a drink at the pub after. And although she was tempted to say yes – she didn't. He had a girlfriend *and* she wasn't about to forget that. That was another one of the reasons she'd been so keen to come away on holiday. It was a good idea to put a little distance between them.

Marvel agreed wholeheartedly. She was delighted her friend had come to visit. They spent most days hanging out with 'the playboys' as they called Chix and Dwight. The youthful-looking – but in reality middle-aged men – relished squiring the two girls around, and they in turn had enjoyed a week of pure indulgence: hanging out on Dwight's boat, having long lunches and afternoon snoozes in the sun and partying into the early hours at D'wine. Charlotte had slipped back into her easy relationship with Chix and she no longer held Dwight's terrible taste against him – he'd become a good friend.

Charlotte had also learnt that Dwight was still in contact with Graham, who, amazingly, had optioned a piece of beach land and was trying to put financing together to build a development. It was strange how both had retained ties with the island, especially when she remembered how much her ex had hated it to start with.

There is something positively insidious about this place. It makes you do stuff you wouldn't normally do. Chad called it 'Fantasy Island' and she had to agree he had a point.

She looked back at Chix. He was leaning over slightly, chatting with the blonde woman on the other side of the bar. It was hard not to appreciate the sight of his pert bottom in artfully faded jeans or the well-groomed locks spilling over his broad shoulders. He was in great shape. *Yes*, she thought, *he really is an extremely attractive man.*

CHAPTER 33
Tracy

Tracy chatted with her half brother about this and that. Nothing important, just stuff. Diver's arm was heavy and hot on her shoulder. She could smell his deodorant and the faintest whiff of hot male armpit – and she loved it. It was a burden she would gladly bear all night.

His finger was gently rubbing the side of her boob and she almost hoped it would slip a little lower. She seemed to be horny all the time! If she was still a tourist, she might have whispered in his ear to do it, drop it lower, but as she was living here now she had to be a little more respectful of his position and local conventions.

As she chatted, she found herself keeping a watchful eye on an attractive, young white woman sitting on the other side of the bar. She came in with a pretty African American girl and their combined beauty lit up the bar as they arrived. Chix, who looked delighted to see them, made their drinks personally.

When the girl was left on her own, Chix excused himself from his conversation with Tracy and moved over, casually purposeful, to talk to her. Tracy's eyes followed her half sibling in fascination. She loved watching him. Trying to figure him out. She hadn't got there yet. He had been friendly, charming to her even. He was great company. But she wasn't close to him yet. Hopefully, that would come.

He definitely had a predatory side to his nature. She could tell she was watching a master at work as she observed him whisper something in the beautiful girl's ear. She smiled at whatever he had said, then lifted her hand up to tuck one of his dreads back on to his shoulder, it was a very natural, affectionate gesture. *If she is touching his hair, it is only a matter of time before she will be touching something else. Good for him, she is stunning.*

It was a special night. They (she loved saying that) had spent the night at Jonathan and H's spectacular villa, discussing the logistics of 'Rosie's' upcoming visit over a delicious dinner. It was great spending time with them – they were such generous, wise people.

I'm so happy Mum's coming to visit. Tracy had told Rosemary that she was welcome to stay with her and Diver but had suggested that H's house would be much more comfortable. Villa Limnisa was on the beach and had air conditioning and a luxurious infinity swimming pool. Diver's house was sweet – the perfect love nest – but was not in the same league. And she really wanted H and Mum to bond again.

Looking back over, she racked her brains, trying to remember where she'd seen Chix's girl before. At that moment, the DJ started playing a popular zouk song and she saw her half brother step out from behind the bar and ask her to dance. The girl accepted and followed him onto the dance floor where they moved gracefully together. Tracy knew the song, it was very romantic with a sexy, slow rhythm: a song for lovers if ever there was one. She swivelled on her stool slightly, so she could watch her new brother and his partner dance. The girl was close to his height, maybe even taller, but that didn't seem to matter – they fit together perfectly. She nudged Diver to have a look. He checked them out and whistled.

"That skinny white girl got moves," he said, and they laughed.

"I recognise her from somewhere. Do you know her?"

"Yes," he grinned, "you've seen her dancing with your brother before – only you didn't know he was your brother then."

"Really? Where?"

"Shell Cay, remember? … there was a long table by the dance floor, she was at the end. You talked about how beautiful she was, and I said I couldn't say because I only had eyes for you, and then I kissed you, and then you kissed me and then when we looked again we both said how sad she seemed."

"Yes, it's coming back to me now. Well, clever clogs. How on earth did you remember that?"

"I remember everything about that day, my love, because that … that was the day I fell in love with you."

THE END

JOIN MY MAILING LIST – PLEASE!

If you would like to read more about Tracy, Charlotte and their friends on Zephyr, I would love you to join my mailing list.

In return I will send you a FREE SNEAK PEAK of the next novel in the series – *Deepest Aqua* – then you'll be the first to know when it's released and receive a special purchase offer.

To receive your free chapters please sign up here: www.trudynixon.com

I look forward to getting to know you.

Trudy

PLEASE REVIEW ENDLESS TURQUOISE

If you enjoyed *Endless Turquoise*, please help me get it noticed so others can enjoy it too.

Reviews are one of the most powerful ways to help a self-published author like myself get noticed, when we do not have the marketing arsenal of a big publishing house behind us.

Reviewing the book benefits me in two important ways.

Firstly, your review will bring my writing to the attention of new readers that I may not otherwise reach. Reviews add credibility and increase visibility. You will improve my ranking in the Amazon algorithm and may even help me to become a best seller!

Secondly, my dream is to build a team of readers who look forward to the release of my books – to do this your feedback is essential. I want to know what you loved (and did not love so much) about my characters and their stories, as well as who or what you would like to read more about.

By spending a few minutes leaving an honest review you could make a difference to my writing career, and I would really appreciate it.

Thank you, Trudy

NEW BOOKS – COMING SOON

In the follow-up novels to *Endless Turquoise*, we discover life in Zephyr is just as colourful as ever and further explore the power a break from our day-to-day lives has to transform and inspire.

DEEPEST AQUA
What happens when you meet the love of your life and follow him to paradise – is it everything you dreamed of?
Tracy's taken a career break and is determined to concentrate on her man, but when he gets a big promotion and she finds out the truth behind his late nights at the office – will the reality of small island life be enough for an independent city girl?

Meanwhile, Zephyr's favourite playboy, Chix, is used to loving and living life to the fullest, until two women from his past arrive on the island to mess with his head and his beloved home. How will he keep his Caribbean cool?

TRUE BLUE
Life is good – but shouldn't she live a little before she settles down for good?
Charlie is happy. She's landed the perfect job and has been getting the green light from (probably) the perfect man for her. But if 'Life is like a box of chocolates' then maybe it's too soon to get serious after her divorce?

Meanwhile, her BFF, Ali, has been behaving strangely and after a night on the tiles that goes spectacularly wrong it's time to stage an intervention. Perhaps a peaceful holiday on a beautiful Spanish Island is the best cure for both of them.

Dive in and hang out with Tracy, Charlotte and friends far and wide. Enjoy a closer look at life in Zephyr and take trips to Spain and Greece in the second and third stand-alone novels in this escapist romantic humour series set in stunning destinations.

Acknowledgements

I have always loved reading, particularly escapist women's fiction, especially when the story is told from different points of view. Mix in some romance, a little humour – and set it in a stunning location I dream of visiting – and you have me hooked. With *Endless Turquoise* I have tried to write a novel that I and others who love these types of books will enjoy and remember.

It has taken eight years to get from writing my first line (which is still there – just in a different place) to publishing. I write professionally, so it shouldn't have taken me so long, but I took a number of different routes to get here and have experienced some challenging times (like all good heroines). I am so glad to be able to complete this particular story arc and publish. I promise the next one will 'soon come'.

I am very grateful to the many people that have helped me along the way.

Thank you to my Anguilla Lit Fest Family: colleagues on the committee, the friends I have made over the years and the professionals I have met who shared their knowledge and input. Special mention to Terry Macmillan whose masterclass was a major catalyst (read my blog post) and to Alafair, Johanna and Krista who all gave me precious professional advice.

Also, to my writing buddies from the early days, Fiona and Rachel, who, one Saturday morning on my balcony, were the first to hear of Tracy, Charlotte and their adventures and encouraged me to keep going. Also, to Jennifer and Laura at Finca Lilo de Biolly, the perfect place to start a novel, Julie W for giving me the copy of *On Writing*, that was my constant companion in the early days and to Annette and Bill for taking a chance on me.

Thank you Beth, Fiona, Liz, Louise J, Nick, Rachel, Sarah, Sheelagh,

Marcy and Mimi for generously reading the first draft – and then rereading it and then, in some cases, re-rereading it again!

And to Julie KH, Lorraine, Louise W, Penny, Risee, Sylvia and Tim for volunteering to be my ARC readers and giving me brilliant feedback.

Respect and praise for the SPF team, Suzy, Mark and James for their courses. You gave me the tools and confidence to dig deep and clear the final hurdle.

I am incredibly grateful to Alex, who, nearly forty years after we first met at university, has become my professional partner in this novel-writing malarky. Her insightful, professional, kind and illuminating editing has been invaluable. And, to her daughter, Esme, a Brighton University Illustration graduate, who created the beautiful cover illustration.

As always, thanks to Andrew for his good taste, design skills and that special touch with type that makes my cover as good as it is. And to my photographer, Kevin Archibald, for making me look younger and smoother than usual in my author portrait!

And finally, love and thanks to all my family, friends and pets, both in Anguilla and the UK, who may or may not spot small elements of their personality appear within these pages and who, I hope, will be pleased that I have finally, finally published that bloody novel I've been going on about for ages. And to the island of Anguilla and the villages of Wiltshire, places to live your best life and where beauty and community co-exist.

Trudy

ABOUT THE AUTHOR

Photo credit: Kevin Archibald, KSharp Media.

I am a British-born writer who grew up on a dairy farm in Wiltshire, studied Art and English at the University of Lancaster (even though that would never get me a job), worked and partied hard in London for years then had a life's-too-short experience and crossed the Atlantic to live in my forever home – Anguilla, British West Indies.

I would love to hear from my readers and am easy to find and reach – either in person, on the beaches and in the bars and restaurants of Anguilla, or online.

www.trudynixon.com
Facebook @TrudyNixonBooks
IG @TrudyNixon
info@trudynixon.com

Made in the USA
Columbia, SC
07 November 2021